Distant Waves

A NOVEL
OF THE *TITANIC*

SUZANNE WEYN

SCHOLASTIC INC.
New York Toronto London Auckland
Sydney Mexico City New Delhi Hong Kong

No part of this publication may be reproduced, stored in a retrieval system, or transmitted in any form or by any means, electronic, mechanical, photocopying, recording, or otherwise, without written permission of the publisher. For information regarding permission, write to Scholastic Inc., Attention: Permissions Department, 557 Broadway, New York, NY 10012.

This book was originally published in hardcover by Scholastic Press in 2009.

ISBN 978-0-545-08584-7

12 11 10 9 8 7 6 5 4 3 2 1   11 12 13 14 15 16/0

Printed in the U.S.A.   40

This edition first printing, May 2011

The text type was set in Minister Light.
Book design by Lillie Howard

Acknowledgments

To my sisters, Regina Weyn Arredondo, Anne Weyn Maloney, and Susan Palubinskas Weyn, women of spirit and compassion. What a blessing to have sisters like these.

With thanks to David M. Young, Jonathan Valuckas, Colleen Salcius, and David Levithan for the generous sharing of their ideas, books, and enthusiasm in the creation of this *Titanic* tale. And thanks to Bill Gonzalez, Diana Weyn Gonzalez, and Rae Weyn Gonzalez — just because nothing would be worth writing without you.

I have had three or four very striking and vivid premonitions in my life which have been fulfilled to the letter. I have others which await fulfilment. Of the latter, I will not speak here — although I have them duly recorded — for were I to do so I should be accused of being party to bringing about the fulfilment of my own predictions.

— W. T. Stead, famed British journalist who did not survive the sinking of the *Titanic* but predicted it

There are more things in heaven and earth . . . Than are dreamt of in your philosophy.

— William Shakespeare, *Hamlet*

Prologue

Dear Friend,

I have never told this story before for fear of not being believed — or, worse, ridiculed. The strange circumstances of my childhood have inclined me to have faith in only that which can be proven by science or verified by research, yet this tale defies both methods of inquiry.

It is difficult to know where to start such a story as the one I am about to recount, but I believe my tale has its roots in events that all occurred on a single day in 1898, well before the even more remarkable happenings of 1912. The things that occurred in 1898 led me on a path that, as I look back on it now, seems predestined.

That day in my early childhood is emblazoned in my mind. All that I know about my life before that, I have been told by others. But the events of that most remarkable day I recall as though they had been photographed.

Now I am on a train headed toward Nova Scotia in Canada. I am propped against my suitcase writing this chronicle, partly in order to make sense of all that has happened, and partly to occupy my time and steady my nerves.

So much is at stake now.

My story, which I believe will have its final resolution in the next few hours, was set in motion on the day I witnessed my mother, Maude Taylor, in a spirit trance, contacting the dead for the very first time.

Chapter 1

NEW YORK CITY, 1898

I edged behind a burgundy drape as my mother raised her arms wide and began to sway rhythmically, eyes shut, head thrown back. An expression of earnest supplication suffused her delicate-featured face. Her reddish brown curls swung behind her. "Speak to me, Mary Adelaide Tredwell," she intoned in her full, throaty voice. "Cease your lonely haunting of this house and come to us!"

She was seated at a round table. To her right were two middle-aged women, their hair plaited high on their heads, lace framing their hopeful faces. Owners of the house, they watched my mother with intense, expectant eyes. To her left was a balding, ill-at-ease man of about seventy.

"Your sisters, Gertrude and Julia, are here," Mother went on. "They sense your presence in this house. They have heard your footsteps at night, noticed the furniture you have moved. Your husband, Mr. Richards, has joined us, as well. It is their dearest wish that you make yourself known to those of us present now."

The luxurious drapes had been drawn, separating the white blast of afternoon light from the elegant, high-ceilinged room. In the deep alcove behind the curtains, I could turn toward the street to see life proceeding as usual: horse-drawn wagons trotting down cobblestoned streets and women walking with parasols to protect them from the blazing summer sun, their male partners properly attired in top hat and coat despite the heat. It was reassuring to be reminded that normal life was going on, especially when compared to the scene unfolding within the darkened parlor room.

I peered back through the break in the curtain and watched as my mother placed her hand on the table and told the others to do the same. "You have been haunting this house of your childhood, Mary Adelaide. Tarry no longer in the shadows of the afterlife. Those who have loved you in life wish to know you still."

A soft hand not much larger than my own reached out to clutch my fingers. My sister Mimi had also been shaken by the eeriness of it all and had come behind the curtain to hide. Ever the protective one, she had pulled our twin two-year-old sisters, Amelie and Emma, asleep together in their large perambulator, behind the drape with her.

How old must we have been then? I am certain it was

the summer of 1898, which would mean I had just turned four and Mimi was six.

Mimi's large, amber brown eyes sparked with terror even as her heart-shaped face radiated its startling beauty. With the hand not holding mine, she nervously twisted one of her curly, raven black locks around her finger, a habit she would retain all her life.

Even though Mimi looked as terrified as I felt, it was a comfort to have my big sister there holding my hand. She might not be able to save me from any horror that could arise from this summoning of the dead, but even at that young age I was confident that she would never abandon me.

With my medium brown hair and more ordinary looks, I would always see myself as a plain brown sparrow next to her glossy beauty. But it never mattered. We were so close that I experienced her glory as simply a reason for sisterly pride.

A woman's sharp gasp riveted us to the scene. The table had begun to tip, first to one side, and then to the other. The two women gazed at it, agape with horror. The man craned his neck below its top, searching for the source of this movement.

The tipping increased in speed. The banging of its three-legged pedestal as it lifted from side to side on the wooden parquet floor created an unsettling clatter. "Mary

Adelaide!" Mother implored, nearly shouting. "Speak to us! Haunt this house no more with coy signs. Instead, let us hear you directly!"

"Yes, talk to us, Mary Adelaide!" cried one of the women. "It's me! Gertrude!"

The table settled into a slow rocking. Mother stood, revealing the round, pregnant belly beneath her flowing vine-print dress.

Mimi's crushing pressure on my hand would have made me cry out if what I was seeing had not already rendered me speechless.

Mother's eyes grew wider than I had ever seen them. With her arms raised, she began to shiver as though a deep, bone-chilling frigidity had descended upon her.

I strained forward with an overwhelming impulse to wrap Mother in my arms and steady her violently convulsing frame, but Mimi's grip held me back. I beseeched Mimi with my eyes to let me go to our mother; surely this couldn't be good for her or for the baby she was carrying. Mimi shook her head. "No, Jane," she whispered. "Stay back." She checked the sleeping twins with a darting glance, and retained her firm hold on my hand.

Mother's eyes rolled back in their sockets as she threw her head back and shook it violently. Then, abruptly, her head snapped forward.

That beloved face, which I had until that moment experienced as being as familiar as my own, was completely

transformed. It had grown timid, the eyes uncertain, fur-
tive. Gone, too, was the confident, bold posture I associated
with her. In its place was a willowy stance that had never
been hers.

"Am I really back home?" she asked in a high, whis-
pery voice, seeming confused. "Gertrude, Julia . . . is
that you?"

"It's us," Gertrude volunteered eagerly.

"How old you've gotten!" Mother said with a gasp.

"It's been twenty-four years since you died," Julia
pointed out.

"Has it?" Mother pressed her hand to her chest in a
gesture of surprise I had never seen her use. "It seems to
me that only a day has passed." She turned slowly to the
man at the table. "My dear, you've lost your hair," she
noted, and laughed lightly.

"This is a fraud!" the man shouted. "I'll not stand for
another second of it!" He pushed back from the table so
fiercely that the chair he had been sitting on toppled
behind him.

A squeal from the perambulator made Mimi and me
turn sharply toward it. The clatter of the chair had stirred
the twins from their sleep. Emma sputtered and fussed,
then settled back to sleep. Amelie, though, sat forward,
wide eyes locked in fascination on Mother.

Mother retained her lithe composure as Mr. Richards
stormed out, slamming the door behind him. She bent

toward Julia and Gertrude confidingly. "The spiritual realm has always made him ill at ease," she said lightly, as if his departure was of little consequence. "He's a captain of industry, and you know how they are."

"Of course we know," Julia said. "What man in our social circle is not?"

Mother looked at Julia, blinked hard, and wilted into her chair, her head bent down on her chest.

Again, I tried to go to her, and once more Mimi held on to me.

A white vapor, like steam from a boiling pot of water, rose behind Mother.

"What is that?" Gertrude asked, looking anxiously from Mother to Julia.

Amelie pointed, leaning so far out of the perambulator that I feared she would fall. I nudged Mimi and signaled for her to pull our baby sister in, which she did.

Mother lifted her head with great effort. "Julia, waste no time. It is short."

Mother slumped forward on the table. This time I wouldn't allow Mimi to hold me back. I raced out of my hiding place and went to her side, shaking her. "Mama! Mama!" I shouted. "Wake up! Wake up, please!"

Mother simply lay there, slumped over, not stirring.

Mimi threw the drapes aside, letting sunlight once more flood the room as Gertrude tried to rouse Mother with shakes and murmurs of solicitude. Julia poured a glass of water from the crystal decanter on the sideboard and brought it to her.

All the activity woke Emma, who reddened and began to cry heartily. Mimi rocked the perambulator, fruitlessly attempting to soothe her. Emma's wails only increased, which turned out to be fortunate, since Mother lifted her head in response.

Relieved beyond measure that she was alive, I threw my arms around her. She stroked my hair and then rose as though everything was perfectly fine. Crossing the room, she lifted Emma from the perambulator and cradled her in the crook of her arm, rocking her gently. The crying stopped.

"Maude, you were magnificent!" Gertrude praised her.

"I have no doubt it was Mary Adelaide that we spoke to," Julia added. "Every gesture and intonation was hers."

Mother seemed bewildered for a moment. "You mean it happened?"

"Oh, yes!" Gertrude told her. "Weren't you aware?"

Mother shook her head. "No, I . . . I suppose I . . . I must have passed out. When I awoke there at the table, I assumed I had fainted."

I looked to Mimi, checking to see if she could make any sense of this. Mimi's eyes had narrowed, and her delicate dark brows were in a ponderous V formation. Clearly she was as confused as I was, and was working hard to sort this out.

"Did you see into the spirit world while you were in your trance?" Gertrude asked Mother. "Did you see Mary Adelaide?"

"No, I did not see your sister," Mother revealed as she sat on a velvet chair, still gently jiggling Emma. "She must have taken over my body and sent my spirit traveling elsewhere."

"You certainly have the gift! I am so happy you have not been neglecting the potential we saw you demonstrate as a girl!" Gertrude gushed.

Mother shook her head. "Not true."

Gertrude cocked her head to the side in a gesture of confusion. "I don't understand. You *have* been neglecting your gifts?"

Mother sighed and nodded. "You ladies know that as a young woman I showed great promise as a medium. When your family visited mine back in Hydesville, you saw the demonstration of my gifts."

"I recall it well," Julia said. "You were being mentored by Maggie Fox then — it's so sad that she has passed over. People said that she and her sisters were frauds, but I never believed it."

"Leah, the eldest, was a fraud, but Kate and Maggie had the gift," Mother insisted.

I did not know it then, but I have since learned that the Fox sisters of Hydesville were famous spiritualists. When the ghost of a dead peddler who had once lived in their house and had stayed around to haunt it contacted them with strange raps and thumps, they became sensations, and started the movement known as spiritualism.

"We remembered you clearly," Gertrude added. "You were so young and yet so impressive when you contacted the spirit of our dead president, Mr. Lincoln."

"Mr. Lincoln was easy to find. He conducted séances in the White House, I am told. His wife was a believer," Mother said.

"Don't be so modest," Gertrude chided. "I have never forgotten your gifts. That is why we sought you out when we needed to speak to Mary Adelaide. We were thrilled to discover you were living in Brooklyn."

"That was indeed destiny, because I have only just arrived in Brooklyn from Massachusetts in the past month," Mother said. "My stay with my mother-in-law is only temporary, God willing. I am at loose ends since the death of my beloved husband and must decide where to take up permanent residence."

"I have of late come to hear about an entire community of spiritualists upstate, just south of Buffalo," Julia Tredwell told Mother. "Now that you are a widow, perhaps it would be a hospitable environment in which to raise your daughters."

"It sounds compelling," Mother allowed.

Julia went to the sideboard and took out a pad and

pencil. She wrote something on the paper and handed it to Mother.

Mother read the name on the pad and put it in a crochet bag she carried on her wrist. Holding Amelie in one arm and Emma in the other, she beckoned for Mimi and me to push the empty perambulator and follow her to the door. "Good day, ladies," she said to Julia and Gertrude as the Tredwells' butler held the door open for us. "Thank you so much for telling me about this town. It might be just the spot I have been seeking."

"Your fee," Julia reminded Mother, hurrying to drop an envelope in the purse.

"Oh, yes," Mother said. "I'd nearly forgotten about it."

"Maude, what do you think Mary Adelaide meant when she said my time was short?" Julia asked, her voice touched with a wavering tremble.

"I have no way to know," Mother said softly. "But time is fleeting for all of us. It is advice we could all use."

"Then why did she not say the same thing to Gertrude?" Julia asked. "Why did she address it to me, specifically?"

Mother pressed Julia's hands in her own. "The mysteries of life and death are as unknown to me as they are to you," she said. "I'm sorry."

When the door of the Tredwells' brick row house was closed, Mother hurried us several buildings down the street. Only then did she stop to count the money in the envelope. A smile slowly spread across her face. "There's money enough here for supper and train fare tomorrow," she told us.

"A train? Where are we going?" Mimi asked.

"I'm not exactly sure at the moment," Mother admitted, stroking her rounded belly. "We need to go somewhere so I can think about it more carefully."

She didn't know it, but we had already stepped on the path.

Chapter 2

Mother chose to think on a bench in nearby Washington Square Park. She arranged her billowing skirts discreetly over her pregnant frame and settled on one of the green park benches. "I'll watch the twins, girls, but you two go for a stroll," she said. "Mother needs a moment to meditate."

The urban park's open space with its imposing white arch, sparkling fountain, and winding cobblestoned paths was a perfectly agreeable spot in which to amble. Mimi and I meandered along, each of us lost in her own reverie.

I was thinking about everything that had happened in the last month: my father's death from smallpox, our mother selling most of our belongings and moving us into Grandmother Taylor's stately Brooklyn brownstone. I sensed without really knowing, as small children often do, that Mother was devastated not only about Father's death but also about her current living conditions. She and Grandmother Taylor did not get on well.

We traveled the circumference of the park and then

headed back to Mother on her bench. I'd always thought my mother made an imposing sight with her long skirt flowing around her. She was not exactly fat, but rather rounded, and now that she had a baby on the way, she was an even larger presence than usual.

Emma was toddling around in front of her, walking several steps and falling backward on her diapered bottom, then getting up to try again. Amelie sat languidly on the bench with her side melted against Mother's, observing Emma's exploits.

Mimi and I joined Mother on the bench. "Have you finished thinking?" Mimi asked.

"I have." Mother took out the note Julia Tredwell had given to her and pressed it flat on her knee. "This is to be our future home."

"Spirit Vale," Mimi read.

I sometimes wonder how much my memory of that day is influenced by the things Mimi and I have talked about through the years and how much of it is purely my own remembering. Being a little older, she had greater understanding of what was going on around us.

Let me promise you, though: I am absolutely sure about the events that happened next. Even now, so many years later, if I close my eyes, I can conjure the scene in every detail. And hardly a day has passed that I have not, for at least a fleeting moment, recalled it.

We were on the wide boulevard called Houston Street. It was a sedate scene with only a few horse-drawn wagons passing by. My head was craned back, ogling the wide four- and five-story buildings. Coming from a New England village of clapboard wooden houses, this city seemed like something conjured from imagination, absolutely huge and wondrous.

Mimi tapped me on the shoulder and hopped forward. It was a game we had begun to play since coming to the city. I would then try to jump farther than she without landing on a sidewalk crack.

I took the challenge and sprang forward. But the moment that I landed, the sidewalk pushed me back with tremendous force, throwing me into Mimi.

Stumbling, the two of us fell over, me on top of my sister.

Looking around, I saw Mother leaning over the twins in the perambulator as though to shield them. She'd lifted one arm over her head and was searching around for Mimi and me. "Stay down. Cover your heads!" she shouted the moment she spotted us.

In the next second, debris of rock, dirt, and plaster showered down on us. A brick crashed to my right. Mimi and I lunged to either side as a narrow opening crack-led between us, traveling fast across the sidewalk. The pavement in front of me jutted forward, disconnecting the two slabs and thrusting them upward.

I tucked myself into a ball, covering up as Mother had commanded.

On every side, the buildings were shaking!

Pow! Pow! Pow! followed by shrill crackling. Three upper windows in a row from the building next to me exploded, raining shards of shattered glass to the street.

Gradually I realized that a terrible pain was burning in my head. It was as if my skull were vibrating at a tremendous speed. My teeth chattered so violently that my jaw ached. I became aware of a high, excruciating whine that seemed to be inside my head.

When I checked on Mimi, she was also wincing in agony, her eyes shut tight, and clutching her forehead.

My eyes pulsated like a heartbeat.

It was horrible!

Terror rocked me, for I imagined that I might literally explode if it didn't all stop right away.

An oncoming clang of an approaching fire wagon mixed with the high whine in my head. Then another set of fire bells from a different direction started up.

I sensed a nearby presence and dared to open my clenched eyes. A man's worn brown shoes were the first thing I saw.

Gazing up the length of him, I took in a tall, gaunt man of about forty. His nearly black hair, parted down the middle, was windblown and askew. The dark mustache above his thin lips twitched anxiously as his onyx eyes darted in every direction, taking in the scene of destruction.

He lifted me to my feet with a strong, firm grip. "Where are your parents?" he asked with a heavy Eastern European accent, his laboratory jacket flapping in the wind that the tumult had stirred up around us.

I located Mother crouched low to the ground with her arms over Amelie and Emma, and pointed to her. The perambulator had fallen to its side. "Oh, no!" the man exclaimed.

Mimi rose unsteadily to her feet. With arms outstretched to keep from falling, we followed the man over to Mother and the twins. "Come! Come inside!" he urged her as another slab of stone crashed in front of us. "You must come inside."

Mother carried one twin in each of her arms as we stumbled after him. The clanging of bells was now all around us. The horse-drawn fire wagons were pulling to rapid halts, mixed with police wagons. A fireman leaped down and was instantly knocked over by the swaying ground beneath him.

We followed the tall man into a nearby building marked forty-six East Houston. Once we were inside, he raced up a staircase ahead of us. "Follow me," he called over his shoulder. "I cannot wait. There is something I must do at once."

Mother seemed unsure for a moment, but a piece of ornate trim from the building's facade crashed down by the front door, and that was all the convincing she needed. The staircase quivered as we climbed, and by the time we reached the fourth-floor landing, we saw an open door that led into a spacious, one-room apartment with sparse furniture and a ceiling that rose about twelve feet high.

In the middle of the room, a metal girder reached about halfway to the high ceiling. Strapped to the girder was a metal box with a gauge and dials, a machine of some sort about the size of an alarm clock.

The man who had guided us into the building did not even notice our quiet, curious entry into the room. He was much too intent on his task.

He held a sledgehammer over his head and violently — smash after repeated smash — destroyed the small, humming machine.

Chapter 3

I wandered to the wall of high, wide windows looking down onto Houston Street. The scene was pure pandemonium. Those who had been inside in restaurants and stores stumbled out wearing dazed expressions to see what had happened. Horses that had been pulling hansom cabs, fire wagons, and police wagons balked at riding down the broken ground, neighing their displeasure and refusing to move forward. This created a jam in the roadway which brought on great bouts of shouting and fighting.

The terrible pain and whine that had tormented me had vanished. But a dull throb had taken their place and my bones ached awfully, especially my jawbone, even my teeth. The twins were draped across Mimi's knees, looking spent by the experience. Glancing at Mimi, I wasn't sure if her dark eyes brimmed with tears or if she was simply squinting against the harsh light that flooded the vast room. She was anxiously twisting one of her curls.

"You made it stop, sir, didn't you?" Mother surmised, standing in front of the man. Her voice was strong, almost accusatory. "By smashing that thing."

He slumped in a beat-up, brown leather armchair, a posture of complete dejection. "Made it stop?" he repeated with weary irony. He glanced at the flattened metal box still strapped to the girder. "Yes, I suppose I did." Having said that, though, he lifted his head and seemed to brighten. "More to the point, my dear woman: I also made it *start*."

"It wasn't a natural earthquake, then?" Mimi inquired in a voice much shakier and smaller than her usual tone.

"Well . . ." He gazed at Mother, as if gauging if he could trust her with further information.

"No need to hesitate, sir. Clearly it was caused by that contraption." Mother broke the stalemate, a note of impatience creeping into her voice. "It's too late to deny that!"

The man threw his arms up and dropped them again on the sides of the chair. With this gesture, he gave up any reticence he may have felt, and from there on was completely forthcoming. "It is my latest experiment: an electromechanical oscillator, a vibratory mechanism. I was amplifying its output to see if it could align with the vibrational patterns of the outside buildings."

"Vibrational patterns? Buildings do not vibrate," Mother objected. "At least, not usually."

The man rose and began to pace, warming to his subject. "That is where you are wrong, madam. *Everything* vibrates! Everything! Vibration is the key to the universe. The very Earth could be split in two given the right vibrations."

"Well, I sincerely hope things won't get that far. None-theless, your demonstration was impressive. Everything out there was most certainly vibrating," Mother said wryly. "But it would seem there are still a few problems left to be worked out in your mechanism. Wouldn't you agree?"

For the first time, the man's mouth quirked into something like a smile. "Excellent point," he allowed. "Nonetheless, it worked. It worked!"

He clapped his hands together gustily, his face becoming radiant with a broad grin. Without intending to, Mimi and I both smiled, too, infected by his glee.

"That was your idea of *success*?" Mother questioned incredulously, gesturing toward the street.

"I am sorry for the destruction, of course. Looking out the window, I witnessed what was happening and was about to stop the machine when I saw your babes in distress. I had endangered you! So I ran down to retrieve you before destroying the machine. By letting the machine run, I caused further ruin, I'm afraid. Regrettably, these sorts of choices are sometimes not so simple."

"Why didn't you just turn it off?" Mother inquired. "Did you forget to invent an off switch?"

"It jammed. I had pushed it beyond its capacity."

"And you still consider the experiment a success?" Mother pressed.

He became nearly giddy with excitement. "Yes! It was an astounding success! I merely intended to create an almost imperceptible quiver, but that's just a matter of tinkering, of getting the calibrations correct. The point is that it works, just as it came to me in my dream."

"You dreamed that earthquake machine?" Mimi asked.

"Earthquake machine! What a wonderful name. That is what I shall call it. Earthquake machine!" he exclaimed as if talking to himself. Then he spoke directly to Mimi, with none of the condescension adults often direct toward children. "Yes, little miss, I dreamed it. Many of my greatest inventions have come in dreams or meditations."

Tilting her head to one side curiously, Mimi studied the tall, highly animated man. "What have you invented?"

"Many, many inventions," he said. "Some of them are still in my mind. But . . . here is one! Three years ago I harnessed the power of Niagara Falls and lit entire cities with electric light running on alternating current! If they had done it Edison's way, with direct current, it would have required a power plant for every mile. Those plants run on coal. Do you realize how that would have fouled the air? At Niagara Falls, through my deal with the Westinghouse Company, we powered Niagara to Chicago, Toronto, Boston, and New York."

Mother gasped sharply and her hand flew to her mouth. "That was you? You're Tesla?"

"I am, indeed, Tesla," he confirmed, bowing gallantly.

Though I later learned that his name was Nikola Tesla, he stayed forever in my mind not as Mr. Tesla or Dr.

Tesla but simply as Tesla, in the same way one would say Socrates or Washington.

"I've read of you," Mother spoke excitedly, moving closer to him. "And about your rivalry with Edison."

Tesla scowled. "Edison invents, while I discover what is already there to be uncovered. He relies on blind chance. He guesses with no regard for theory or scientific formulation. He stumbles upon his inventions."

"I take it you don't like Mr. Edison," Mother observed.

"Almost fifteen years ago, when I first came to America from Austria-Hungary, I worked for Edison. He offered me fifty thousand dollars to revamp his generators and machinery. Do you know what kind of laboratory I could have set up with fifty thousand dollars? So I did what he asked, working myself into a state of exhaustion. When I was done, the efficiency of all his machinery was many times what it had been. And do you know what he told me when I asked for my money?"

"What?" Mother said.

"He laughed and said: 'Tesla, you don't understand our American humor.' Later that year, I resigned."

"But surely you have recovered that money many times over in your work at Niagara Falls?" Mother remarked.

"The electricity was derived from the power of Niagara Falls, not from me. I do not believe in making money from naturally occurring resources. It should be free, like water or air. For a few to claim it as theirs to sell is wrong."

"What a unique perspective," Mother remarked. "Clearly you are not American."

"I *am* a citizen," Tesla informed her. "I became a naturalized citizen in 1891 when I was thirty-five years of age."

"But your thinking is not American," she clarified. "You are not a capitalist."

"So I have been told. Edison is the great American!"

By now, we had almost recovered from the shock of what had happened on the street. And Mother was clearly intrigued by this encounter with Tesla, admiring his intelligence. Still, I was a little surprised by what she said next.

"Mr. Tesla," she said, walking around to the window so that she was standing directly in front of him, "I am not educated like yourself, so I would appreciate your thoughts on a subject that has been much on my mind lately."

I sat forward, as did Mimi, both of us fiercely interested to hear what she would ask.

"I am at your service," Tesla obliged.

"What do you think of ghosts, Mr. Tesla?"

He did not seem in the least surprised by her odd question. "Well, madam, as I have said previously, everything vibrates."

"I don't follow," she said.

"Have you ever seen a hummingbird?"

"I have."

"And do its wings seem to disappear as it hovers near a red, tubular flower?"

Mother considered for a quick moment. "I suppose they do, yes."

"Yet the hummingbird's wings are still there despite the fact that we cannot see them," Tesla said. "The rate of the vibration of the hummingbird's wings renders them invisible to our feeble human senses."

"So when a person's spirit passes over, that person might begin to vibrate on a different level?" Mother said, struggling to follow.

"Vibrate at a different *frequency*," he corrected, "in the same way in which one can tune in different channels on a wireless communication, one may be able to tune in different spirit *frequencies*."

"Do you mean like in Marconi's radio invention?" Mother asked.

"I invented it first," Tesla said sternly, looking out the window. "Marconi merely beat me to the patent and the credit. I'm fighting him in court."

"I'm so sorry for you," Mother sympathized. "It's a terrible injustice not to receive credit for one's work."

"No matter," Tesla said quietly, continuing to gaze out the window. "The point is that science bears out a belief in what *cannot* be seen. In physics there are many things we cannot see directly: the underwater transmittal of sound; power from above surging along wires and through the ground in waves of electricity."

"So then, you believe that the existence of ghosts —
spirits who hover in this dimension after their physical
incarnation has ended — is a possibility?" Mother asked.

Tesla turned dramatically from the window and faced
Mother. "Madam, I believe that *everything* is a possibility."

This was the last bit of convincing Mother had needed.

For the first — but not the last — time, Tesla had
changed our lives.

Chapter 4

That night, Mother commanded us to assemble our few belongings and pack them. While Mimi and I stuffed rag dolls and nightgowns into our carpetbags, I could hear my mother and grandmother downstairs engaging in a conversation that quickly escalated to a full-scale shouting match.

"If you engage in this lunacy, you will disgrace the Taylor name!" Grandmother Taylor shouted, her voice barbed with indignation.

"This is my life, and I shall live it as I see fit!" Mother shot back at her.

With Grandmother Taylor irately barraging Mother with phrases that contained words such as *unstable*, *unfit*, *disinherit*, and *disown*, we scrambled down her front steps, our carpetbags thumping behind.

At Grand Central Depot we boarded a train for Albany and then changed at that city for a different train. I recall eating sandwiches and sleeping slumped against Mimi as we rumbled at great speed through the night. I remember being alert with excitement coupled with anxious worry over what lay ahead but also suffused with relief to be away from Grandmother Taylor's disapproving eyes.

My giddy, thrilled state slowly gave way to a deep exhaustion. What a day it had been! Yawning widely, I slumped in my seat next to Mimi and let the train lull me.

Mother sat rocking the twins in their perambulator with one hand, engrossed in a slim novel she'd bought at the newsstand at Grand Central Depot in New York City.

"What's the story about?" Mimi asked as I stirred drowsily beside her. "Tell us."

Mother put down her book. "It's an adventure tale titled *Futility*, by a man named Morgan Robertson," she said. "It's about a very, very large ship called the *Titan* that hits an iceberg and sinks on its very first voyage. It seems that most of its passengers are about to drown."

"I don't like that story," Mimi said. "Is it true?"

"No, it's not true. It's just fiction that the writer made up from his imagination," she answered.

"It's too sad," Mimi declared.

"You're right. I don't much like it, either." Mother closed the book and set it aside on her seat. "It's putting me in a melancholy frame of mind and I hadn't even realized it. That's not what I need right now. I must entertain only the most positive of thoughts if I am to move forward effectively."

Finally we reached the bustling city of Buffalo, New York. We spent a night in a rather shabby hotel there. It was newly morning, still almost dark, when Mother roused us and we hurried down to the street without even telling anyone we were leaving. There she hired a horse-drawn cab to carry us as close to Spirit Vale as the last of her money would allow.

That wasn't far enough, apparently, because I recall us walking for quite a long time along a dirt road — I pushed the twins, while Mother and Mimi dragged our bags.

In memory I see us passing under a tall wooden arch, atop of which was a sign with the words SPIRIT VALE WELCOMES THE LIVING AND THOSE GONE BEYOND all written in birch branches. The words had a pinkish tone in the early morning's new light. We made our way down a wide dirt road lined with wooden buildings, each one sporting an open front porch decorated with intricate gingerbread latticework.

The hour was so early that no one was around. Mother paused at a four-way intersection and gazed in each direction, looking unsure of where to go next. On one corner was a two-story, red wooden hotel with a porch wrapping around both levels. The sign over the entrance to the front porch read THE SPIRIT HOTEL.

Mother lifted the twins, cradling one in each arm and, with a nod of her head, beckoned us to follow her up the hotel's steps. Pulling at the front door, she found it to be locked. "Someone's got to come along eventually," she said with a sigh, then directed us to rest on some wicker chairs set around a table on the porch. We were all instantly asleep — Mother, too, with the twins nestled on either side of her.

The sun was fully up when, through sleepy, slatted eyes, I saw a petite woman of middle age pop her head out the front door and eye us owlishly through thick, rimless glasses. She cleared her throat loudly to rouse us from our slumber.

"Hello there," Mother said, instantly bright. "Are you the proprietor of this establishment?"

"That I be," the woman replied in a way that was not especially friendly.

"I see from your nameplate that you are Aunty Lily," Mother observed.

"Correct. Ya need a room?" Aunty Lily asked, inspecting us with a suspicion that I am sure was understandable given our bedraggled condition.

"Yes, please," Mother answered. Presumably she had some magic way to pay for this, since I knew from our long walk there that she had run out of money.

"Well, that's unfortunate, since we're booked up. August is our biggest month. Plus, we don't take children. Too noisy. They disturb the mediums. Mediums require tranquillity to contact the beyond," Aunty Lily told us without a hint of apology.

"Perhaps your husband there might know of a place where we could stay," Mother suggested, looking over the woman's right shoulder.

Aunty Lily's eyes narrowed, and her lined lips drew together angrily. "What did you say?"

A shard of vivid morning light cutting across the porch required me to squint up at Aunty Lily. Actually, I was trying to see over her shoulder for any sign of a man who might be standing behind her. I saw no one.

Mother's hand went to her mouth in an apologetic gesture. "Oh, I am so sorry. He looked so real that I naturally assumed . . . Can you forgive me?"

"Ya say he's right next to me? And ya saw him?"

"I see him still, clear as day," Mother confirmed. "He's recently passed, hasn't he? I feel it was somewhere between last April and now."

Aunty Lily continued to hold Mother in a skeptical gaze, but her hard face softened a touch as she nodded. "It was just this past June."

"And he was very far away when he died, wasn't he?" Mother sighed sadly. "You told him he was too old to go fight in Cuba but the dear, stubborn fool insisted. Did his name start with an *H*? I'm sensing an *H*."

"Yes! Yes, it did!" Aunty Lily took a lace-trimmed hanky from her pocket and dabbed her wet eyes. "It weren't even the fighting that got him. It were the malaria."

I noticed that Mimi was twirling one of her curls, a sure sign that she was finding something amiss here.

Mother put her arm around the stricken woman as she leaned close, speaking confidingly. "He says to tell you it was the grandest adventure of his life, and he wouldn't have missed it. He thanks you for understanding why he had to go, and he misses your warm touch, but he is always by your side in spirit."

Aunty Lily stepped away from Mother's grasp. "Hiram, can ya hear me? Did ya leave any cash stashed anywhere? Ya left me here sort of strapped for money." Aunty Lily turned to Mother. "Well, ask him!" she said. "Hiram, tell the lady — did ya leave any money?"

Mother held up her hand to quiet Aunty Lily. "It's no use. He's gone off to rest. The malaria left him weak, and crossing over drains him. He'll be back, though. He's sworn to never leave your side again."

Aunty Lily became teary-eyed once more. "That's a comfort. A real comfort. I can see that ya got the gift."

"The gift?" Mother questioned.

"The ability to see those that have crossed over, to predict, to channel spirits. It's Spirit Vale's main industry."

"Oh, yes, that gift," Mother said. "Yes, I have studied mediumship with the Fox sisters of Hydesville. It was my hometown."

That impressed Aunty Lily greatly. "The Fox sisters,

ya say! Well, mercy me. Have ya come here to set up shop?"

"If that were possible, it would be a dream fulfilled," Mother told Aunty Lily, her voice a silken river of sincerity. "But since you have no room, we will go look for other —"

"No! No!" Aunty Lily quickly stopped her. "There's not a proper guest room available, but I've been looking for a helper and I've set aside a little back cottage for such. Would ya mind doing some housekeeping and working the front desk when I can't? It won't pay much, but the cottage would be part of the deal."

"When would I do my medium work?"

"We could work around that," Aunty Lily offered. "None of the other mediums in this town have been able to contact Hiram — and him right beside me all the while! For some reason, he trusts ya, and my Hiram was *not* a trusting man. I wouldn't want to see him go away again."

"It's wise to be cautious," Mother murmured.

"Mayhaps it's 'cause you're with child," Aunty Lily conjectured. "Hiram always liked babies, perhaps 'cause we never had none of our own. If Hiram trusts ya, then so do I." Aunty Lily's lower jaw began to quiver with the effort of controlling her emotions. "Things have been so hard, but ya've made me feel better just knowing my Hiram is here."

"I know how it is. I, too, am recently a widow," Mother confided.

Aunty Lily linked arms with Mother and guided her toward the door. Pausing at the threshold, Mother instructed Mimi to wake the twins and bring them in. Eager to be helpful, I aided her in rousing Amelie and Emma, who were slow to waken.

"Bring in that mail, would ya, children?" Aunty Lily pointed toward a roll of letters bundled together on the wicker table.

I held on to Emma while Mimi took the mail in one hand and Amelie in the other. We entered a large, open lobby. On the right-hand side, a long, wooden counter was positioned against the wall. Aunty Lily led us behind the front counter, through her office, and out the back door. We instantly saw a wooden cottage with the same gingerbread scrollwork on its small porch that I had observed on the other buildings.

"It's small," Aunty Lily allowed, "but it's got a wood-burning stove for warmth in the winter, and the outhouse isn't too far a walk into the woods in the back. Or ya can come to the hotel to use the indoor facilities, if you're particular."

"It's perfect," Mother declared. "I feel excellent vibrations here."

"I don't feel *no* vibrations," Aunty Lily said, looking confused. "This cottage ain't vibrating."

"Aunty Lily," Mother said in a confiding tone, "*everything* vibrates."

Chapter 5

There was only one double bed with a wooden headboard in the bigger of the two bedrooms. Though we would all eventually get our own beds, that night Mimi, Amelie, Emma, and I all snuggled together. Emma snored and Amelie slumbered silently between us. We'd put them in the middle for fear that they would fall off the sides during the night.

Silver light from a bright full moon streamed in the curtainless window. That in combination with the loud chirping of crickets kept Mimi and me awake. Or perhaps it was simply that we were so excited about everything that had happened.

We had spent the day trailing Mother as Aunty Lily introduced us to so many people that they became a blur of faces. We went into storefronts and private parlors, each the scene of some séance, mystical reading, or strange bridge between the living and the dead. It was impressed upon us that we were not to call them *the dead*. No one was truly dead, at least not in Spirit Vale; they had passed

on, gone over, were living elsewhere — and were still emi-
nently reachable.

Despite my high-strung state, slowly I began to drift.
Glancing at Mimi, I saw that she was still wide-awake,
twirling and untwirling one long curl with so much energy
I was reminded of a woman knitting.

As I replayed the remarkable events of the previous
two days, I thought of Tesla. Strangely enough, I felt that
I missed him.

"Do you think Tesla misses us right now?" I
asked Mimi.

"He doesn't even know us," she said to me.

"He knows us," I disagreed.

"I miss Father," she said softly.

"Me, too," I said, resting my head on her shoulder. The
truth, though, which I didn't dare tell her, was that I was
already beginning to forget what Father had looked like. I
recalled his outline: tall with broad shoulders and dark hair.
And I remembered kind eyes. But the rest of him was starting to fade away.

It was easier to picture Tesla. In fact, the image I held of
him was extremely vivid, and it somehow merged with the
recollection I had of Father. This refreshed image comforted
me, for it meant somehow that I wasn't forgetting Father,
after all. I know it might sound odd, but I don't believe
such peculiar thinking is really unusual in small children.

"Tesla misses us," I said earnestly. Then I yawned. "I like this place," I added sleepily. "Do you?"

"It will do, I suppose," Mimi replied with a reserved air.

"It was lucky Mother saw Hiram's ghost," I said.

"I could have seen Hiram's ghost, too," Mimi said.

I was suddenly up on my elbow. "Did you see him? I tried to, but I couldn't."

"No, but I could have pretended to see him, just like Mother did."

"What?"

Mimi turned on her side so that we faced each other. Bending her head, she dropped her voice. "The top letter in that bundle on the table was addressed to Mrs. Hiram Miller, widow. It was from the U.S. government, veteran affairs, but it was postmarked from Cuba. On the bottom of the envelope was a typed line about widow's benefit forms being enclosed."

"I don't understand," I said.

"Mother knew Aunty Lily's husband was dead because it said she was a widow right on the envelope."

"How did she know where he was when he died?" I challenged.

"That's where the war that's on now is taking place. Grandmother Taylor told me about it. It started last spring and is almost over now. That's how Mother guessed where Hiram was and when he died."

"She lied to Aunty Lily?"

Mimi nodded sullenly.

Mimi had been reading since she was four and was already starting to teach me, so I trusted that she had really seen what she said she did. But I was not as accepting of the conclusion she'd drawn.

"She didn't see the letter," I protested. Mother wouldn't do such a thing.

"She saw it," Mimi insisted.

"No, she didn't," I stated firmly.

"You're just a little girl," Mimi said offhandedly, as though my opinion was of no importance to her. She had made up *her* mind.

I flipped over onto my other side, facing away from her. Mimi had annoyed me. I wasn't ready to give up my unqualified faith in Mother. Not just then, at any rate.

Chapter 6

SPIRIT VALE, NEW YORK, 1898-1911

Within a day of arriving in Spirit Vale, Mother let it be known she had been taught by the famous Maggie Fox, and — coupled with Aunty Lily's often teary-eyed endorsement — it made her an instant celebrity, revered among the other mediums and sought after by many clients seeking contact with lost loved ones.

Mother's approach was what she called "scientific and mystical" — modern yet rooted in traditional spiritualism.

Everything vibrates.

It became Mother's motto. The phrase was mysteriously enigmatic, yet sounded so knowing and wise she was almost never questioned further. It seemed to explain so much even when no one really knew what she meant.

Her delivery was artful. Eyes narrowed with a distant gaze, she would nod a little as she conveyed her message in a voice thick with portentous meaning: "*Everything* vibrates." Then she would incline her head forward in a gesture that asked, "Now do you understand?" She didn't wait for a reply because it was to be tacitly understood that one *did* understand.

My sister Blythe was born at the end of 1898, right there in Spirit Vale. Mother was aided by a medicine woman midwife from the Oneida tribe, Princess Running Deer, who doubled as a baby channel, a medium specializing in contacting children who had passed on as babies. "I think I'll name her Blythe Oneida Taylor," Mother considered one day while rocking on the porch with baby Blythe in her arms.

"Tesla is also a nice name," I suggested. "Blythe Tesla Taylor."

"Tesla? The scientist we met?"

I nodded.

"What has he to do with us?"

"You say his words — *everything vibrates.*"

She nodded, seeming to consider the idea for a moment, and then shook it off. "Oneida is more fitting. I think all our middle names shall be Oneida from now on. It will befit our new life here."

And so my mother put a wooden sign on the porch of our white cottage, like so many other plaques around town, advertising MAUDE ONEIDA TAYLOR — MEDIUM, CHANNELER.

Mimi, Emma, Amelie, little Blythe, and I became known as the Oneida Taylor sisters. Mimi said she didn't like it. And if Mimi didn't like the new name, then neither did I. Blythe was too young to care. And Emma claimed it was all right by her.

Amelie said nothing.

She never did.

From the day of the séance at the Tredwell home, I never heard Amelie speak another word. She made sounds — laughed, cried, even hummed. But never a word would she speak.

As soon as we were settled in Spirit Vale, Mother took Amelie to a specialist in Ontario, Canada. As far as he could tell, Amelie *could* talk. She understood what words were and what they meant. She just chose not to say anything.

After that, the five of us went to Syracuse so Mother could talk to a psychologist about Amelie. He suggested that a severe trauma might be at the root of her refusal to speak. It had been known to happen. Could we think of any such trauma?

"I can," I volunteered, and told all about the séance and how baby Amelie seemed to be seeing something that none of us could and from that day on never spoke again.

"You are telling me that your sister was frightened by a ghost?" the psychologist inquired skeptically.

"No, that's not when it happened," Mother said. "It was the earthquake. The vibrations must have shaken her vocal cords loose."

"You were in an earthquake? In New York City?" Again, the psychologist seemed very doubtful, as I would have been myself, had I not been there.

"Yes, indeed. You are correct. It was highly unusual," Mother said, disarming him with her most charming smile.

"I don't believe her vocal cords were shaken," the psychologist ventured. "More likely, she was traumatized by the tremendous fear she felt during the quake."

So that became our official story on Amelie. She had been rendered mute by the ordeal of the quake. Mother preferred that story, I think, because it absolved her of all blame. If she had conjured something from the spirit world that had so affected her baby, her guilt would have been too enormous to bear.

As I grew older, I took to watching Mother carefully, trying with all my powers of observation to discern if she could really contact the spirit world or if she had simply hit upon a way to use her innate powers of showmanship to make money. She would sometimes do something that many of the mediums in town did, called *automatic writing*.

In an apparent trance state, she would hold up a blank slate, and the spirit being contacted was supposed to imprint a message on the slate.

It had become my habit to sneak under her table once the lights were out. More than once I caught sight of her writing feverishly on a second blackboard on her lap and then producing that board as though the spirit had written the message on it.

One time, as a joke, I scribbled, *Hello Mother*, in the corner of the board when it was resting at her feet, waiting to be produced. Luckily her client took it as a message from a child who had died as a toddler and was delighted to see that her son had learned to write in the afterlife. Nonetheless Mother was not amused and made sure to kick around under the table before every séance to be sure I wasn't lurking there, waiting to cause mischief.

Still, among the townspeople there were those mediums thought to be mostly fraudulent and others who were revered for their ability, and my mother was among the most respected. Due to her Everything Vibrates motto, she was even considered something of a scientist. "Maude Oneida Taylor has studied with the great minds of our times" was an oft-voiced rumor around town. "She believes there are layers of reality, much like the skin of an onion. The afterlife is one of those layers, and Maude is able to vibrate at the same speed as the afterlife and shake those layers loose."

Mother had made the most of her brief meeting with Tesla and did nothing to dissuade anyone that she was, indeed, a deep student of science and that her mystical methods incorporated the latest theories.

"There is an intersection of science and spiritualism," she claimed to her clients. "The journey of the spirit can be thought of as a science we do not yet understand, in just the same way as Nikola Tesla is forging new frontiers in the field of electricity. He pulls electric power from waterfalls and the sky. I pull spiritual power from the Beyond."

It was a persuasive speech, and she seemed sincere when she told it to every one of her clients. But when I showed her the articles I was pulling out of the papers about Tesla, she was fairly uninterested. "That's nice, Jane. Interesting, I suppose, though I don't quite understand it," she would say, and then go about her business without further comment.

When I was eight, I found an article in which Tesla claimed he had invented a wireless telephone. Though we had no telephones yet in Spirit Vale, the landscape of the outside world was more and more strung with ugly telephone wire, festooned from pole to pole along the main roads. When I told Mother, she was attentive and took the article from me.

By the next day she had acquired a telephone receiver. "I'm incorporating it into my . . ." I was sure she was about to say *into my act*. ". . . into my spirit work. It will be a fine tool for contacting the Beyond."

Through the years, just when I decided that Mother was a complete fake, she would do something so uncanny that I was sure she had *the gift*. When a letter came from Gertrude Tredwell telling Mother that her sister Julia Tredwell had passed on, as Mother had predicted, Mother sighed. "The gift feels more like a curse sometimes," she commented.

One time I listened at the door and heard a séance in which a woman and her husband sought to speak to a wealthy aunt who had passed on. There was trouble over her will that they wanted cleared up. The aunt failed to show herself, but the woman's deceased first husband came by to reveal that the woman had once been a snake charmer in a carnival act.

My hand flew to my mouth to stifle the rising giggle this delicious and unexpected revelation inspired. There was a drawn-out pause, and I could easily imagine the poor husband gaping at his wife in stunned horror. "But, Maybelle, you told me you'd been living in a convent up until we met!" he cried at last.

I sputtered hard into my hand, clutching my mouth to stifle my laughter, desperate not to reveal that I was there eavesdropping.

Then Maybelle, the wife, broke down and admitted the truth when the spirit — speaking through Mother — began to recall details of their carnival life together. I jumped away from the door as Maybelle abruptly hurried her living husband out before her chatty spirit ex could reveal too much more.

"How did you know all that?" I asked Mother after they had left.

Mother simply stared at me, perplexed by the question. "I didn't know it. The spirit of her late husband told me."

Despite my confusion about the validity of its main industry, in those days Spirit Vale was a child's dream. For one thing, folks swarmed to the town — often as a stop on their trips to see Niagara Falls, only an hour away — seeking consultations with their loved ones who had passed on and advice from spirit guides.

One time, when I was ten, I sat on the porch beside Mother as she rocked in a rocker. "Can you contact our father?" I asked.

She shook her head. "No. I've tried. I believe it means he's moved on. It's what a spirit should do. Only restless spirits with unfinished business stay behind."

"Didn't he want to stay with us?" I wanted to know. This was more a matter of curiosity than heartfelt longing on my part.

Mother looked down at me and smiled a little sadly.

"Your father could move to the Beyond because he knew we'd be fine. You're fine, aren't you, Jane?"

"I suppose so," I replied after a moment's thought.

"You don't sound certain," she noted.

I shrugged. "It might be nice to live in a place where the dead stay dead and don't speak."

"Don't call them *dead*," she corrected me.

"Sorry. I meant those who have passed over."

"Better."

"I'd like to go to school, I think," I mentioned.

"You'd be bored in school. I've taught the five of you to read, write, and do figures better than you'd have learned in school." But it wasn't the learning that appealed to me. It was the sheer ordinariness of the situation. I was slowly developing a burning desire to be *normal*.

"Don't you want to get married again?" I inquired slyly, with a sidelong glance to gauge Mother's reaction to this question.

"No, Jane, I don't," she said. "I'm happy with no husband to give me orders. It's bad enough that as a woman I can't vote. At least not being married gives me some autonomy. I am my own woman, at last."

From June to late August every year, the town boomed with visitors and there were not enough rooms

to accommodate them. Even the huge Spirit Hotel was filled to capacity. Residents of Spirit Vale pitched tents for their children in order to rent their rooms out to the tourists.

Imagine, if you can, children running freely through the summer woods in night shirts, catching fireflies in jars, not chaperoned by any adult at all, while the streets were illuminated in a carnival atmosphere of people walking from home to home, shop to shop, sampling the various mystical services offered.

Tarot and palm readings were given on the porches. In some shops, spirit photos could be purchased whereby a person had his or her picture taken with a "special" camera. More times than not — in fact, almost always — a hazy, white blur of a spirit figure would be captured by the lens as it hovered around the photographic subject.

Princess Running Deer's husband, Wild Elk, owned one of these studios. Mimi and I ran errands for him one summer, which gave us access to the darkroom where he processed his photos. One day Mimi found his collection of spirit negatives, pictures of other people that could be superimposed on a photo to make it appear that spirits hovered in the air around the person being photographed. Some kind of wiping technique had been used to blur the distinctive features of the people in the spirit negatives so that they might be almost anyone.

In the square outside town hall, free readings would be

given by several mediums at once. We would hover at the fringes of the crowd, unabashed by being dressed only in nightclothes, hugging our blinking jars with care, watching the mediums work their trade. "I'm getting a J.R. — either initials or a junior. I can't be sure. Does this make sense to anyone? *Junior* or *J.R.* It's a male."

Invariably someone would respond, something like, "My son was John Robert Junior!"

"He was young when he died!"

"Yes! Yes!"

On occasions when we watched scenes such as that, Mimi would roll her eyes — something I was noticing her do with increasing frequency the older we grew — and make a droll comment, such as, "No kidding. Anyone could have figured that out. Look how young the mother is."

That we were flitting about in the shadows like so many fairy spirits on these nights was not lost to several enterprising mediums. We were often bribed with promises of fresh-made ice cream or fried dough that was served from carts on the street for performing simple services.

One night several of us — Mimi, Amelie, Emma, me, and a number of other local children — were assigned to stand at a window and stare at the black shade covering it. We had been instructed to uncap our jars of fireflies the moment the shade went up. When we did this — releasing a rising cloud of shimmering fireflies in front of the window — shrieks erupted from the room within. Following orders, we then sped off into the woods behind, like so many escaping ghosts.

This was how I grew up.

Chapter 7

By the summer of 1911 we had moved into a larger home, a white Victorian in the center of town with a large front yard separated from the road by a picket fence. Like the others, it had a wide porch and its trim was a riot of elaborate scrollwork. It was a far cry from the small cottage we had started out in.

Mother no longer worked for Aunty Lily at the hotel because her medium business was so good, but Mimi and I had started to work there as helpers, doing whatever Aunty Lily needed. We were at the hotel the night it became the first building in Spirit Vale to be wired for electricity. After months of renovation, gas jets were capped and electric wiring was installed.

"In 1893, Tesla demonstrated wireless electricity at the Chicago World's Fair. Why aren't they using that?" I asked Mimi as we stood with Emma and Amelie, looking at the hideous wires defacing our beautiful town.

"I don't know," Mimi replied. Suddenly, she clasped her hand over her mouth, and her eyes went wide.

She was looking at Amelie, whose hair had become electrified and stood practically on end, thousands of small wisps dancing around her face. It made her laugh.

"Amelie, you look so funny!" Emma cried as she hugged her. Instantly, Emma's hair began to dance around her head, as well.

Mimi and I tried touching them but nothing happened. "Why didn't our hair stand up like that?" I asked Mimi.

She shook her head, mystified. "Those two are on a wavelength all their own" was the only explanation she could offer.

Nearly everyone in town came out to see the spectacular sight of the Spirit Hotel glowing like a giant firefly in the night.

I stood there with the others and wondered at the magic of electricity. If light could travel through wires, perhaps a spirit really could find a way to move along secret paths, as well.

An article I showed Mother one day talked about how Tesla felt that disease could be cured by vibration. He claimed that if one could calculate the correct vibration of a virus, one could match it and smash the vibration in the same way he had caused the buildings to crumble years before. This sparked Mother's interest more than the other articles.

The next thing I knew, VIBRATIONAL READER AND HEALER had been added to her list of talents on our front sign. Her "vibrational readings" became extremely popular.

Her readings were always preceded by the story of how she and her girls had been caught in the freakish earthquake of 1898 and met the great Tesla. She embellished on how the brilliant scientist Tesla had imparted to her the secret of harnessing the earth's vibratory patterns, adding that Tesla had studied under Swami Vivekananda. She had found a picture of the swami in a magazine, framed it, and put it in our parlor beside the scientific manuals I never saw her open. I half expected her to autograph it: *To my good friend, Maude, Love, Swami V.* But she didn't.

The vibrational reading consisted of Mother tracing an outline of her client at about a hand's length from his or her body. From this she would make all sorts of predictions — most of them medical — based on the vibrations she was detecting. I couldn't make any sense of it, but these readings became all the rage, and customers lined up in our front yard, especially during the summer months.

She was, one might say, the queen bee, in a town occupied predominantly by mostly single women. Feminist feeling was strong and it probably added to the lack of male presence. There were a few men who were practicing psychics, most of them elderly. And in terms of young men my own age — I was due to be sixteen on April fifteenth of that year — there were a few, but nobody who interested me romantically.

At eighteen, Mimi was easily the most beautiful female in Spirit Vale, with her dark, luxuriant hair piled high on her head and her dresses cinched to accentuate her tiny waist. I was still the plain brown sparrow next to her glossy raven beauty. I'd taken to wearing my shoulder-length brown hair up in a bun atop my head, as she did, but I could never have matched her dramatic, abundant locks. Just the same, I didn't mind, content to bask in the shadow of her glory.

Men who came in with the summer crowd always looked twice when they saw her walking down the street. She claimed to pay no attention to them, but more than once I'd caught her looking back quickly before averting her eyes modestly. I couldn't blame her. Living in Spirit Vale was like being in a convent. Mimi, I knew, couldn't wait to leave.

I had kept up my interest in Tesla by scouring the newspapers in the dusty, small, dimly lit Spirit Vale library. I learned that after we had seen him in New York, he had moved to Colorado Springs and built a huge radio tower. He claimed that the tower had received signals he thought must be from extraterrestrial beings living on Mars or

Venus. I did not find this hard to believe; in Spirit Vale, people regularly claimed to get signals from locales much farther than outer space. He had invented something called a *Teslascope*, meant to aid in communicating with other planets.

In a yellowing issue dated 1900, I read that he had left Colorado Springs — the article alluded to a suspicious fire in his lab — and that his equipment had all been sold because he was deeply in debt. Then, in an issue from later in 1900, I learned that he had built another huge transmission tower on Long Island, New York, in a town called Shoreham. He had found a wealthy banker and lawyer named James S. Warden to back him this time; the tower was thus called Wardenclyffe Tower. Many other wealthy financiers were funding the project, as well. I cheered silently for my hero, the father figure who had saved me from the shaking ground. He hadn't been down for long.

In 1905 he invented something called the Tesla coil and then the Tesla turbine, but as I continued on in my reading, I saw that by the end of 1905, his tower had been shut down because his backers had lost faith in it. By 1908 the property had been foreclosed by the bank.

All these articles, the favorable and the disappointing, I clipped and kept in a scrapbook — to what purpose, I wasn't sure. I think that secretly I harbored a fantasy of one day meeting the great man again and showing him how I'd followed his career. I also, on a more practical note, was beginning to think I might like to become a journalist someday and thought, perhaps, Tesla could be my first subject.

It was in that summer that I also discovered a tall, dusty stack of a British magazine, the *Strand*. The Spirit Vale library's collection went back to 1901. While perusing it, fascinated by the comical fashions of the decade just passed, I came across the first installment of a detective story called *The Hound of the Baskervilles*.

I couldn't stop staring at the color drawing on the cover of the magazine. The main part of it showed a scene from the story. But in the right-hand corner, in a red, outlined circle, was a close-up drawing of the story's main character, Sherlock Holmes. He was Tesla — I mean, he looked just exactly like him, with sharp features and piercing eyes. I could hardly believe it!

Settling down to read, I soon discovered that the story inside did not disappoint. It featured a detective of supreme logic who noticed everything and worked out his solutions with a cool attention to detail untainted by emotion or superstition. His name was Sherlock Holmes.

I couldn't get enough of Sherlock Holmes. He was erudite and polite, brave, and even witty at times. And so smart! A genius! I knew that the real genius, of course, was the author, Arthur Conan Doyle, but it was not him I mooned over — it was the fictional character.

One hot afternoon in 1911, I was scanning the papers

while Mother was inside trying to contact a spirit for a husband and wife client when a Haitian couple came to Spirit Vale. I was sprawled out, my legs dangling from the end of the front porch swing, when Mimi approached me at a fast clip.

I'd been distracted from my Tesla search by an article about the largest cruise ship ever built. It had been constructed in Ireland by the British White Star Line. It was to be four city blocks long, built for luxury, and remarkably unsinkable. I was so engrossed in imagining it that I didn't notice my older sister until she was right in front of me.

Glancing up, I saw instantly that she was in a state of agitation. "What's wrong?" I asked, laying my newspaper aside.

She plunked down on the front steps. "Oh, it was just so strange. I had to get away," she cried.

We had become so accustomed to the *strange* that for Mimi to find anything this unsettlingly out of the ordinary garnered my instant attention. I came down onto the step beside her. "What's strange?"

She told me that a couple had arrived that morning. They were dark-skinned Africans of about middle age and appeared to be husband and wife. "They were in a motorcar."

A motorcar! Although I knew from the newspapers and magazines that automobiles had been around for a few years, they were just starting to show up in Spirit Vale and it was still a cause for excitement. "Did you see it?" I asked, eager for every detail.

"Yes, but that wasn't the strange part," she replied.

The couple had parked their Model T Ford and were headed for a reading with Madam Anushka, a medium from Russia who was said to have studied magic with Rasputin himself. "They had just gotten out and I stopped, curious to see the motorcar," Mimi said. "The woman looked over her shoulder and noticed me. She suddenly turned around and stared right at me as though I had terrified her. She clutched her husband's arm as though she was about to faint."

In my mind I was ticking off the details in an effort to be like Sherlock Holmes. *Black African couple. They have a motorcar. Locks my sister in a piercing stare.* "What happened next?" I asked.

"She kept staring at me and staring at me as though she knew me," Mimi recalled. "I just rushed away. I can't tell you how she unnerved me."

"Who unnerved you?" Twelve-year-old Blythe came up the path wearing a pretty, white ruffled frock. Her blond ringlets were tied back in a pink satin ribbon. Even at twelve, Blythe believed that appearances counted, and she was determined to become someone of note.

Mimi once again relayed what she had just told me. "Oh," Blythe said, "I know who you mean. She was asking Madam Anushka about you. They came out on Madam

Anushka's porch as I was going by. Madam asked me to come get you."

Mimi's hands crossed her chest in alarmed surprise. "Me?"

Just then Mother appeared on the porch with her clients. "Thank you again, Mrs. Oneida Taylor," the woman gushed, red-eyed from crying. "Your words have been such a comfort."

"Pleased to have helped," Mother said as the husband handed her a stack of cash. As her clients went down the path away from the house, Mother surveyed Blythe's and my serious expressions and Mimi's stricken one. "What is going on?" she asked.

Blythe excitedly told her what had happened. As she spoke, Mother slowly grew so pale that she could have been a spirit herself. "Come inside, Mimi," Mother said firmly, bending to pull my sister up. "There's no need to see this woman. Stay home until she's gone."

"But Madam Anushka said for her to come," Blythe protested. "What should I tell her?"

"Tell her your sister went to Niagara Falls on a sight-seeing trip," Mother replied with an agitated wave of her hand. "Tell her she'll be gone for the rest of the month."

Mimi resisted my mother's pulls on her arm. "Mother, what is going on?" she demanded.

"It's nothing you need to know," Mother insisted. "Nothing at all. Come inside. You, too, Jane. Inside right now and go straight to your room. Do not come out until I say you may. And Blythe, gather Amelie and Emma, then return here as soon as you give the message to Madam Anushka."

"Why are we being punished?" Blythe demanded. "It's not fair."

"I have my reasons."

Mother marched us inside. We were full of questions, but she silenced us by turning away and pointing to the stairs. We obediently ascended, though in minutes we had crawled out our window and were sitting side by side on the back porch roof outside the bedroom we shared.

"I have to know," Mimi said, restless.

"Mother is dead set against it," I reminded her as I wrapped my arms around my knees.

"Why should she be?" Mimi demanded.

I furrowed my brow thoughtfully. "I wonder why this stranger wants to see you so badly."

"Why does Mother *not* want her to see me so badly?"

Emma came out onto the roof with Amelie behind her. "There you are," said Emma, seating herself beside Mimi. At fourteen, the twins were willowy and long limbed with straight, blond brown hair that would never hold a curl no matter how long they wrapped it in rags or wound it around hot curling tongs. Their greatest beauty was their four identical, limpid, violet blue eyes, surrounded by incredibly long, dark lashes.

After some time, Blythe climbed out to join us. "Mother is arguing with Madam Anushka," she reported. "She and her clients are in front now with Mother."

That was it. We had to know what this was about. One by one, the five of us descended the rose trellis that was attached from the ground to the porch roof, fairly well demolishing Mother's yellow roses, and scurried along the side of the house to peer around the corner and try to see what was happening.

"*Eef* it is true, she has *de* right to know," Madam Anushka was insisting in her thick Russian accent.

The black woman was dressed elegantly in a yellow dress with black lace trim. She wore a quite spectacular matching hat above a dark, attractive face. Her husband seemed somewhat older than her. He, too, was dressed well in a summer suit.

The woman spoke with a melodious French accent. "I would only like to see the girl for the briefest moment," she pleaded.

"I have told you, she is gone." Mother held fast to her lie.

Mimi shocked us all by stepping forward from our hiding spot. Mother placed her hand on her cheek and hung her head, beaten.

The moment Mimi stood beside the woman in the yellow dress, I drew in a sharp gasp of surprise. Except for the difference in the color of their skin, Mimi was a younger version of this woman. They shared the same luxuriant mane of black hair; they were very close in height and of a similar slim build; the large, black eyes were exactly the same.

"Marguerite?" the woman asked, calling Mimi by her given name.

Mimi nodded cautiously.

The woman turned to her husband and spoke excitedly in French. Then she turned back to Mimi. "Marguerite, you do not know me because I have not seen you since you were an infant."

"You know me?" Mimi asked.

The woman nodded. "When I saw you on the street, I thought I had seen the ghost of my sister." She laughed in an embarrassed way. "I thought you were so pale because you were dead. But by the time I reached Madam Anushka's, I had done the mathematics and figured it out. I came here to find my sister's spirit, and her spirit led me to you. I am your aunt Yvonne. Your mother was my sister."

Mimi's head snapped around to find Mother. We all looked at her as she stood with tears overbrimming her eyes.

"It's true," she whispered.

Chapter 8

"Here's the truth," Mother said about an hour later. She and Mimi were seated in the front parlor, side by side on the window seat. Both of them had eyes puffed and red from crying.

Emma, Amelie, Blythe, and I hovered outside the room, crushed together behind the narrow right-hand wall of the arched entry, holding our breath for fear of being discovered. We all felt guilty about listening in on their private talk, but we had to know what they were saying. Our entire reality had been rocked. Mimi had a different mother? It just didn't seem possible.

"Your father had a first wife whom he married while doing missionary work on the island of Haiti in the Caribbean. The wife was named Louise, and she was a black Haitian. She died of malaria when you were an infant. Father returned to America with you."

My sisters and I looked at each other, our eyes wide with amazement. Father had a first wife? A black wife?

"You were less than a year old when I married your father. I had known and loved him ever since I was a girl, so the decision was easy for me. You were such a sweet and lovely baby that it was easy to love you as my own, as well," Mother went on. "And you *are* my own daughter in every way but biology."

"Why didn't you tell me?" Mimi asked quietly.

"We thought it would be better if you grew up thinking of me as your mother. Your complexion was so fair that it was possible that you were mine by birth."

"Does anyone else know?"

Mother shook her head. "My parents knew before they passed. Grandmother Taylor never approved of the marriage, so Father didn't tell her about you until after he and I were married and living in Massachusetts."

"He was ashamed of me," Mimi deduced sadly.

"He didn't want her to know that . . ." Here Mother's voice trailed off as though she wasn't sure how to express what she wanted to say.

"That I'm black," Mimi supplied.

"Half black."

From behind, Blythe tugged on my sleeve. "How can she be black when she looks white?" she whispered.

"Shhh," I replied sharply.

I'd tried to be quiet, but both Mother and Mimi looked in our direction. "Show yourselves, ladies," Mother commanded.

Sheepishly, we emerged from our hiding place. Then, seized by an overwhelming rush of love for my older sister,

I dashed forward and threw my arms around her. Emma, Amelie, and Blythe followed my lead.

"Nothing has changed," I gushed. "Nothing at all!"

We clung together there, rocking, a pile of teary-eyed females, consumed with sisterly love for one another, desperate to assure Mimi that it didn't matter if she was a half sister. Our love for her was whole, complete, and unconditional.

After several minutes of this, we loosened our grips and settled into our own seats, apart yet still sitting close together. "It can be our secret," Blythe suggested. "No one need ever know."

An expression of indignation swept across Mimi's face. "Why should it be kept secret?"

"I wouldn't tell anyone I was black if I didn't have to," Blythe replied. "No one would ever know unless you told them."

"It might make your life harder if people knew," I said, thinking only of Mimi's happiness. "You know how things are in this country."

"Then maybe I shouldn't live in this country," Mimi countered, a note of anger creeping into her voice.

"Not live in America!" Emma said with a gasp. "Where else would you live? How would you even get there? How would we see you?" Amelie, too, appeared stricken by the very idea.

"I don't know yet," Mimi admitted.

It was the word *yet* that struck fear in us. When Mimi set her mind to something, she made it happen. She might not have our mother's blood in her veins, but she had spent her life observing the mistress of self-actualizing determination, and she'd learned well.

Mother's eyes glistened as she stood. "Jane's right, Mimi," she said. "Nothing has changed."

Mimi nodded in agreement but I saw something in her eyes — a confusion, a distance — that had changed already.

The rest of that season was a summer of reading. My involvement with Sherlock Holmes grew ever deeper as I finished *The Hound of the Baskervilles*, devouring a year's worth of *Strand* back issues in just weeks. Then I moved on to "The Adventure of the Empty House," "The Adventure of the Norwood Builder," and "The Adventure of the Dancing Men." I gleaned from my reading, and also from talking to other people in town, that the character of Holmes had been killed off back in 1893, but the demand for the sharp-witted detective was so great that he had to be revived. Given my circumstances in Spirit Vale, where the dead routinely returned, this did not strike me as odd.

Emma and Amelie were also engrossed in reading. They would sit side by side and read *The Way of an Eagle*, a new romance by Ethel M. Dell. Blythe was sobbing her way contentedly through *Anne of Avonlea*, the sequel to her favorite book, *Anne of Green Gables*.

For her part, Mother had discovered a treasure trove of back issues in the library, as well. *Borderland* was a quarterly newsletter that had been published in Britain by the famous journalist W. T. Stead. He had made his reputation as a straight-ahead reporter but had come to believe in contact with the spirit world. He was also a psychic who made predictions about the future.

In *Borderland*, W. T. Stead spoke about his spirit guide, a young woman named Julia. Julia had warned Stead to be wary of ice, so he rarely went out in winter, fearing that he would slip and die by hitting his head.

By the time Mother had read every single issue of *Borderland*, she'd decided Stead had misunderstood Julia. The threat, she was sure from reading Julia's words, was that Stead might freeze to death, not that he would slip. She sent him a lengthy letter stating why she felt that way, and was thrown into a state of near-delirious joy when she received a response. From that moment on, Mother adored W. T. Stead as much as she revered the Fox sisters.

After the Haitian couple left, Mimi no longer wanted to work for Aunty Lily at the hotel. "It's too much like being a maid" was her only explanation, but it wasn't hard to tell what was on Mimi's mind from her reading list. She put her head into *Narrative of the Life of Frederick Douglass, An American Slave* and hardly took it out all through July. By the end of August she was onto the brand-new work by Booker T. Washington, *My Larger Education*. Then she went to a collection of essays that had been published in 1903 called *The Souls of Black Folk* by W. E. B. Du Bois. One hot early September afternoon, while we were both reading on the porch, she lifted her head to tell me, "Du Bois says, 'The problem of the twentieth century is the problem of the color-line.'"

"But it's not a problem here," I pointed out. Spirit Vale had been an active abolitionist town just as it was now full of sympathy for the women's movement. Frederick Douglass had even visited seventeen years earlier in 1894 with his second wife, a radical white feminist named Eva Pitts. They both spoke at the town center, and their speeches had been met with the warmest applause. It was a fact of which the town was very proud.

"It's fine that this town isn't racist, but I won't be staying here forever," Mimi stated with calm firmness.

"Well, me, neither," I agreed uncertainly. I was determined to go at the first chance, but where to or how I was going to accomplish this was still a mystery. Plus, I wasn't really ready to wrench myself away from my mother and sisters, or even from the town itself, truth be told. Weird though it was, it was still the only home I knew.

"That reminds me," Mimi said as she took a torn-out square of a newspaper from the back of *The Souls of Black Folk*. "This morning I found this item in a paper one of Mother's clients left on the porch. You weren't around, so I tore it out and stuck it in my book. I can't believe I nearly forgot to give it to you."

I read over the advertisement she handed to me. It was a notice of a journalism contest sponsored by the *Sun*. The winner would receive five hundred dollars and an internship at the *Sun*, complete with board "at the home of a family of impeccable repute."

Mimi and I looked at each other, bursting with possibilities. "But Mother would never let me go, even if I did win," I pointed out.

"I'd go with you," Mimi said.

"You would?"

She nodded vigorously. "Think of what fun we'd have on our own in New York City. And there are all sorts of different people in the city: black, white, people of all shades. I could discover how I want to deal with this new news about my . . . heritage. Not telling anyone just seems so . . . wrong. It's deceitful. Inauthentic."

"What could you do differently in the city?" I asked.

"In a city like New York, I could figure things out. I could tell people who I really am, maybe get to know other black people."

"I suppose," I conceded. I didn't really understand why she couldn't go on just as she was, but I wasn't in her shoes and couldn't feel it as she did.

"You're a great writer, Jane, and you say you want to write for a newspaper someday. You have to enter this contest. I know you could win it," Mimi insisted. "I don't want either of us to stay in this town forever."

Her confidence was contagious but I still wasn't sure.

Did I have the nerve to try for this? Was I really good enough?

"I've been wanting to write an article about Tesla," I admitted to Mimi. "But I'd need to interview him, and I have no idea where to find him. He's not on Houston Street anymore, and I read that he had a Fifth Avenue lab but it also burned down. His project on Long Island is closed."

Mimi's eyes lit with excitement. "I can't believe this! I know where he is. It was meant to be!"

"How do you know?"

Mimi got to her feet. The *Sun* was still on the porch table, held from blowing off by a rock. She retrieved it and paged through until she found the article she sought in the society page. She handed it to me with a triumphant smile.

The photo showed Tesla inside eating alone at a round table in a gorgeous dining room complete with high windows and enormous, lavish bouquets of shining porcelain flowers. The mention of Tesla in the gossipy article was very short, and I scanned it quickly.

September, 1911. Scientist and inventor Nikola Tesla was spotted looking dapper but dining solo at the world's tallest hotel, the swanky Waldorf-Astoria on 34th Street in New York City today. The creator of the Tesla coil and famed rival of Thomas Edison has lived at the Waldorf-Astoria for some years now. It's rumored that despite several recent crushing financial setbacks, the eccentric genius is able to afford such posh digs due to his long-standing friendship with his occasional financial backer, the hotel's co-owner and the world's richest man, John Jacob Astor. The two men met back in 1893 at the Chicago World's Fair and have been fast friends ever since.

I gazed at Mimi blankly. What good was this information when he was hundreds of miles away? "I couldn't even get a letter to him in time," I pointed out.

"This town is so backward we don't even have phone service yet," she said.

"Even if we called him at the hotel from Buffalo, what would we say?"

"You're right — I'm sure he would never remember us. That's why we have to go there to talk to him as he leaves the hotel or has a meal in the dining room," she said, as if it should have been obvious.

"Go there?" Had she lost her mind?

She hooked her arm through mine conspiratorially. "We have to leave immediately. I have some money saved from working at the Spirit. Do you have any?"

"Yes, but Mother will never let us go off to New York City on our own," I reminded her.

"I know. That's why we're not going to tell her."

Chapter 9

Seventeen hours later, Mimi and I were in the palatial lobby of the Waldorf-Astoria hotel in New York City.

We had taken a ride to Buffalo with Aunty Lily in her new automobile, a crank model of which she was very proud. Mimi misled her to think we were going with Mother's blessing. Mother was in the midst of another heartfelt letter to W. T. Stead and paid no notice of anything else when she was involved in this correspondence. We wrote her a hasty note that we left on the front porch table, assuring her we'd be fine.

We'd slept for the whole trip down, so we weren't feeling too tired when we arrived. Even if we had stayed awake the entire time, we were so high-strung with excitement we'd have barely noticed the fatigue.

We encamped on two of the velvet-upholstered chairs in the Waldorf-Astoria's lobby. We had decided that Tesla had to come down at some point to eat; we would connect with him when he did.

I didn't exactly mind waiting there, fascinated as I

was by this grand hotel. The lobby couches and square chairs were exquisitely rich and vibrant in color, their walnut-wood arms and backs gleaming with high polish set off by their gold details. The elaborate wooden moldings on the ceiling were illuminated by the glowing white globes of chandeliers set in a long row. A mixture of cinnamon and rose petal fragrances infused every inch of the lobby.

An hour passed quickly as Mimi and I goggled at the parade of high-fashion guests who passed by, dressed in the latest styles. Not far off, the desk manager started stealing suspicious glances in our direction. My stomach growled. We'd eaten cheese sandwiches on the train, but it was getting close to lunchtime. "I don't think they'd let us eat here, but maybe I could sneak a snack in," Mimi proposed. "You watch for Tesla. I'll go see what I can find."

I was once again observing the dazzlingly rich saunter through and marking each face to make sure Tesla didn't slip past unnoticed when a young man rushed by. I guessed him to be in his late teens, maybe early twenties. He caught my attention because . . . well, to be absolutely honest, it was because he was so good-looking. He had short, sort of tousled, light brown hair and a slim, athletic build. His pants were gray and his summer jacket was light blue. Although he was neat, his attire did not bespeak the kind of wealth that typified the place.

He hurried to the front desk, and his words put me on full alert. "Could you tell Mr. Tesla that Thad is on his way up?" he requested.

Instantly, I was on my feet, frantically wondering what Sherlock Holmes would do at such a moment as this.

Follow him! Of course.

It was difficult to hang back inconspicuously, as Holmes would have done, since Thad was heading for one of the elevators. If I let him get on and go up without me, I'd have conducted the briefest tail in the history of all detective work. So I picked up my pace and scooted into the car alongside him, just as the white-gloved elevator operator closed the gated door.

"Floor?" the operator inquired, looking first to me.

My mind raced. I had no idea what to reply. Then it came to me. "Top floor, please," I said, trying to sound confident. If I went all the way to the top, I could claim to have changed my mind and jump off when Thad got out.

The operator nodded and looked to Thad. "Mr. Tesla's room?" he inquired.

"Yes, thank you, Charles," Thad replied.

As we began to move, I turned my attention to Thad. I gazed up at a set of vivid blue eyes, beneath a forehead that bore a faded white scar, which I felt gave just the right note of character to a face that might have been too blandly handsome otherwise.

He nodded and smiled slightly. "Hello."

"Hello," I said, relieved that he had spoken first since it wouldn't have been seemly for me to have started speaking to him.

A moment of silence passed between us during which I felt consumed with panic and had not a clue as to what to do next. *Do what Holmes would do; observe something,* I thought. "That looks heavy. What's in your package?" I asked, noticing that he clutched to his chest a parcel wrapped in brown paper.

He laughed lightly. "If I told you, you wouldn't believe me."

"Let me guess," I ventured. "Will it light all of Manhattan?"

His smile faded into a look of startled suspicion. "No."

"Will it contact alien life on other planets?"

Thad tightened his grip on the parcel, as though fearing I might snatch it away from him. His eyes darted nervously to the lights on the ascending elevator, no doubt checking to see how long it would be until he could escape me. "No," he replied.

"Is it an earthquake machine?" I persisted.

"Charles, forgive me, but I think I'll get out here on the fifth floor," Thad said abruptly.

"As you wish," Charles complied.

The elevator doors slid open and Thad stepped out quickly.

"I've changed my mind, too," I said as the doors closed once more. "Please let me out on the next floor."

Charles hid whatever annoyance he must have felt beneath a mask of polite professionalism. "Very well."

On the sixth floor I hurried out, my eyes darting frantically around the quiet, elegant hallway in search of stairs to take me back down to the fifth floor. If I was fast enough, I could continue to follow Thad, though now that he was onto me, I would have to hang back even more than before. This wouldn't be easy but I was determined to find Tesla.

At the end of the hallway was a stairway and I ran to it. I was only a few steps down when I came face-to-face with Thad, who was running up.

"Who are you, anyway?" he asked.

"Jane Oneida Taylor."

"Mind telling me how you know so much about my parcel?"

Talking fast, I told him everything, starting with that day back in 1898 when we were caught in the Tesla-induced quake and continuing with how I'd avidly followed Tesla's career. I finished up by telling him about the *Sun* contest. "And what better person to write about than someone I've been researching all my life — so if I could only meet him and get a quick interview . . . Do you think you could get me in to see him?"

I don't think Sherlock Holmes would have been impressed with my approach, so completely lacking in subtlety or cleverness. Just the same, Thad was much more relaxed once he heard my story. "An aspiring journalist, huh?" he said, seeming impressed as he leaned against the banister and looked me over. "You sure picked a great guy to write about. Tesla's the smartest guy alive, even brainier than that Einstein, if you ask me."

"Can you get me in to see him?" I pressed.

"Maybe," he said. "Come back here in an hour. I'll meet you."

"Can't you just tell me what room he's in?" I asked.

He shook his head, still studying me as though he hadn't yet decided if I could be trusted. "No. If he says it's all right, I'll come back and take you to him."

He continued on up the steps, and I went with him. He stopped at the top step and faced me. "You can't keep following me," he said.

"Is it wonderful being his assistant?" I asked.

He shrugged. "He's a weird guy. Brilliant. But sort of nuts."

"In what ways?" I asked, a little disturbed at this.

He grinned mischievously. "You'll find out."

He turned to leave, but I found it hard to let him go. "You never told me what's in the parcel," I reminded him.

He glanced at it, then back at me. "You're right. I didn't."

In exactly one hour, Mimi and I were standing by the stairs on the sixth floor waiting for Thad.

"He's not coming," I fretted.

"He'll be here," Mimi insisted optimistically, but I noticed she was twirling a curl at her neck that had fallen from her thick, upswept hair.

Just when I was despairing of Thad's ever arriving, the elevator door opened and he stepped out. He spied us and, with a quick wave of acknowledgment, headed our way.

"He's handsome, isn't he?" I quickly whispered to Mimi.

With a sly smile she pinched my waist. "Jane's in love."

I pinched her back. "No!"

In the next moment Thad was standing in front of us. I introduced Mimi and then asked the burning question: "Will he see us?"

"Yes. I'll bring you to him but you can't say a word until his meeting is over."

At the same time, Mimi and I both put our index fingers over our lips in a gesture of assured silence.

"Come on," Thad said, waving for us to follow him. We went into the elevator and Thad directed the operator — no longer Charles — to take us to the private floor. Mimi and I exchanged darting, thrilled glances — the *private* floor!

We got out at the very top of the Waldorf-Astoria. There were many fewer doors — only about four — than in the hallways of the lower floors, and the ceiling was easily three times the height. I clutched Mimi's wrist as we followed Thad down to the farthest of the doors. "Is this where Tesla lives?" I whispered to Thad.

Thad shook his head. "It's Astor's guest suite. He uses it for meetings," he answered quietly.

My heart bounced with excitement the moment I spied Tesla sitting at the end of a long dining room table in the spectacularly lavish suite. The two-story-tall windows beside the table framed Tesla in a field of blue sky that made him seem to be sitting in some heavenly realm. After so many years of seeing him frozen in newspaper photos, it hardly seemed possible that he was a real, moving, living person. But there he was.

Tesla was deep in quiet conversation with an elegantly dressed, middle-aged man in a suit. The man's hair and beard were close-cropped. Frameless pince-nez glasses were propped on his straight nose, attached with a black silk cord. "That's George Boldt," Thad whispered to us. "He runs this place for the Astors."

We couldn't hear their low-pitched conversation, but I deduced it wasn't going well from all the head shaking going on. After another terse exchange, Tesla rose abruptly and headed straight for us.

My mind went blank. This was the moment I'd waited so many years for . . . and I hadn't prepared anything to say! What had I been thinking — or *not* thinking?

I stood there smiling eagerly like an empty-headed fool, but Tesla did not seem to even notice Mimi or me. Instead, he spoke only to Thad. "I am having one of my flashes," he stated in a dull, lifeless voice, not at all the animated man I remembered from so long ago. With that, he returned to the suite.

"What was he talking about?" Mimi asked Thad.

"He gets these flashes, where everything kind of overloads. He feels like he hears smells and sees sounds," Thad explained, keeping one eye on Tesla as he disappeared into one of the bedrooms. "This day has probably been very stressful for him. Astor was supposed to be here to talk to him, but he hasn't shown up yet."

"Will he be all right?" I asked.

Thad nodded. "He'll lie down in one of the guest rooms until the flashes pass. When they're over, most likely he'll have a brilliant idea."

"How long does that usually take?" I asked.

"As long as it takes," Thad said with a shrug.

"Hours, days, months?" I pressed him for some kind of parameter. "Should we return home and come back in two years?"

"He's usually knocked out for two to four hours," Thad estimated, which was a bit more helpful.

Someone rapped on the door and Thad opened it. A somewhat heavyset man in his late thirties with black, slicked-back hair entered. Behind him was a much younger woman, with curly brown hair swept up onto her head. She was slim and beautiful; her dress was a floral crepe de chine adorned with a black lace collar that climbed up her neck all the way to her face. She wore rouge and red lipstick. I guessed she was about twenty-five.

The man strode past us and went directly to Mr. Boldt, who still sat at the table.

"Mr. Guggenheim!" Boldt greeted him in a heavy German accent, surprised to see him.

Guggenheim! It had to be Benjamin Guggenheim, one of the richest men in New York, if not the world. I had seen his picture in many papers. And now here he was, in the same room as me! I was glad Mimi was there, because there was no way Amelie, Emma, or Blythe would have believed it without a witness.

"What's this? I arrive to find my suite is in use," Mr. Guggenheim said. "Aren't I Jack's favorite guest?"

"We weren't expecting you," Mr. Boldt explained.

"Does that make a difference? Jack said I could always count on having this room."

"By Jack does he mean John Jacob Astor?" I whispered to Thad.

"John Jacob Astor *the Fourth*," Thad replied with a nod. "He owns the place."

"I know," I whispered, remembering the newspaper article I'd read.

"Why is this person so important that he got my suite?" Benjamin Guggenheim demanded.

"Mr. Tesla had some business to discuss with Mr. Astor, and I thought this suite was available. Regrettably, Colonel Astor has been delayed in Rhode Island."

Guggenheim snickered as if he knew some secret about John Jacob Astor that was too embarrassing to mention. "I'll bet he's been delayed. Say no more. Tell this Tesla that Benjamin Guggenheim has arrived and he has to clear out!"

"I'm afraid Mr. Tesla is presently feeling ill and lying down inside. He has his own apartment in the hotel but I'm reluctant to disturb him in his current state."

"Oh, I know who you mean now! Weird Tesla. That nutty inventor pal of Jack's!" Mr. Guggenheim threw an unhappy glance toward the closed bedroom door. For a moment, I thought he would storm in and pull Tesla out.

I bristled, disliking Guggenheim intensely. How dare he call Tesla names!

"May I offer you Colonel Astor's suite down the hall? He is apparently remaining in Newport this night and will not be using it," Mr. Boldt suggested in a conciliatory tone.

"I wish Jack wouldn't insist on being called *Colonel* Astor," Mr. Guggenheim cried. "It's so ridiculous. He donated his yacht and bought himself a brigade of volunteers just so he could have that ludicrous title! It's absurd."

"Colonel Astor served his country with distinction during the Spanish-American War," Mr. Boldt insisted loyally. "Shall I prepare his suite for you?"

"Very well, I suppose," Mr. Guggenheim agreed grudgingly. "I think Jack's suite is bigger than this one, anyway."

"Somewhat larger, yes," Mr. Boldt agreed.

When I turned to check on what Mimi was making of all this, I discovered she'd stepped out into the hall with the young woman who'd come in with Mr. Guggenheim. She was showing Mimi the lacework on the underslip of her dress. They were laughing and appeared to be getting on quite well — amazingly well, I thought, for two people who'd only just met. When they noticed me watching, they came back into the room.

"Benjamin, *mon chéri*," the young woman said to Mr. Guggenheim in a charming French accent when he returned to the front door, "can we invite these lovely people to our suite to have a bite to eat? The trip here has been *très* dull and I would so love to be *amusée*."

"I'm tired and I want to unpack, Ninette," he grumbled.

Ninette pouted prettily. "You sound like an old man," she complained.

Her barb must have hit its mark because Benjamin Guggenheim relented and invited Mimi, Thad, and me to the suite of John Jacob Astor the Fourth.

I caught Mimi's eye and opened my mouth just enough to express my total disbelief. She stifled a grin and nodded. She felt the same as I did:

Could this really be happening?!

Chapter 10

If possible, John Jacob Astor's private suite had even more floor-to-ceiling windows than the one we had just left — and more crown moldings, and a larger fireplace, and an even more spectacular view of the city. One of the windows was actually a door that opened out onto a terrace of greenery overlooking the city. The furniture was fit for royalty.

A bellhop arrived with an overloaded luggage cart. A strikingly handsome, dark haired man in his early twenties entered the suite behind him. He handed the bellhop a tip and instructed him to bring the suitcases to the master bedroom.

"*Bonjour*, Mr. Giglio," Ninette greeted him.

"*Bonjour*, Mrs. Aubart," he responded with a quick, polite bow.

Mimi was trying not to stare, but I caught her looking at him. I could understand why. He reminded me of an actor one might see on stage playing a prince or a knight, broad shouldered and tall.

He departed with the bellhop, but not before noticing Mimi. Their eyes met, and then Mimi looked away
shyly.

"You like him, eh?" Ninette whispered to Mimi mischievously when he was gone.

"He's very . . . handsome," Mimi whispered. "Who
is he?"

"Victor Giglio, Benjamin's new valet. Come, Mimi. I
will show you the dress I was talking about," Ninette said
as she pulled Mimi with her deeper into the suite. "It is the
latest from Paris. You are going to adore it!"

Then, as though remembering her manners, she hurried back to Thad and me, scooping two menus from a side
table and handing them to us. "Order what you would like
for lunch. I will have the lobster. You should, too. Order
everything on the menu!"

"Yes, order us a fine lunch," Mr. Guggenheim agreed.
"If you'll excuse me, I must go call my broker."

When he disappeared into an office off the main living room, Thad and I were left alone to look at each other
and down at the hotel telephone on the table. I burst into
incredulous laughter at the sheer fun of it all. "Well, I never
expected this," I remarked.

"Me, neither," he agreed, unsmiling. "It's all so . . .
obnoxious."

"Obnoxious? I thought it was kind of . . . marvelous.
We've stumbled into the life of luxury."

"Yeah, for us it's a lark. But don't you think the way these people live is ridiculous?"

Ridiculous? I didn't see anything ridiculous about it. I thought it was all too good to be true.

Thad gestured around the room. "Why do they deserve all this when the rest of us have to struggle? Are they better than us?"

I'd never thought about it before. "Luckier, maybe?" I ventured.

"You bet they're luckier. They're lucky their fathers were born before they were. John Jacob Astor and William Waldorf, his cousin who also owns this place, inherited their money. They didn't work for it."

"They run this hotel," I pointed out.

"They hire guys like Boldt to run it for them."

"What about a man like Thomas Edison who's earned his fortune from his brains?"

Thad waved me off dismissively. "Don't talk to me about Edison. He's a greedy industrialist like the rest of them. If anything, amassing wealth through your own ruthlessness and treachery is even worse than inheriting it."

I recalled how Tesla felt Edison had wronged him. "Tesla's not like that, though," I said.

"And look what it's gotten him. He's constantly on the brink of bankruptcy because he's not out to build a personal fortune. He wants his inventions to serve the people. He wants to pull energy down from the air and light the world for free. Do you think guys like Edison and his backers will ever let that happen? Not when they're making fortunes charging people for electricity!"

"You sound so bitter," I remarked.

"I'm sorry," Thad said. "It's not directed at you. I can tell that *you're* not wealthy."

I was suddenly painfully aware of the plainness of my blue cotton dress and the scuff marks on my well-worn boots. But Thad seemed to think they were superior to the lavishness surrounding us, so I didn't feel as bad as I might have otherwise.

"It's just that I see what Tesla's up against every step of the way. These rich guys won't let him succeed in his work," Thad went on. "The only reason he gets anywhere at all is because he finds wealthy backers who hope that Tesla is smarter than the other guys — which he is, by miles — and that he'll invent something that makes them a fortune. But then Tesla finds ways to produce his inventions inexpensively and they decide there's not enough profit in it, so they withdraw their funding. Even worse — they trip him up, mess up his work, set fire to his labs."

"Do you really believe that's true?"

"I know it's true!" he exploded. "I've seen inventions work perfectly; then he goes to demonstrate to a crowd and it's all a bust!"

"How do they get away with it?" I asked.

"The police don't bother them because they're rich. Edison or his backers hire thugs who disappear into the back alleys they crawled out of. These rich guys have no ethics. They just love money and don't care that Tesla's the greatest genius of our time."

"But, before, you said he was a nut."

Thad nodded. "He's also a nut . . . in some ways."

"What ways?"

"He's crazy about germs, always cleaning his silverware, even in restaurants, yet he loves pigeons, which are just flying rats, if you ask me. He loathes women's jewelry, especially pearl earrings. Don't wear any pearls around him or he won't talk to you."

"I don't have any."

"Good. You don't need them."

I wondered what that meant — *You don't need them.* Was it a compliment toward me . . . or just an insult to women who bothered with pearls?

"What should I wear, then?" I asked.

"What you have on," he replied. "You look perfect just the way you are."

I felt heat at my temples and turned away. The last thing I wanted was for him to see me blush like some silly schoolgirl. Perfect? Did he really think so?

When Mimi and Ninette returned to the living room, Mimi had put on a gorgeous deep purple dress with a hobble skirt. "How do you like it?" she asked me, turning with tiny steps required by the ankle-length, narrow skirt. "Ninette says everyone in Paris is wearing this."

"That skirt would drive me insane," I remarked.

Thad chuckled approvingly.

"Why?" Mimi asked.

"You're completely hobbled by it."

"What do you mean?" Mimi asked.

"It cripples you," I offered. "It's no accident that they call it a *hobble* skirt. Hobbled means crippled."

"I see you have not the love of fashion that Mimi and I share," Ninette said lightly, as if my disapproval was unimportant. She draped her arm around Mimi's shoulders as though they were old friends. A pang of possessive jealousy welled up in me. How dare she presume this kind of familiarity with *my* sister?

"Are the lobsters here yet?" Ninette asked.

"We haven't ordered," I admitted. "And I've never used a telephone before, so I'm not really sure how to do it."

"Never used a telephone!" Ninette cried incredulously. "How quaint! Here, I will show you."

She lifted the conelike receiver off its black metal pedestal, but before she could speak into it, Thad raised his hand to stop her. "Come to think of it, we're not really hungry for this rich hotel food," he said. "Jane and I are going to have lunch in a good little restaurant I know of in Chinatown."

I glanced at him in excited surprise. This was news to me.

"Would you ladies care to join us?" he offered halfheartedly.

"No. I have my heart set on the lovely lobsters," Ninette declined.

"Me, neither. I'll stay here with Ninette," Mimi said.

Did she know what she was doing when she made this choice?

Was she doing it for me . . . or for herself?

Chapter 11

That afternoon I had my first ride on a train, which ran up- and downtown on an elevated track. The train took us to a part of the city known as Chinatown because the vast majority of its citizens were from China.

Before arriving at the restaurant, Thad and I got off at Fourteenth Street at a place called Union Square. "Come on," Thad said. "There's something here I want to show you."

"What is it?" I asked.

"You'll see. You'll like it."

I hurried behind him down the metal stairs to an open area dominated by a statue of George Washington on horseback. In front of it, a band of five scruffy boys, one with a homemade drum, another with an actual harp, played an off-beat song while the others danced and sang for the coins passersby threw in their rusted pot. I tossed in a few pennies of my own, not because their music was good but because they were so adorable.

It wasn't easy to keep up with Thad's long strides as we crossed the bustling square, but we quickly came to a sort of theater on the side. A large sign over an arched door-way declared: AUTOMATIC ONE CENT VAUDEVILLE. "What is this?" I asked him.

"It's a nickelodeon, which is a kind of kinetoscope."

"A what?"

"They show short films," he explained. "This is the biggest one in the city."

My hands flew to my mouth with excitement. I'd read about these in the papers. They were like films, only shorter and less expensive.

"Come on," he said, and I followed him in. The place was gigantic, with row upon row of shoulder-high machines lined up along the walls and forming center aisles. Each one of them displayed a placard that told the name of the brief film it played.

"I've never even seen a movie before," I told him excitedly. This was true; although I read all about the movie actors in them and devoured the reviews, I had never actually seen a movie or a nickelodeon.

"Well, now's your chance," he said with a smile. "Tesla believes that someday every home will have its own private nickelodeon."

I hurried off toward a bank of nickelodeon machines on the right but Thad grasped my shoulder firmly. "Not those," he said. "They're not suitable for a young lady."

A second glance made me realize that they were all being used by young men dressed in boater hats with their suit jackets slung over their shoulders. "Oh, I see," I said, trying to sound worldly wise and knowing.

"There are some good ones over here," he said, directing me to the wall on my left. "This is my favorite," he told me as he dropped a penny in a machine marked: BOATING DISASTER. "Take a look."

A funny little man was taking his rather large girlfriend for a canoe ride on a lake. He had trouble with the oars, turning the canoe in circles at first. Then his girlfriend readjusted her seat and the canoe tilted so that the little man was lifted up along with the canoe's bow. He frantically rowed in the air. Finally, the two of them slid into the lake, looking none too happy.

The film lasted no more than three minutes. "Funny, huh?" Thad said, wanting my reaction.

"It is funny, but I felt sorry for them," I replied, smiling despite my sympathy for the characters.

"Don't. They're only actors," Thad said. "Come on. I'll show you some of my other favorites."

We spent the next half hour working our way down the line of nickelodeon machines, watching film after film. It was such fun!

We came to a film called *Dance of the Ghosts*. Five women in white, hooded, flowing robes did a sort of ballet around a glowing ball in a darkened room.

"Isn't that one crazy?" Thad checked enthusiastically.

"Crazy," I agreed. I didn't dare tell him how much it reminded me of home.

Eventually we got back on the train and took it to Canal Street. It was the most amazing place! Every sign was in Chinese. Vendors sold all manner of exotic clothing, toys, and even baby turtles out on the street. We browsed in small shops that sold exotic carved knickknacks and porcelain curios. We passed a Chinese apothecary with bizarre items such as dried wings and powdered rhino horn displayed in the window. With a little imagination, I could easily believe I was really in China.

We reached an electric neon sign that flashed the name Wo-Hop, and Thad took us down a flight of stairs to a belowground restaurant of plain chairs and tables set with white dishes on white paper tablecloths. Nearly everyone there was Chinese, many more men than women, dressed in traditional Chinese garb.

A small man in a white shirt and black pants ran out to greet Thad. He clearly knew him and was delighted at his arrival.

"Jane, I'd like you to meet Mr. Wang, a friend of my family's. Mr. Wang, meet Jane Oneida Taylor. She's a journalist writing about Tesla."

Mr. Wang shook my hand enthusiastically. "Mr. Tesla a very great man. Very big brain. I am pleased to meet you."

Once we were seated, Thad ordered for us both, speaking Chinese to the waiter. "I hope you don't mind," he said to me when he'd finished. "I think you'll like what I ordered. I never met anyone who didn't."

"Where did you learn to speak Chinese?" I asked. Thad, it seemed, was full of secrets and surprises.

"I was born in China. My parents were missionaries."

"My father was a missionary, too."

While we waited for our food, we had a lively conversation. I told him that Father had passed and all about our life in Spirit Vale, even admitting that the *Dance of the Ghosts* nickelodeon made me think of home. In the hours since we'd first met, I'd grown increasingly at ease with him. "Does it sound insane?" I asked.

"It sounds like a lot of fun," he replied. "What a great place to grow up."

"It's not meant to be fun," I said. "They take it very seriously. Being a scientist, you must think it's a lot of rubbish."

He shrugged. "Who knows? I believe in life after death but I don't know how long a soul hangs around before it moves on."

Thad told me that he'd lived in China until the age of ten and then he'd returned with his parents. At seventeen his parents had wanted him to go to seminary college to become a minister, but he'd had other ideas.

Thad was interested in science even though his parents

were adamant that science was the enemy of religion. Thad thought that was absurd. "They're so behind the times," he said. "They don't realize that we're on the brink of a new, modern age. Everything will soon change. Everything!" He and his parents had fallen out bitterly over this. And so he'd come to New York to live on his own.

"The greatest thing that happened to me was being hired as Tesla's assistant," he told me. "In the last three years I've learned more about science than I would have in Harvard and Yale put together."

I realized that made him twenty. I decided to make no mention of my own age. There were only four years' difference between us — not really so much. We were getting on so well and I didn't want anything to spoil it.

"Do you want to be an inventor like Tesla?" I asked.

"I could never be like him. I'm no genius. But I *have* invented a few things."

"What?" I asked eagerly.

He pushed the white plates to the side and took out a pencil. He began to draw an airplane different in every way from the propeller planes I'd seen.

"It's a glider," he told me. "Tesla is working on something he calls a flivver plane, which is a cross between a gyroscope and a plane, but it needs fuel. This is a glider that would ride the air currents like a hawk. I believe that we can't be so reliant on fossil fuels. It's going to run out someday."

Tearing off a piece of paper tablecloth, he began to fold it in intricate ways. "I learned origami in China," he said with a grin as he folded. When he was done, he got up and opened a high window. "Have to let some air currents in here," he explained. Then he shot his paper plane into the room.

Everyone stopped eating and gasped as it sailed over their heads. Every second, I thought it would crash into someone's food, but it kept going. I couldn't believe it.

Finally, the little paper plane glided in for a landing on the windowsill. The entire restaurant erupted in applause, and so did I. "That's wonderful. How can you say you're not a genius?" I praised him sincerely.

"I'm not," he said, retrieving his plane. "But I would like to take what I'm learning from Tesla about magnetic resonances and apply it to aeronautical design. Planes are going to be huge."

"Do you think so?" I asked. "They seem so clumsy right now."

"They won't stay that way for long," he said. "There are guys like me everywhere who are working on sleeker, better designs. You'll see, Jane. It's the future."

Our meals came, interrupting us. They were a sort of egg pancake with shrimp, onions, and vegetables cooked in and topped with gravy. "Shrimp Egg Fu Young," he told me. "What do you think?"

"I'm sure this is better than anything Mimi and Ninette are having back at the hotel," I said. "I still can't believe I met Benjamin Guggenheim."

"All those rich backers are like that Guggenheim guy," he said as he ate with chopsticks. "They're so full of their own importance. And it's absurd that he has that young girlfriend, Ninette Aubart. She's divorced or something. People gossip about them. She's not his wife. She's his side girlfriend. He's forty-six and she's about twenty-four or -five."

"I suppose it's the trend with wealthy men," I suggested. "I read that John Jacob Astor is marrying a woman twenty years younger than he is next month."

"Madeleine Force. Yeah. She's twenty! He's getting married next month *if* they can find a minister to marry them. Nobody will do it."

"Because of their age difference?" I asked.

"*And* he's divorced," Thad said, nodding. "Their problem might help Tesla, though. He's trying to get in to see Astor before he sails off on his honeymoon. Ever since the last World's Fair, they've been great friends. They have a lot in common because Astor is a sort of amateur scientist himself. He's had articles published and even holds a patent on a moving sidewalk he invented. Astor was one of Tesla's backers on the Niagara Falls project."

"If they're such good friends, why is Tesla having so much trouble communicating with Astor?" I asked.

"It's this Madeleine Force romance. Astor and Madeleine are lying low in his mansion in Rhode Island to avoid the press. The papers are having a field day with the scandal."

I put down my fork and attempted to use the chopsticks by my plate. Studying Thad, I gave it my best attempt. I didn't have much luck.

He chuckled good-naturedly and took them from my hand. "Like this," he instructed, arranging my fingers in the proper position. With his hand on mine, he worked the sticks, scooping up the food and lifting it to my lips.

To tell the truth, I was so pleasantly unnerved that I forgot to open my mouth!

"Oh! Sorry!" I said, laughing nervously when I realized the food was hovering in front of me.

"Now you try," he advised.

My second attempt went more smoothly.

"I guess the timing is bad for Tesla," I remarked as soon as I was eating well enough with the sticks.

"There are rumors that Astor is going to run off and get married," he replied. "If Astor disappears on a prolonged honeymoon, it will be a disaster for Tesla. He won't be able to catch up with Astor to persuade him to finance his next idea."

"What is his next idea?" I asked, finally spearing a piece of egg pancake with the end of my chopstick and getting it to my lips.

Thad shook his head sadly. "I can't tell you that."

"I won't tell anyone," I promised.

"Oh, no?" He smiled. "Aren't you writing a newspaper article?"

"I guess so." I smiled back.

Electricity.

Thad held it for a moment, just the two of us looking at each other, the air charged between us. Then, just before it went on a beat too long, he said, "When we go back, Tesla will probably be awake. I'll ask if he'll talk to you and see what he says. Then, if he wants to tell you, it will be up to him."

Chapter 12

My long walk from Thirty-fourth Street to Central Park went quickly because I was so fascinated by the variety of people passing me. No doubt I was conspicuously the gaping rube, drinking in every face that passed. New York City seemed to me like a reflection of the entire world. I loved its excitement.

Thad had instructed me to meet Tesla at the entrance to the park at Columbus Circle. I was to walk with Tesla while he fed the pigeons in the park, a ritual he carried out every day, rain or shine.

As I stood by the grand entrance to the park with my Tesla scrapbook tucked under my arm, my mind wandered . . . and I have to admit that it was Thad whom it veered toward. Our lunch together had been the first time I'd sat alone with a fellow and, honestly, I'd found it exciting. I liked everything about him: his sympathy for the common person; his interest in science; his independence in striking out for New York City on his own. And I couldn't get those vivid blue eyes out of my mind. Or that white scar on his forehead, that handsome imperfection.

I spied Tesla hurrying across the traffic circle carrying a brown paper bag. With a nervously pounding heart, I hurried toward him as he came near. "Sir, I'm Jane Oneida Taylor. You agreed to let me interview you?"

He stopped and scrutinized me. "Is Oneida really your middle name?" he asked.

"My mother adopted it in honor of the native people who lived near us," I explained.

"You are from northwestern New York, then," he surmised.

"Not far from Niagara Falls. I know you're familiar with that," I said.

This brought a fond smile to him. "Indeed, I am. You have done your homework."

"Yes," I replied. I had been doing it for the last twelve years. "I know everything that has been printed in the newspapers, at least." I lifted my scrapbook to show him. "It's all in here."

He took it from me and perused it briefly. "Then, no doubt, you know many things that are not true," he commented. "Newspapers are not renowned for their accuracy."

"That's why I wanted to talk to you."

"Come. We will walk while I feed the pigeons." He nodded toward his paper bag. "This is my own blend of birdseed. A pet store makes it to my specifications. It has all the nutrients a pigeon needs. Sometimes I feed them at Bryant Park behind the New York Public Library and other times here in Central Park."

We entered the park, ambling along the winding paths as I asked him questions and furiously scribbled his replies in the blank pages of my scrapbook. I learned that he'd been born in Austria-Hungary in 1856. I quickly calculated that it meant he'd been forty-two when I had first met him and was fifty-four now. He spoke Serbo-Croatian, Czech, French, Hungarian, Italian, and Latin, as well as English. He loved animals, especially cats and pigeons, and was a vegetarian.

He explained to me why alternating electrical current was superior to the direct current advocated by Edison. "This is something the public has come to agree with me about," he said with a hint of pride, "even though Edison did his best to convince them otherwise. Even to this day, Edison has not forgiven me for this defeat. It eats at his arrogant soul. All he cares about is making a profit."

"Don't you want to make money?" I asked.

By then we had stopped at a boulder along a path. At the first sight of their faithful benefactor, the pigeons immediately fluttered to Tesla's feet, and he began scattering seed for them. As he swung his arm in a smooth semicircle, an expression of such far-off absorption crossed his face that I could not tell if he was considering my question, was ignoring me, or had forgotten about my presence altogether.

Finally, after several minutes, he spoke. "Jiva is Shiva," he said.

"Excuse me?"

"It means each person is divinity itself," he explained without taking his gaze away from the pigeons. "I met Swami Vivekananda when I was demonstrating at the Chicago World's Fair back in 1893. Between demonstrations of my rotating egg, which turned by magnetism, I went to the pavilion where the swami was speaking. It was his belief that only tireless work for the benefit of others is the true mark of the enlightened person. No one can truly be free until all of us are."

I thought of the framed photo of the swami that sat in our front parlor, his dark, piercing eyes staring out at us. "And what the swami said influenced you?" I surmised.

"Profoundly," he replied earnestly. "It was at the fair I also first demonstrated wireless lighting. As the globes lit and my experiment was a success, I knew that wireless technology was the wave of the future and that energy from space could give all nations the advantages of free power."

"Give?" I questioned.

"I could be a rich man, Jane. Right now, just like the rest of them. George Westinghouse, the owner of General Electric, wrote me an extremely large check to develop electric power for him. But I knew that by accepting that money I would immediately elevate the cost of providing the electricity, so I ripped it up. No one wants to invest in free power, because then how would the investors become rich?"

In my life I had always accepted that there were rich and poor and those in between. I had never questioned the right or wrong of it nor what kinds of things all people should be entitled to. Now Thad and Tesla were changing that.

Was charging for electricity truly like charging for air?

The subject seemed larger than I could really comprehend, and I suddenly wanted to get off it. "Is it true that you made contact with creatures from another planet?"

"Alien life forms? I believe so."

"Do you think that's really possible?" I questioned skeptically.

"It is certainly possible. Probable, even," he confirmed. "Do you not think your mother would agree?"

"My mother?"

"Does not she want to contact other life forms, though in her case it is the other side, those who have passed over?"

"You know who I am?" I cried, gasping.

"It was the sight of you that brought on my episode and sent me to my bed," he said. "My mind was struggling to locate your first appearance and it was causing a sensory overload. But I got it eventually, once I was able to dream. I saw you as a little girl. You were caught in my earthquake."

"Yes! Yes! That was me — and my sister who's with me, too."

"I know. I placed her, as well. I have a photographic memory, and you do not look so different than you looked then, more mature, of course. Is that why you have come to see me now, Jane? Does it have to do with that day?"

I'd thought I was merely there to interview him, but I suddenly realized that it was more than that. "I don't know," I admitted softly, an unexpected emotion in my voice. "I have always remembered you and felt that somehow you would be important in my life, in my future."

His eyes locked on me as though he were peering into my mind — or my heart. "Do you want to travel with me to the future to see if I make a difference to you?"

"What?" I asked, not understanding. "What do you mean?"

"It comes down to physics, and there are several theories about this. My thinking on it is that, using something I created called a magnifying transmitter, I could create electrical waves that travel one and a half times the speed of light. Once you pass the speed of light, time changes."

"In what way? I don't understand."

"Of course you don't understand. Few people do. It's an extremely complex application of quantum physics. But, it's too dangerous still."

"Can you really travel to the future?" I asked.

"Forget I mentioned it. We're all inevitably traveling toward the future," he said vaguely, rolling the top of his seed bag shut.

"That's not what you meant, though." I was sure of it.

He wiped off seeds that were clinging to his coat. "It does not matter what I meant. I must end our interview now because I am due to catch a train and meet up with Colonel Astor in Rhode Island at his summer estate in —"

Abruptly cutting his sentence short, he grasped my upper arm and leaned forward, speaking in an urgent whisper. "A sinister character is loitering behind a boulder several yards behind us. He is an agent of one of my competitors."

Despite being warned not to, I shifted my gaze over my shoulder and did indeed catch sight of a stocky man wearing a full-length brown coat and a bowler hat pulled low on his forehead. "How do you know?" I asked in a whisper.

"I have glimpsed him before, several times," Tesla replied in a low tone. "In the Colorado Springs lab, I saw him fleeing the flames as I scrambled to save my research notes from the inferno."

Still holding my arm, Tesla began to walk, hurrying me along beside him. "This part of the park is very isolated," he explained under his breath. "For safety's sake, I think it best to get out among the general population."

For the first time I noticed that we'd wandered down a

shady cobblestoned walkway thick with foliage but most definitely off the beaten path. Were we to be attacked, there would be no one to come to our assistance.

Quickly glancing behind us, I saw that the man had left the boulder and come out onto the lane. I noticed he wore leather gloves and carried a walking stick with an ivory knob at its handle end.

"I feel like Sherlock Holmes in 'The Adventure of Central Park,'" I whispered, just to lighten the mounting tension and lessen my fear.

"Sadly, this is not a detective mystery. It is all too real," Tesla replied.

The man quickened his pace, and we also began to walk faster. "What do you think he wants?" I asked.

It was only when we reached the safety of the general population that Tesla answered: "The destruction of my work. Which is, inevitably, my own destruction."

Chapter 13

When we arrived back at the Waldorf-Astoria, Mr. Boldt was waiting for Tesla in the lobby. "Colonel Astor married Miss Force this morning in Newport," he reported. "They left immediately on his yacht for a honeymoon."

"When will he return?" Tesla asked, clearly troubled by the news.

"He is planning an extended tour of Europe with his new young wife. The bad press and scandal have been very draining for both of them, and they need to get away for a while. I would venture to say he will not be back for the better part of the year."

"A year!" Tesla cried, throwing his arms out in frustration.

"You might send a telegram," Mr. Boldt suggested, "though it will be difficult to reach him since he will be moving from hotel to hotel."

"This is terrible!" Tesla said. "I must go upstairs to my apartment to lie down."

"Are you all right? Can I help?" I asked.

"Excuse me, Jane," he said to me. "I am overcome." I thanked him for talking to me. "It was my pleasure," he replied politely, despite the fact that his complexion had grown nearly white and a purple vein in his forehead throbbed visibly. "You are a courageous young woman with intellectual curiosity. May you never lose either trait."

"Thank you, sir. I hope you feel better."

With a courtly bow, he strode off toward the elevators. I was sad to see him go.

I gazed around looking for Mimi or Thad, but did not see either of them. I sat a few minutes looking over the notes I'd taken and then went up the elevator to John Jacob Astor's suite to find Mimi.

Ninette answered my knock and bade me to enter. "Come, look at your sister," she said to me. "She is *très chic*."

Mimi stood in the middle of the living room. Naturally, I recognized my own sister, but barely. Her hair was piled high atop her head, jeweled barrettes sparkling in the black sea of carefully sculpted curls. She had on a new satin dress so deeply blue that it seemed to shimmer. It boasted puffed sleeves from shoulder to elbow that narrowed dramatically as they continued down to her wrist. The long skirt, formed out with a black under crinoline, revealed her black-stockinged ankles. On her feet was a brand new pair of shining leather high-button boots.

Dressed like a young society woman, she was completely ravishing. "Ninette bought this for me," she said. "What do you think?"

"You're gorgeous!" I cried.

"Isn't she?!" Ninette said. "The moment I saw Mimi, I knew that she was a diamond in the rough. Now that she is polished, she will be a perfect companion."

"I think she's already a perfect companion," I said.

"Perhaps for you," Ninette allowed. "But now she is just right as a companion for me."

I looked to Mimi, confused.

Mimi's voice was bright but strained. "I'm going to Europe, Jane. Ninette has hired me as her assistant and companion. Isn't it wonderful?"

"Wonderful?!" I cried. "Have you gone crazy?"

Late that evening, I stood on the train station platform still sniffling into a handkerchief. How could Mimi do such a thing? I had pleaded with her not to go off with Ninette Aubart to Europe but she insisted. She said fate had brought her this chance and she had to take it. She'd found an escape hatch, a way to discover who she might be in another sort of world. My mind reeled with the possibilities. Would she ever come home? Might she jump ship, deserting even Ninette in some exotic port on the other side of the planet?

How would I live without the big sister who had always been my best friend?

It was going to be hard enough to face Mother as it was. Now I would have to tell her something immeasurably worse — that I'd lost my sister.

I heard another announcement for a train bound for Washington, D.C. I considered taking it and just running away altogether, but I knew I couldn't do it. Not to return to Spirit Vale would have been to further compound the hurt my mother and sisters would endure at the loss of Mimi.

"Jane!"

I looked toward the shout to see Thad hurrying toward me, his blue summer jacket flying behind him. His hair was mussed and his brow was sweaty from running. His worried expression transformed into a smile of relief as he neared me.

"Were you going to leave without saying good-bye?" he asked.

I smiled through my tears, glad to see him. Even in my misery, this was an unexpected pleasure. "I didn't know where you were," I explained. "How did you find me?"

"I saw Mimi at the hotel and she told me you had left."

My tears started to fall heavily once again at the

mention of her name. "Did she tell you why she's not with me?" I asked.

"She did. And I also see she's upset you badly."

"She says she wants to see the world," I spoke through my salty tears. "She's not sure what her future holds — claims that this is her fate."

He fished a worn but clean handkerchief from his jacket pocket and handed it to me so I could mop up the tears soaking my face. "Oh, don't worry," he said soothingly. "She's just dazzled by all the stuff. You know, the dresses, the suites, the decoration. A free trip through Europe is pretty hard to resist; don't you think?"

"But to travel with those two; they're not even married," I objected.

"'Judge not that ye may not be judged,'" Thad quoted the scripture lightly.

I hung my head in despair. "It's just wrong."

Thad took hold of my hands comfortingly. "We can't control what other people do," he commented. "I bet she'll be back home in no time. You'll see."

Hanging my head, I nodded and sniffed. "Do you really think so?"

"Sure," he said. His unconcern and confidence were contagious and my spirits lifted a bit. He left hold of my hand and gently whisked a lingering tear from my cheek. "I'm not concerned about Mimi. She'll have a great time," he went on. "It's you I was worried about."

I looked up into his steady blue gaze. "Me?"

Despite my upset state, my heart did a quick, delighted bounce. He was worried about me? Then the full realization of his unexpected appearance here hit me. He'd run the more than twelve blocks uptown to the station because of me. Me!

Thad had heard from Tesla about the man with the bowler hat. "Are you all right? Were you scared?" he asked.

"Terrified," I confirmed. "But Tesla is going ahead with his project, anyway. Do you think that's wise? Will he be safe?"

"I'll stick close to him like a bodyguard," Thad said confidently. I wasn't sure he'd be any match for the bowler-topped thug. "Maybe you should start carrying a walking stick," I suggested.

"I was a wrestling champ back in school," he boasted with a playful wink.

"Were you really?" I asked, impressed.

"Sure. I'm a preacher's son, remember? I wouldn't lie."

"Be careful, anyway," I counseled.

He looked deep into my eyes. Without meaning to, I leaned in closer, irresistibly drawn to his energy and warmth. I think he must have moved toward me, as well, because we somehow came to be standing very close to each other — he still holding my hands, I looking up at him.

"I don't know exactly where you live, Jane," Thad said

as steam from the newly arrived train billowed around us. "I want to write to you."

I want to write to you. Six simple words. But there was an unspoken multitude of words that could spring from them.

On a day when I felt I'd lost so much, suddenly I had a brief glimpse of something being gained.

Spirit Vale was so small that any letter addressed to me there would arrive at my house, and I told him so. "Would you really write?" I asked hopefully.

"I'd like to," he replied. "I've enjoyed talking to you, and it would be good to keep it up, even if it's only through letters."

"That would be great," I said.

"You'd write back, wouldn't you?" he checked.

"Of course I would. With Mimi gone I'll really need someone to talk with, and I also find it easy and interesting talking to you."

We stood there a moment, smiling at each other like two fools. For all our talk of talking, we were romantically speechless.

The train broke the spell by sounding a warning blast. "All aboard for Albany and connecting points on the northwest corridor," a conductor yelled.

"You'd better go," Thad said.

"I suppose so." It was so hard to leave.

We began walking together toward the train. "How did your interview with Tesla go?" he asked.

"Wonderful. It should be a great article," I told him, climbing up the metal stairs to the small platform between train cars. "And the most amazing thing happened — he remembered me from all the way back in 1898! Can you believe it? I was only four at the time."

The train's engine chugged and a white mist of smoke rose up around me. "Better take your seat, miss," a conductor advised.

Thad jumped nimbly onto the train, grabbing hold of the railing between the cars just as the train moved forward.

I gasped — but with a touch of delight at his daring. "You'd better get down," I cautioned.

"I have a few minutes before it leaves the station," he said.

The train slowly chugged, blowing its whistle as it inched up the tracks.

"Wait! Did you say you were only four in 1898?" he asked.

I nodded. "Why?"

"I just assumed you were older."

The train continued moving forward, slowly picking up speed. Thad leaped easily to the ground.

I wasn't prepared for how wrenching his jump away from me would be. I'd felt so safe with him. Now it was as though he'd jumped out of my life altogether. I was abruptly on my own again.

He waved, but an uneasy expression played on his face, and mine probably mirrored it.

"Don't forget to write," I called back to him, waving as the train carried me off.

He waved back but did not say anything.

A conductor came to the doorway. "You must take your seat, miss. It's not safe to stand here."

With a last wave to Thad, I stepped inside. I slumped into the seat, despondent. Tears once again wet my eyes.

The grim reality of my dismal situation — which had momentarily been cushioned by my delight at Thad's arrival — surged back on me with full force. I was on my way to a certainly angry mother and sisters who would probably be bewildered and feel caught in the middle. Would they all blame me for letting Mimi run off as she had? How could I face it all without her?

And now I worried that the one bright spot I had to look forward to — letters from Thad — would not arrive. The last three minutes of our time together had, I feared, completely changed his view of me. In a second, he had gone from seeing me as his contemporary to viewing me as a child! Why couldn't I ever keep my mouth shut?

The train was now running at full speed, racing into the blackness of a tunnel that would carry me away from this exciting city — and away from Thad. Shutting my eyes, I lost myself in the motion of the train carrying me forward. What would it be like to travel on and on and never arrive, simply to keep moving with no endpoint?

I remembered what Tesla had said about traveling into the future, but for the moment, I was in no rush to get there. The future would be fully upon me the moment I arrived back in Spirit Vale.

Chapter 14

My recklessness in taking off for New York was almost forgotten in Mother's shouting and weeping over Mimi's departure. Why hadn't I stopped her? How could I have let her go? I must not have tried hard enough to talk sense into her. It was as if I had been the older sister and could have somehow controlled Mimi. Mother decried the terrible loss of Mimi as "irresponsible" of me.

The entire town took up my disgrace. Aunty Lily said I had been the one who tricked her into driving us to Buffalo, when in actuality it had been Mimi's idea. Princess Running Deer did a Native American spirit ceremony to try to contact Mimi's living spirit to make sure she was safe. When no response came, Mother went into fits of distress, crying for days, certain some harm had come to her.

Amelie and Emma provided unexpected comfort in a weird sort of way. One night at dinner, Emma suddenly stood up at the table and began to rock slightly as a faraway look came into her eyes. The same strange distance appeared in Amelie's expression.

"I have found her," Emma spoke in a trancelike voice, softer and gentler than her own normal tone.

"Who are you?" Mother asked cautiously.

"It's me, Mother. Amelie."

We all looked to Amelie, but she gave no indication of being aware of us. Why had Emma said she was Amelie?

We shifted back to Emma. "Mimi is over water. It's night where she is," Emma said, still in her trance state. "She is staring up at the moon. She is in love."

"In love!" Mother cried and jumped up so forcefully that her dinner plate fell to the floor. "With whom is she in love?"

The commotion had the effect of breaking Emma's trance. Her eyes blinked rapidly and lost their distant gaze.

"Whom is your sister in love with?" Mother demanded.

"I don't know what you're talking about," Emma replied. "Who is in love?"

We looked to Amelie, but she had rested her head on the table and was now snoring lightly.

"You said you were Amelie," I told Emma. "Why?"

Emma shrugged. "Did I? How odd."

This news that Mimi was safe, derived from *wherever*, comforted us all, except for Mother, who seemed to think that this impending romance simply upped the level of peril involved. Every time she looked at me, she seemed reminded of it anew and shook her head darkly.

Only Blythe, recently turned thirteen, thought Mimi was brave and adventurous. "She would have been an idiot not to have gone," she stated boldly to us one night when everyone was in the parlor and Mother was once again engulfed in tears and recriminations. This took everyone by surprise, since Blythe was not usually one to buck the tide of prevailing opinion. "We're not rich. There is no wealthy young man for her to meet in this town. The only young men at all are ones who have died and speak through other people. When else would she have a chance like this to see the world and find romance?"

"Don't you go getting any ideas, Blythe," Mother chided. "Your sister is involved with scandalous people. Who knows what this will do to her reputation or to her chances of making a suitable marriage — not some ship-board fling with who knows what manner of man."

"What do you care what people think?" Blythe spoke to Mother with unforeseen defiance. Her words seemed so at odds with the cherubic face that it made me see her in a new light, as a surprisingly independent person, no longer a child. "Most people think everyone in this town is crazier than a loon," she continued. "And they're probably right! That doesn't seem to bother you."

"Crazy . . . why . . . craz —" Mother cried, sputtering incredulously. "No one thinks that. People flock here for guidance!"

"Crazy people," Blythe insisted.

For being so insolent, Mother banished Blythe to her room, punishing her for the first time any of us could recall. She then confined me to my room, simply because I had brought all this on in the first place.

This blame did not relent, making that autumn of 1911 one I did not particularly enjoy. But, like waves, events roll in with a crash-bang, then recede, leaving the waters calm — at least until the next wave comes along. That's what I discovered in the weeks of being constantly confined to my room, a confinement during which I worked on my article about Tesla while thinking about Thad unceasingly. After a while, Mother stopped crying and quit noticing whether Blythe and I were in our rooms. The townspeople gave up looking at me with condemning glances.

Late that November, teams of workers descended on Spirit Vale in flatbed trucks loaded with timber. It seemed that nearly the entire town came out each day to watch them work as, in a remarkably short time, giant poles were erected along Main Street. The workers then scrambled up the poles and strung great lengths of telephone cable between them.

Once again, as with the electric lighting, the Spirit was the center of our first experience of the telephone. The first words spoken over the telephone cable in Spirit Vale were voiced by Aunty Lily. She was proud to be the one to speak them in front of a fascinated crowd that included Mother, Blythe, Emma, Amelie, and me, as well as many of the other resident mediums. "Hello," she said. "Is this the Buffalo police station? It is? Well, we are pleased to report that all is calm here in Spirit Vale. Thank you."

When Aunty Lily hung up, Madam Anushka lifted the tall, black metal phone, turning the speaker piece in her hand. "I vonder eef de spirit vorld can be contacted in dis way?" she pondered aloud.

"It is a mite like talking to a spirit," Aunty Lily remarked. "There's this voice talking at ya, but no body."

"What if Hiram called you up one night?" Blythe suggested with a touch of mischief.

"Now why would he do that when he's right here?" Aunty Lily asked. "He is still here, isn't he, Maude?" she checked with Mother.

"Yes, and he says you were very intelligent to have this phone installed," Mother reported.

Aunty Lily beamed proudly.

By December I had stopped checking the mailbox, continually hoping for a letter from either Mimi or Thad. It had never been easy to secretly check the mail at the box out by the white picket fence. When Mother wasn't busy with clients or helping Aunty Lily with her hotel accounts, she was nearly camped there. She and W. T. Stead had begun a lively correspondence. To receive a new letter from him was the greatest pleasure of her life.

I think it was safe to presume that Mother had developed a crush on the noted journalist. He told her of Julia's Bureau, an institution he'd established in 1909 where inquirers could obtain information regarding the spirit world from his spirit guide, Julia. He had on staff a group of mediums who could contact her.

He also sent Mother small gifts: a pack of tarot cards, a crystal ball made of real crystal, clusters of amethyst stone for channeling and focusing energy. Another gift that arrived in early December was a Ouija board, which Mother immediately set about mastering and using with her clients. The plaque in our front yard soon read: MAUDE ONEIDA TAYLOR — MEDIUM, CHANNELER, VIBRATIONAL PATTERNS INTERPRETED, TAROT READ, CRYSTAL ENERGY FOCUSED, EXPERT PRACTITIONER OF OUIJA BOARD CONTACT.

On Christmas Eve that year, my sisters and I each played a role in Spirit Vale's yearly production of *A Christmas Carol*, held in the town center. As one might imagine, in a population focused on the spirit world, this play about Christmas ghosts and prophetic, transformative dreams was held in very high, nearly worshipful esteem. I had been cast as Mrs. Cratchit. Blythe was the beautiful young woman Scrooge almost married. Emma and Amelie were the Ghost of Christmas Past, played as one entity, which was how people were starting to consider them. Aunty Lily made a wonderfully cranky, if somewhat effeminate, Scrooge, and Princess Running Deer was an ominous presence as the Ghost of Christmas Future. Madam Anushka accompanied the scenes with haunting performances on her violin. The final bows were met with rousing cheers.

All that was missing was Mimi.

Afterward, snowflakes began to fall as my sisters and I headed across the empty main road toward home. The fast-falling snow required us to flip up the hoods of our woolen capes. The light blanket of whiteness that quickly accumulated added to the quiet beauty of the town, with all its gingerbread porches strung in tiny, white electric lights for the first time ever. "It's so magical," Blythe commented wistfully. "I hope it's snowing wherever Mimi is, and that some handsome fellow is holding her hand."

"Me, too," I answered, picturing Mimi in a Swiss mountaintop chalet with some prince by her side.

The image also made me think of Thad. What was he doing this Christmas Eve? Was he at a party paying attention to a girl — one prettier than me and closer to his age? Or was he deep in Tesla's laboratory, unaware of the celebrations outside?

When we arrived home, Mother, who had left the show at curtain call, was waiting with hot chocolate and candy canes. She'd put our wrapped gifts under the tree that, despite the general embrace of electricity, was still lit with delicate, tinfoil-cupped candles on its branches.

We were about to begin opening our gifts when we heard the new motorized mail truck stop at our box and then move on. "He's arriving late," Mother commented. "He must have an overload of holiday mail."

"I'll go get it," I said, unable to resist, despite the fact that I had convinced myself neither Mimi nor Thad would ever write. I threw my cape over my shoulders and ran out the front door, once more into the snow, which was falling even more heavily than before.

At the mailbox I pulled out a stack of letters, mostly Christmas cards from our neighbors and one from W. T. Stead, sure to delight Mother. But also included in the delivery was a package wrapped in brown paper and addressed to me. Its postmark was from New York City.

With excited, trembling hands, I ripped the paper apart right there.

It was a book. Without even reading the title, I flipped inside, looking for some kind of inscription or note, but there was none.

Closing it, I read the title: *The Time Machine* by H. G. Wells.

It could have come from only one of two people — Tesla or Thad.

"What's taking so long?" Mother called from the front porch. "Are you all right?"

"I'm all right," I assured her, heading back toward the house.

She waited for me on the porch. "Anything from Mimi?" she asked hopefully.

"No, but Mr. Stead has sent you a card."

"How wonderful," she said, extending her hand for it.

She glanced down at the card, smiling fondly. Then she looked back to me. "Merry Christmas, Jane. What do you say we put all our disagreements behind us and start fresh for the new year?"

"I would like that," I said with a catch in my voice.

"So would I." With her arm around my shoulder, we turned back to the house.

Neither of us had any idea what the new year was soon to bring.

Chapter 15

And so we lived through the cold months of January and February, when business was always slow in Spirit Vale and the winter wind wailed down Main Street like so many spirits despondently wondering why their loved ones were not seeking their attention.

The Time Machine stayed on my shelf, its spine unbroken. It had probably come from Tesla, I decided. I had given him our address before we'd parted. That he had thought of me at all touched me. His words *Jiva is Shiva* repeated in my head, but only because I liked the sound of them, much as a popular tune becomes lodged in your brain.

Of course, I pondered why he'd sent me that particular book. I recalled him mentioning traveling to the future and I was eager to see if I could find a connection in the story. But to begin reading the book would make me think of Thad and Mimi, and I didn't want to dwell for too long on either of them. It was too painful.

I could well imagine why Thad hadn't written — in fact,

I imagined it incessantly, reliving over and over the disappointed look on his face when he realized my age.

But where was Mimi? Why hadn't *she* written? My thoughts ran from horrible anxieties about terrible perils that might have befallen her to an even more horrifying thought: What if she'd decided to embrace her new life by cutting all connection to her family? I couldn't imagine that she would do such a thing . . . but it was a possibility.

It was easier on my emotions to stay close to my fictional companion Sherlock Holmes and *his* friend, the sensible Dr. Watson. Holmes was logical, rational, and impeccable in scrutinizing every detail. Watson and Holmes were both men of science clearing a path of reason among the murky depths of crime and passion. They did not talk to the dead — nor did they run off to Europe on a whim or make a promise to write and then not do so!

I continued to follow Tesla in the papers. I saw a picture of him at a press conference when his radio tower in Long Island was foreclosed once and for all. He promised the gathered press that he was working on a new invention that would be so successful it would enable him to personally finance a new, higher tower with a stronger signal. He didn't look well. In the background behind Tesla was Thad, listening to his employer with intense interest. I took that photo out and studied it often with a painful mix of longing and anger until it was a worn, nearly translucent shred.

With my accumulated collection of articles and my original interview, I wrote an article titled "Through the Eyes of a Genius." Just in time for the contest deadline, I mailed it — painstakingly typewritten and bound with a blue ribbon — to the *Sun*. Then I tried not to think of it again.

The Spirit Hotel was all but empty at this time of year, so Aunty Lily didn't need my help as a chambermaid anymore. Mother decided I no longer needed schooling, so I was given the responsibility of tutoring Blythe, a task I enjoyed more than expected. It seemed Blythe, who had always seemed so contented to play with her dolls, was now chomping at the bit to get out of Spirit Vale. "Boarding school would be lovely," she told me with a longing sigh. "Imagine an entire school where the dead just kept their mouths shut."

"Why would you possibly want that?" asked Emma from her straight-backed chair in the parlor. She and Amelie would sit as heavy snows fell past the window beside them, at a narrow table in the parlor, facing each other, knees touching and working with the Ouija board sent by W. T. Stead. With their wispy, light brown hair caught in identical loosely bound knots atop their heads, their matching slim, willowy frames bent over the board in intense concentration, they looked like lovely fifteen-year-old bookends. Emma asked the questions and Amelie worked the triangular disc, in theory letting the spirits spell out their responses. Sometimes the two sets of violet blue eyes they focused on that board didn't waver from it for hours at a time.

One day I stood behind Emma. "Amelie, ask the spirits why you won't talk," I said.

Amelie looked directly at me as though startled by the question. Then she placed her hands on the disc and it began to move. I was never sure if it was pulling her fingers along or if she was pushing it. Before long it had spelled out a sentence that read: *I am talking.*

"Then why can't I hear you?" I asked.

"You're not listening," Emma replied.

"Do you hear her?"

Emma nodded. "I hear her in my mind."

"It must be because you're twins," I decided.

"Amelie has the gift," Emma said. "It drains her. It's easier if she doesn't speak."

Blythe had been paging through the fashion section of the *Sun* but broke from her perusal of the latest ankle boots. "That's one gift I don't want. Give me a pair of these boots any day."

That same night, I was awakened by a strange sound outside my window. Lifting my head to listen, I decided it must be a branch blown loose, banging in the winter wind. I returned to a light sleep, only to be reawakened by the noise, which was now louder.

I was proud of my logical mind and did not allow

the ghostly goings-on in town to frighten me. But that night, I shrunk low under my covers. Had Mother summoned some spirit who had decided to stay? And if so, why was it walking around outside Blythe's and my bedroom window?

I looked to the twin bed beside me where Blythe had decided to sleep since Mimi had vacated it. She claimed the room she shared with the twins was too crowded, and I didn't object because I hated staring at Mimi's empty bed at night.

I heard the sound again, and this time I realized it sounded like a footstep out on the roof. Once this thought hit, I was instantly wide-awake, every sense alert. Blythe continued to sleep, so, tight with fear, I crept out of my bed and jostled her awake. "Listen!" I whispered. The creaking from the roof had become unmistakable.

Wordlessly Blythe left her bed and went to the window. I followed behind her.

There was, indeed, a pale, ghostly figure standing on the roof.

Blythe pushed up the window. "Amelie!" she called in a harsh whisper. "Come inside."

"What's she doing out there?" I asked.

"I don't know," Blythe answered. "But it's freezing outside!"

Moving Blythe aside, I raised the window sash and leaned out. Amelie was indeed out there, barefoot on the icy roof. The moonlight poured down on her. With the winter wind blowing her hair and nightgown, she made an eerily ghostly figure, but of course, she was no ghost.

What could she be doing? Had she gone crazy?

Instinctively I looked for Mimi to take charge and then remembered that she wasn't there. I was the oldest now. It was up to me.

"Go get Mother," I instructed Blythe as I began crawling out the window.

Amelie was perilously close to the end of the roof. She didn't seem to know it, though. As I drew closer, I realized that she was in some sort of trance. I would have to pull her back without startling her and causing her to tumble off. And I had to act quickly — she might fall at any moment.

With my arms wide for balance, I inched slowly toward our sister. "Amelie, stop," I said softly, needing to keep my voice calm. "Come back toward me."

Amelie walked along the edge of the roof with the sureness of a cat. "Amelie, look at me!" I commanded her.

But Amelie didn't acknowledge me. She didn't even seem aware of my presence.

And then, suddenly, she tottered, arms windmilling crazily.

Frantic, I clutched her nightgown, then lunged forward and gripped her wrist tightly with my other hand.

For a horrible second, I was sure she would go off the

roof and pull me over with her. Bending my knees, I threw my weight backward as hard as I could.

Both of us fell back hard onto the roof, hitting with such force that we rolled to the very edge. If I hadn't been able to keep hold of her and jam my heel in the wooden gutter to stop our slide, I'm sure we would have sailed right out into the night.

Looking to the house, I saw Mother at our open bedroom window with Blythe hopping about anxiously behind her. Mother's expression was shocked and confused. "Come in here this minute!" she scolded. "What are you girls doing?"

Amelie blinked hard and recognition returned to her face. She shook her head, seeming as bewildered that she was out on the roof on a winter's night dressed in her nightgown as we were to find her there.

"Follow me," I instructed her, crawling back up the cold roof on my hands and knees. Amelie obeyed, and soon Mother was pulling us inside. "What were you doing out here?" Blythe asked her, but Amelie just blinked with confusion. Clearly, she didn't know.

Once inside and wrapped in blankets, I explained to Mother what had happened. She sat beside Amelie on Blythe's bed and stroked her tangled, windblown hair. "I'm afraid you were sleepwalking, my love," she said.

"You mean she was asleep out there?" Blythe cried. "She could have walked right off the roof!"

Emma appeared in the doorway. "What's happening?" she asked, rubbing her eyes.

"We'll tell you in the morning, dear," Mother said. "Go back to sleep."

"I can't," Emma said. "I just had the strangest dream. I dreamed I was walking around somewhere that was very high up and the stars were all around me — stars everywhere as far as I could see. I was flying into the starry night when I suddenly woke up."

Blythe and I stared at each other, wide-eyed. Had my sisters been dreaming the same dream?

Mother held Amelie closer to her side.

That was the first night that Amelie began sleepwalking — but it would not be her last.

I passed the remainder of that winter with my head buried in my Christmas gift from Mother, a collected volume of Sherlock Holmes stories starting from the very first, as well as a single installment of the most recently published addition, "The Terror of Blue John Gap."

It was the end of February, on a particularly frigid morning, when the whistle of icy winds down from Canada reminded me to stoke the wood-burning stove, that Mother received a letter from W. T. Stead. "Girls," she announced after she'd read it, her face lit with excitement, "Mr. Stead is gathering all the greatest spiritualists for an international convention in London in April, and we've been invited to attend."

"All of us?" I said hopefully.

"There are five tickets for a transatlantic crossing on an ocean liner in this envelope," Mother said, taking out the tickets and holding them for us to see. "I have a cousin outside London in Brighton. I will contact Agatha immediately to see if she is willing to have us stay at her house."

"It's too wonderful! We'll meet all the great spiritualists," said Emma. She looked to Amelie, whose face was as illuminated with anticipation as her own.

"We leave in a little over a month," Mother told us. She held Mr. Stead's letter over her heart and closed her eyes, smiling beatifically. "Isn't he the most generous man alive?"

"We're going to London!" Blythe shouted, twirling around the room with her arms spread wide, nearly delirious with joy.

Chapter 16

LONDON, APRIL 3, 1912

The voyage across the Atlantic was uneventful, but I adored every minute of it just the same. Much of the time I hung at the sides, gazing out over the ocean, mesmerized by its rolling waves. I had never seen the ocean before, and now I wondered how I had ever lived without it.

Nothing had ever imparted such a keen sense of how small a part of a larger universe I was. At night, the feeling was amplified by the addition of stars more immense and seemingly closer to Earth than I had ever seen. Standing there with the sea breeze in my hair, the black, glittering fields of both ocean and heavens before me, I felt lifted from my own body and happy. I had to assume it was an experience akin to being in a state of grace.

Blythe shared my fascination with the ocean, but for different reasons. To her it was sea of possibility. One afternoon she joined me at the ship's side. "Think of all the places we might go on this ship," she said. "Imagine all the things Mimi is seeing right now."

"Well, hopefully we'll find a better way to travel than as the maid of some rich man's mistress," I remarked sourly.

"She's a *companion*," Blythe corrected.

"What's the difference?" I quibbled.

"It's probably easier and more fun," she conjectured in the straightforward manner that was more and more becoming a hallmark of her personality. "Besides, *she's* not doing anything wrong. What Ninette Aubart does is on her conscience. It's not up to Mimi — or you, for that matter — to judge her."

Judge not that ye may not be judged. Blythe's comments made me think of Thad. Just about everything made me think of him. It was so odd that a person I had known so briefly could get so stuck in my head. I had done a similar thing with Tesla, but it didn't feel the same. When I thought of Thad, I recalled the fresh smell of his jacket, his white scar, the brightness in his vivid blue eyes. The power of my longing was so great that I could almost conjure an image of him standing right beside me.

Sometimes I talked to Thad in my mind, upbraiding him for being so foolish about the few years between us, telling him how much I wished to see him again, begging him to get on a train and come to Spirit Vale. I would insist that he felt as much for me as I did for him. Why else would he have run down to the train station to see me off on the train? These mental conversations became so animated that I sometimes listened for a reply — and half thought I heard distant words. But it was all wishful thinking.

A strong wave slapped the ship, rousing me from my reverie. It apparently did the same for Blythe, who had wandered off on a path of thought of her own. "Do you think Mimi is really in love, as Emma predicted?" she asked.

"Who knows?" I replied. "Blythe, do you think it's Emma or Amelie who does the predicting?"

"What's the difference? They're one person."

"No, they're not," I disagreed. "There are differences. Amelie is off in her own world but Emma is very much with us."

"Maybe," she conceded with a shrug. "They're both in our cabin bathroom being violently seasick right now," she pointed out.

"This ship does rock a bit," I allowed. "I feel my stomach lurch sometimes."

"Wouldn't it be great if we could be on one of the new White Star Line luxury liners?" Blythe suggested. "At dinner all the people were talking about the *Olympic* and the *Titanic*. The *Olympic* was launched last year and everyone raves about it. It's the biggest ship in the world and it's number one in luxury and speed. The *Titanic* hasn't even gone out yet. They say it's even better."

"Tickets must cost a fortune," I said.

"The other passengers are saying second class on the *Titanic* is better than first class on other ships," she replied. "How I would love to see it!"

It didn't matter to me. Any ship that would bring me out onto these rolling waves would suit. I think it was on this voyage that the word *vast* became my favorite word.

I had packed *The Time Machine* by H. G. Wells and finally felt ready to tackle it again. In it a scientist known only as the Time Traveller creates a machine that carries him far into the future. He tells his friends that time is a fourth dimension to which one can travel.

Sitting there on a deck chair with a blanket tucked around me, I often put the strange tale down on my lap and let my thoughts drift back to Tesla. Like the Time Traveller, he was such a genius and said so much that I simply didn't understand. Was time travel really possible?

I continued reading, immersing myself in the adventure of the story and accepting — for at least as long as I was reading the story — that time travel could be achieved. Once I suspended my doubts about that, I found the story very engaging.

Finally, we arrived at port in Southampton, England. From there we took a horse-drawn cab to Waterloo Station in London. As soon as we stepped outside the station, we were greeted by a woman with blazing carrot hair in a sporty red motorcar with no roof. "Darlings!" she gushed, getting out of her car and greeting us with open arms. "What richness to have you all here with me!"

Horse-drawn carriage drivers shouted at her to move her automobile, which she'd abandoned in the road, but she serenely ignored them. Agatha's family resemblance to Mother was easy to see. She was much heavier and her orange hair was brighter — I suspected an artificial tint — but she had the same delicate nose and sparkling blue eyes.

Needless to say, we all loved her instantly, even though we wished she had a bigger automobile. Mother sat in front alongside Agatha while the rest of us crushed together in the small backseat, clutching what bags wouldn't fit in the back storage compartment.

Cousin Agatha's adorable little house was in Brighton, just over an hour south of London. It was one block from the Atlantic Ocean. The moment Agatha parked the motorcar, Blythe was out and running toward the water.

I was eager to see the beach, too. It was another first for me. "Come on," I said to Emma and Amelie as I climbed out, about to follow Blythe.

"We'll stay here," Emma declined. I noticed Amelie had covered her face with her hand as though the very thought of going to the ocean was disturbing her greatly.

"All right, then," I said turning away from them. I caught up with Blythe on the boardwalk. A chilly, wet April wind blew a moist, salty spray around us. At home, there was not yet any sign of a thaw, but here the first notes of spring played in the air.

"Let's go down to the water," Blythe suggested. Without waiting for my reply, she hurried across the rocky beach to the water's edge. Down by the shoreline, the wind was stronger and whipped her blond curls around her face. "Oh, isn't it wonderful!?" she cried exultantly.

"It is," I agreed. "I wonder why Emma and Amelie don't want to see it. They're frightened of the ocean."

"They're probably afraid there are spirits floating in the sea," Blythe said flippantly. "On the way over it probably wasn't seasickness at all. It was sheer terror. They didn't even want to look at the ocean once."

Her remark made me think about all the shipwrecks throughout time. Were Emma and Amelie seeing something there that the rest of us could not?

After we walked along the shore, we returned to the boardwalk and then to Cousin Agatha's house, straightening our wind-tossed hair as we went.

Inside, in the front parlor, Mother was telling her cousin about the reason for our visit. "The subject of the conference is nothing less than the fate of the world," said Mother, sitting at a cloth-covered table as Agatha brought in a tray laden with a porcelain teapot and cups. "Stead has been invited by President Taft to attend a world peace conference in America this April."

"A world peace conference?" Agatha asked. "Whatever for? Don't we have peace already?"

"Taft feels that world peace is in a precarious state at the moment and that a world war could erupt at any time," Mother said, relaying what Stead had told her in his last letter.

"A world war?" Agatha questioned skeptically. "There has never been such a thing, and it seems less likely to occur now than ever. Queen Victoria's granddaughter Alexandra is the czarina of Russia and her husband, Nicholas, is a cousin. Our George the Fifth is the first cousin of Kaiser Wilhelm. Victoria's granddaughter Ena is queen of Spain. Marie is queen of Romania. Victoria's daughter-in-law is the daughter of the Danish royal couple. She had nine children and forty-two grandchildren and most of them married into royal families. They rule the world."

"You certainly know your royals," I remarked.

"Oh, we English love the royalty," Agatha replied. "And I could go on from there. Everyone is related to everyone. My point is that the world is one big, happy family affair these days."

"Families quarrel," Mother pointed out. "Stead says they've been playing a political chess game that's about to explode into a violent fight. As it is, things have not been entirely peaceful. Last year Italy declared war on Turkey, and this year war broke out in the Balkans."

"Wherever that is," Agatha said.

"Stead says that conflict's not over, even though there's been a truce," Mother said. "You'll be hearing more about the Balkans, maybe even this year. A world war could very easily happen."

Agatha's bright expression darkened as she poured the tea. "Oh, well, I do sincerely hope not."

"So does President Taft. Such a conflict would surely affect America one way or another," Mother said.

"England is our ally," I added. "We'd have to get involved."

"This is terrible!" Blythe cried. "I don't want a war."

"No one does," said Mother. "That's why Stead has called together the best spiritualists. He wants to be armed with whatever the spirit world can tell us by way of predictions."

"Can the dead see the future?" Agatha inquired.

"Sometimes," Mother answered, sipping her tea. "There will be psychics in attendance who make predictions. Stead himself is a psychic."

"Then why doesn't he simply tell your president what he knows?"

"It's not that simple," Mother said. "Psychic predictions come in flashes and are subject to interpretation." She used the example of Stead thinking he would die by ice. "But will he slip on ice? Will he freeze to death? No one knows for certain."

"I should move to a sunnier clime altogether, were I he," Agatha suggested.

"Perhaps so. Nonetheless, he is as brilliant a psychic as he is a journalist."

"I don't know about all this," Agatha said uneasily, "but I wish you all success. Heaven knows that the last thing any of us wants is a war."

That evening, Mother shared the guest room with Amelie and Emma. Blythe and I settled in on the couches in the living room. From our improvised beds, we could hear the ocean waves crashing against the shore.

"I love it here," Blythe whispered to me.

"Mmm," I murmured in agreement, half asleep.

"I don't think our lives will ever be the same after this trip," she said.

"Why's that?" I mumbled.

"I don't know," Blythe replied. "It's just a feeling."

Chapter 17

*I*n the morning, Agatha drove us back into London even though we offered to take the train. "I wouldn't hear of it," she said. "I have many friends in London whom I might visit." She used a map of the city to guide her and in little over an hour we pulled up in front of an elegant town house in the heart of the city. Clearly, we had arrived at the right place, for a steady stream of men and women were entering.

"Good-bye, darlings. I will return for you at about five," Agatha said as we climbed out of her motorcar. Suddenly she went pale and pointed. "What is it, Agatha?" I asked, concerned, for she was trembling with excitement.

She pointed at a short man with a white mustache and beard. He wore a black suit and black stovepipe hat. "That's the great playwright George Bernard Shaw who just walked out of the building you're about to enter," she said in a voice filled with awe.

"How do you know it's him?" Blythe asked.

"I follow the theater avidly, darling," she explained. "I see his picture in the paper after every opening. Either he's written the play or he's accompanying some famed thespian."

"Yes, he's a good friend of Mr. Stead's," Mother said.

"Really?! And look whom he has stopped to speak to," she said with a gasp.

I looked in the direction she was pointing and saw that on his way out of the house, Shaw had, indeed, paused to speak to two men walking toward the house. One was a portly but dignified-looking gentleman with an impressive mustache but thinning hair on his head whom I guessed to be in his early fifties.

The other man was short and clean-shaven, with curly black hair. He was much younger, probably in his early thirties. He looked somehow familiar to me, but I couldn't think of why that should be.

"Who are they?" Emma asked.

"I don't know who the younger gentleman might be, but the older one is none other than Dr. Arthur Conan Doyle."

"What?" I cried. Surely I'd heard her wrong!

"Indeed," Agatha confirmed. "He's the author of the Sherlock Holmes mysteries. Do you read him in America?"

I would have answered her if I could have found my voice. At the very moment, I had the newest Holmes story, "The Speckled Band," tucked away in my carpetbag. Now it was my turn to tremble in awestruck amazement.

"It's practically all Jane reads," Blythe informed her. "I didn't know he was a doctor."

"Oh, yes, darling. He's also a physician."

I watched while Conan Doyle and his friend bade good-bye to Shaw and continued on. My heart began to pound as I realized they were entering W. T. Stead's house.

Why would this man of science, this paragon of rational deductive logic, be entering a convention of renowned spiritualists?

There could be only one answer: He had come to debunk these mediums as frauds. Using his brilliant powers of observation, he would expose the tricks they used to work their wonders.

This was my chance to learn the truth from a man whose word I could never doubt. It was as though Sherlock Holmes himself had come to deliver the final answer to my questions.

When we entered the main front room of the building, I didn't see Conan Doyle or his companion. But W. T. Stead appeared from one of the side rooms and instantly approached Mother. "William," Mother greeted him warmly by his first name; I had never heard her use it before.

He had a broad, open face with dark brows and piercing eyes. He was a man of middle years, probably in his fifties, and wore a full, white beard. "Maude, at last we meet," he said, taking Mother's hands in his. "You are just as you described in your letter, only more lovely by far. And these, of course, are your daughters. I can guess their names from your descriptions."

He greeted my sisters each correctly by name. "And you must be Jane, the aspiring journalist," he surmised when he got to me.

"Yes, sir. It's an honor to meet you. Thank you so much for the tickets," I replied. "If you can spare the time, I have so many questions I would love to ask you."

"It would be my pleasure," he said.

He led us to a ballroom where all the invited guests were assembled. There were approximately a hundred or so men and women. I caught sight of Conan Doyle sitting in the far corner with his dark-haired companion.

After a few moments, W. T. Stead appeared in the front of the crowd and announced that rooms had been set up throughout the house for the conducting of séances. Additionally, there would be sessions of tarot, Ouija board, and automatic writing. Throughout the rest of Stead's address to the crowd, I couldn't take my eyes off Conan Doyle.

I imagined a scheme for meeting him in which I dropped my copy of the *Strand* and pretended I didn't know who he was but praised "The Speckled Band" extravagantly, causing him to like me so much that he made me his assistant. In another flight of imagination, I fantasized being invited to join him in solving a crime that took place there at the psychic convention. "The Adventure of the Meddling Mediums" is what it would be called, and I'd be featured as the American Girl.

After Stead's speech, a paper was posted announcing the morning's events, with different mediums and psychics being assigned to various rooms. Mother was to join a circle of mediums in the attempt to contact Queen Victoria herself, in the hope of getting her to comment on the present situation and perhaps give a word of sage advice for her quarreling descendants.

I noticed Mother engaged in conversation with a balding, pleasant-looking man in his early fifties. "This is Mr. Robertson," she introduced when I approached. "This is my daughter Jane. She would also like to be a writer like yourself."

"Pleased to meet you," I greeted him. "You're not a medium or psychic, then?"

"No. My experience is as a merchant marine and later a writer of sea stories," he said. His speech immediately revealed him as American. "Have you read any of them?"

"No, I don't think so." I couldn't recall ever reading a sea story. "But your name is very familiar to me," I said truthfully. I struggled to recollect where I'd heard of him.

"Perhaps you've read *Sinful Peck*?" he suggested.

"I should think not," Mother demurred. "Not with a title like that."

"It's not as scandalous as you might think," Mr.

Robertson said with a laugh. "It's a sea story like my others."

"What brings you to this conference?" Mother asked him.

"Well, madam, it's a funny thing. Although I have a great deal of personal experience of the sea, and my father was also a captain on the Great Lakes, I always have the sensation that my stories are coming to me in visions of the future."

"You're psychic," Mother said.

"I don't usually admit this freely, but I believe I am," he said. "I confided this to my fellow writer Mr. Stead, and he invited me to come to the conference to explore the possibility further."

"Best of luck to you, Mr. Robertson," Mother said, departing to meet the other mediums in her Queen Victoria séance in a library on the second floor.

"Since you are both writers, I was wondering if you knew Dr. Conan Doyle," I said.

"I met the man once, though I don't really know him," Mr. Robertson replied. "He's Sir Arthur Conan Doyle, you know. He was knighted for his service as a doctor in South Africa during the Boer War, and for writing about it."

"Do you know why he is here?"

"I do know he is with the British Society of Psychical Research. That is a most respected group that researches all occurrences of the supernatural."

"Is he a believer?"

"He calls himself an agnostic, which means one who does not know."

I suddenly had a name for what I was — an agnostic. It was reassuring to know that it could be named something other than confused, bewildered, unsure.

I spoke about writing a bit further with Mr. Robertson and about the difficulties of getting published. He agreed to make some time to discuss professional writing with me on the last day of the conference. Thanking him profusely, I hurried off to Mother's séance.

When I reached the second-floor library, Amelie, Emma, and Blythe were already inside. Mother had talked her fellow mediums into allowing the twins to join them as they linked hands at a round table. Stead was one of the participants along with two other, very average-looking middle-aged men and an elderly woman. A large glass ball was in the center of the table.

Blythe and I were permitted to observe if we promised not to interfere with even the slightest sound. We sat on the straight-backed chairs lined up against the wall.

Just as the séance was about to begin, Conan Doyle slipped quietly into the room and took a seat right beside me. I was dying to say something to him but had promised my silence.

With the lights very dim, Stead began the session by summoning the queen to come and help her country one last time. Conan Doyle leaned close to me. "There's no rest for the weary, I take it," he quipped irreverently. "The old girl ruled for over fifty years and they still want her to work."

Stead stopped talking and all the mediums looked at us in annoyance. "Sorry," Conan Doyle apologized. "Proceed."

Stead resumed his attempt to summon the queen's spirit. After a few moments, one by one, the other mediums, including Mother, joined him. The elderly woman grew forceful, raising her voice and demanding that Queen Victoria appear in the same tone one might command a dog to sit. I didn't imagine a queen who had once ruled half the world would respond well to that approach.

All this calling, conjuring, and commanding went on for the better part of fifteen minutes. Blythe sat forward and watched. Conan Doyle had slid low in his chair, his arms wrapped around his belly. "This could go on all day," he complained to me under his breath.

"You don't think she'll show up?" I whispered.

"I hoped she would, so I could expose them in some fakery," he confided.

"You're not a believer?" I asked.

"Not for a second," he answered in a low voice. "Stead asked Ehrich Weiss and myself to observe and alert him to signs of fraudulence. He must give Taft accurate information."

Just to hear him speak was heaven. It was exactly like I imagined the voice of Dr. Watson in the Holmes stories. Forevermore I would hear that rich, resonant voice speaking when I read the text of a Sherlock Holmes adventure.

"If it's a fraud, why is nothing happening?" I quietly inquired.

"My intuition is that these particular people are honest, but misguided. They've set out to do something impossible and thus derive no result."

I looked over to Mother, whose eyes were shut and her brow furrowed with concentration as she quietly tried to summon the queen. Emma and Amelie had also closed their eyes and were gently rocking back and forth.

And then, abruptly, Emma lurched to her feet, breaking the chain of hand holders.

"Surging rivers of gushing blood!" she cried, throwing her arms open. Her eyes were now wide as though viewing the horror she spoke of.

Amelie's face was also contorted into an expression of absolute terror as she sat ramrod straight in her chair.

"Do not do this thing, my children! Stop it now, I say! It is chaos! It is suicide and damnation!"

This was not Emma's voice! Not even if Amelie was speaking through her.

Her right arm swung around like a compass finding true north, and she pointed to Conan Doyle. "You will suffer! Such unbearable pain! I weep for your intolerable loss."

The color drained from his face as Emma locked him in a fierce, wild stare. "Brace yourself, man. Your son will go to fight in France and he will not return."

This was too much!

I hoped fiercely that he did not have a son. I wanted to scold Emma, demand that she stop saying such awful things.

I stood to admonish her but I never got the chance.

"Heed this warning from a queen to a boy king!" Emma shouted.

Conan Doyle let out a strangled cry of surprised anguish.

At the exact same moment, Emma and Amelie both crumpled to the floor.

One of the mediums threw the light switch and everyone rushed to their aid, lifting them by the shoulders, patting their cheeks. "Give them room to breathe," Mother commanded. "Step back."

I noticed Conan Doyle, his palm pressed over his eyes and a trail of tears running down his face from either eye. Was it possible that this paragon of logic had been reduced to such a state by Emma's prediction?

Apparently it was so.

$\mathcal{E}$mma and Amelie came to consciousness pretty quickly but seemed dazed. Cousin Agatha was telephoned to collect them along with Mother, Blythe, and me.

While we waited in the lobby of the town house, I saw no sign of Conan Doyle, though I did catch sight, from time to time, of the dark-haired man, Ehrich Weiss.

While Mother went off to tell W. T. Stead why she was leaving, I spied Weiss looking at some oil paintings hanging on the wall across the way. Leaving my seated sisters and summoning my courage, I approached him. "Excuse me," I said. "Do you know if Dr. Conan Doyle is still here?"

"He is not," Weiss responded, studying me with his intense, nearly black eyes. "Are you a friend of his?"

"No, only a great fan, like so many others," I replied. "I was at the séance where the medium spoke to him and I saw how upset he was."

"Yes, he was completely rattled. He rushed home, desperate to see his teen aged son, Kingsley."

My hand flew to my mouth. *A boy king?* Was it a reference to Kingsley?

Weiss snapped his fingers in annoyance. "Just like that, he has shifted his position completely from that of arch skeptic to a total belief in spiritualism."

"That one séance convinced him?" I asked. I tried to hide the fact that I was scrutinizing him. Why did he look so familiar?

"He recalled once attending a speech given by Queen Victoria. The medium, he claimed, spoke in her voice. Plus, she knew of his son. I reminded him that he is a figure of public note. It would be easy enough for a charlatan to learn that he has an adolescent son."

"My sisters are not charlatans and they know absolutely nothing about Dr. Conan Doyle," I assured him, probably sounding more than a touch defensive.

"Your *sisters*?"

"They were the ones who spoke to him."

"And do you also have" — and here he rolled his eyes derisively — "*the gift*?"

"No, I do not."

"But you're a believer," he assumed.

I hesitated, caught between loyalty to Mother, Amelie, and Emma, and my first response, which was to be truthful. "I am searching for the truth," I said at last. "I am an agnostic," I added, proudly trotting out my new word.

"Commendable," he remarked. "Don't be fooled, young lady. As a magician, I have traveled Europe, completely convincing audiences that I have conjured magic which I know to be no more than sleight of hand, clever machinery, and the ability to misdirect. I began learning such tricks as a boy, and do you know who my first teachers were?"

"Who?"

"Mystics and mediums. I trained as an assistant. They let me in on all their secrets. Did you ever hear of the Fox sisters?"

"One of the sisters trained my mother," I said.

He chuckled. "The Fox sisters could make loud cracking pops with their toe and finger joints. They traveled the U.S.A. performing that little stunt, passing the sounds off as contact from another world, and got rich doing so. These women founded spiritualism, a mumbo-jumbo religion millions of gullible dupes now believe in, including, alas, as of yesterday, my poor, misguided friend Dr. Arthur Conan Doyle."

"But they found the skeleton of the dead man who contacted the Fox sisters in the wall of their house," I said, reminded of the firework celebration that had followed this event back when I was a child.

This caused Ehrich Weiss to laugh uproariously. "My dear girl, I merely said the Foxes were dishonest; I never implied they were stupid. They could well have heard tales of a man dying or disappearing in that house; maybe it was a story that someone murdered him and hid him in the wall. Many fake mediums are extremely clever — they have a sharp eye for the *tell*."

"The *tell*?" I questioned.

"It's a physical tic like a mouth quirk, a jerk of the elbow, a quiver of the eyebrow — something a person does that indicates an emotional reaction. Usually the person who does it is not even aware of it. But the medium is aware, and it directs the medium to keep pursuing that line of inquiry until a nerve is struck."

I thought of Mother seeing Aunty Lily's dead husband back so many years ago. Had she simply read the envelope addressed to Aunty Lily or had Aunty Lily given hints, shown a *tell*, that she missed Hiram? Maybe both things had happened.

"Conan Doyle must have displayed some *tell* when there was talk of war," Weiss went on. "The medium picked up on it and targeted him, assuming that he was too old to be a soldier but probably had a son he was worried about."

Was Emma really that cunning? I had never seen any sign that she was ever anything other than sweet and sincere.

"Jane," Blythe called to me, "Agatha has arrived."

I said good-bye to Ehrich Weiss and hurried to join Mother and my sisters. Together we piled into the motorcar and headed back to Brighton, all of us uncharacteristically silent, lost in our own musings. When we arrived at Agatha's house, Emma and Amelie headed straight to bed. "That sort of genuine contact saps one's energy completely," Mother commented.

"So if a person doesn't collapse, then he or she is a fake?" I asked cagily. I had seen Mother collapse only that one time when I was very small.

"Not at all," she replied. "Mediums have varying degrees of stamina and strength. Emma and Amelie are young and inexperienced."

Only after they had gone up did Mother tell Agatha everything that had happened.

"So the twins have inherited your gift," Agatha surmised.

"There can be no doubt after today," Mother replied.

"How can it be, though?" Agatha wondered fretfully. "In what way can a spirit travel back from the spirit realm to communicate with the living?"

"You know, Agatha, everything vibrates," Mother said. I hadn't heard her use her famous Tesla-inspired phrase in a while, and was mildly surprised.

"When a person passes over, that soul begins to vibrate at a different rate from those of us still on this earthly plane," Mother continued. "A medium is like a wireless transmitter simply tuning in the correct frequency. The gift is no more than a talent for discerning the correct spirit frequency."

"Fascinating," Agatha murmured.

It made so much sense when Mother spoke. But Ehrich Weiss had almost convinced me *he* was right. Which was it? I was more confused than ever.

"Say, Maude," Cousin Agatha said uneasily, "I would so love to speak to my late husband, Reginald. Do you think it might be possible to contact him?"

"We can certainly try," Mother agreed.

That night, after supper, Mother, Cousin Agatha, Blythe, and I sat around the table in the parlor. Mother produced her glass ball and set it in the center.

Close as I had always been to séances, I had never before participated in one; neither had Blythe. We exchanged nervous glances.

With the room almost completely in darkness, Mother began calling on the spirit of Reginald to come to us.

A silvery beam glowed in the glass ball.

The shades had been drawn, but my eyes darted to a sliver of moonlight that had found its way through a crack between the window and the shade creating a line of light. Was the ball reflecting *that*?

"I see him!" Cousin Agatha cried, nearly screaming. "He's there in the ball."

I leaned forward, peering into the glowing ball. In the center, a shape of dark silver wavered. I squinted at it and saw how it could be interpreted as the shape of a tiny man.

"Reginald, it's Agatha. Are you all right?"

The shape kept wavering and Agatha looked to Mother for guidance.

"Reginald is telling me he is fine," Mother said.

"Can you hear him?" Agatha asked urgently. "He had a rather squeaky voice for a man."

"It's a little squeaky, yes," Mother confirmed.

Was she being honest? Would she deceive her own cousin?

"Is he in the ball?" I asked Mother.

"His essence is inside the glass," Mother replied. "He does not choose to speak through me but rather to me."

"He always was such a gentleman," Agatha remarked, as if this was something gallant she was proud of Reginald's spirit for doing.

"He's being very polite," Mother confirmed. "He's keeping his distance somewhat so as not to burden me."

"No doubt he doesn't want to tax your strength too much." Agatha leaned in until her nose almost touched the glass ball. "Reginald, do you know if there will be a war coming?"

Mother cocked her head to one side as though listening intently. She frowned, and then pursed her lips in distress, listening to Reginald speak to her in a voice that only she could hear. "Do you mean naval ships?" Mother asked Reginald. "No? What kind of ship?"

"Navy!" Agatha cried. "Then there is a war!"

"No," Mother said. "No war — at least, he doesn't know for sure. He's warning me about danger from a ship, but I'm not sure what he means."

"Mimi might be on a ship," Blythe offered.

"Oh, dear," Mother said with a gasp. "She might be. Reginald, is Mimi in danger from a ship?"

At that moment, a face appeared above the glass ball. Underlit from the ball below, it seemed to hover there, disembodied and glowing.

"It's Mimi!" Blythe shouted and then screamed.

She was right. It *was* Mimi.

I sprang back and groped the walls in the darkness, desperate for a light switch. I overturned a vase that splashed water on me as it crashed to the floor. I found a switch, and the room was once again ablaze with light.

"You're not dead!" Mother cried in an emotion-filled voice. "You're not dead." A tremble ran through her and she began to cry with relief.

"I'm very much alive," Mimi assured us. "I'm so sorry to scare you all. I was waiting quietly in the dark but I only meant to stick my head into your circle to say I was not on a ship and quite all right."

"Are you really all right?" I asked. "What are you doing here?"

It turned out that Mimi had traveled to France, Spain, Italy, Germany, and Holland — in that order — and had just arrived in England with Benjamin Guggenheim and

Ninette Aubart and their entourage of about fifteen other servants and friends. "I telephoned Aunty Lily at the hotel and she told me you were here," Mimi explained.

Blythe ran from the table and threw her arms around Mimi's waist. "I'm so glad to see you!" she shouted, squeezing tightly as Mimi stroked her yellow curls.

I was also ecstatic to see Mimi, but unresolved resentment kept me frozen where I stood.

It took Mother only minutes to switch emotional tracks from the most joyful relief at seeing Mimi alive to a white-hot fury. "Has it never occurred to you in all these months to write to us to tell us that you were alive!?" she shouted.

"I sent a telegram from France when I arrived," Mimi defended herself.

"We never received it!" Mother shouted, turning red.

"The nearest telegraph office is in Buffalo," I offered. "They might not have bothered to deliver it." I felt the same mix of relief and anger as Mother was expressing, but an instinctive sisterly bond compelled me to come to Mimi's aid. "You should have known it wouldn't reach us," I added, ambivalent about exactly how much help I was willing to offer.

"Well, at first I planned never to come back," Mimi blurted.

"Never come back?" I echoed, outraged.

"What?!" Mother hooted in a voice more shrill than any I'd ever heard her use. "If I had known that insanity was playing in your head, I would have gone to Europe myself and dragged you back personally."

"Mother, I'm a grown woman," Mimi said in a dignified voice.

"Then behave like one!" Mother shouted. "Do grown women run away from home like Huckleberry Finn?"

Mimi threw herself into one of the chairs despairingly. "I thought it would be better for all of you if you could be rid of me," she admitted in a voice choked with tears.

"Whyever would you think that?" Mother asked incredulously.

"You know why," Mimi shot back.

"I do not," Mother insisted.

"Because I'm a person of black descent."

Agatha gasped at the news.

"No one knows that!" Blythe pointed out.

"But I don't want to live a lie," Mimi said passionately. She dropped her head and began to cry. "I'm so confused."

Mother came and sat in a chair beside Mimi. "Has something happened, Mimi?" she asked gently.

"No. Well . . ." she replied, wiping her eyes. "Only that I've fallen in love."

Mother threw her arms wide. "We knew it! Emma and Amelie predicted it months ago!"

"Fallen in love!" Blythe shrieked happily. "Then it's true! With who? Is he a prince? A duke? Tell!"

"He's Mr. Guggenheim's valet, Victor," Mimi told us.

"The valet?" Agatha echoed, clearly chagrined.

"With all those rich people around, you fell in love with the *valet*?" Blythe could not hide the disappointment in her voice.

"How old is this Victor?" Mother asked.

"Twenty-three," Mimi answered.

"Does he love you, too?" Blythe asked.

"He says so."

"Then what's the problem?" I asked.

"It's the issue of race," Mimi revealed. "What if we marry and have a child with dark skin?"

"Have you told him about your background?" Mother asked.

Mimi shook her head and began twirling a curl that had escaped from the elaborate, upswept style she now wore. "I've been too frightened."

"You must tell him," Mother advised firmly. "If he is a man of character and truly loves you, it won't matter to him."

"Mother, that's naive," Mimi argued.

"It's not," Mother disagreed. "Not everyone in the world is a bigot. You can come live in Spirit Vale where people are open-minded about such things."

"I don't want to live in Spirit Vale. I've been living in the real world and I like it there. I want to stay there."

"Even when this so-called *real* world is so cruel as to deny true love because of its own small-minded bigotry?" Mother shot back.

Mimi slumped lower on her chair. "Even then," she said.

The conversation came to one of those natural lulls where no one knew what to say next. Finally Agatha turned to Mother. "I suppose Reginald is gone," she said. Mother nodded, causing Agatha to sigh sadly. "That's a shame. He was always a good problem-solver. I wonder what he meant about the ship being dangerous."

"Speaking of ships, I have some exciting news," Mimi told us, brightening a bit. "I'll be traveling home on the maiden voyage of the most fabulous ship ever to cross the ocean — the *Titanic*!"

hat night Blythe and I stayed up deep into the next morning, talking with Mimi, who curled up with a quilt in one of Agatha's overstuffed armchairs. The twins had woken up earlier and weren't nearly as surprised as the rest of us to see her. Then they returned to bed with Agatha and Mother, who made Mimi promise not to run off again without saying good-bye.

"Tell us everything about Victor," Blythe requested eagerly now that the adults were asleep.

Mimi sat forward in the chair. "Jane has already seen him. Do you remember, Jane?"

I did, and I told her so.

"Who could forget him?" Mimi went on. "He is so handsome with large dark eyes. He's slim with broad shoulders. For some reason Mr. Guggenheim assumes he's Egyptian."

"But he's not?" I asked.

"No! He thinks it's funny that Mr. Guggenheim just jumped to that conclusion by looking at him, so he doesn't tell him otherwise. But Victor was born in England and his ancestry is Italian."

"Will you continue traveling with the Guggenheims?" I asked, trying to keep tones of disapproval from my voice and not completely succeeding.

There was tension in the air as Mimi looked me in the eyes. "I know you don't approve of Ninette," she said after a long pause.

"Have I ever said so?" I replied.

"You don't need to *say* anything," she snapped.

"That's your business. I only asked if you'd be traveling with them." Really, I didn't want to fight.

"Mr. Guggenheim is here in England. We left Ninette behind in Paris with her maid so she could see family and friends. She'll board the *Titanic* when it docks in Cherbourg to pick up passengers. It looks better."

I scoffed. "Who do they think they're fooling? Everyone knows what's going on between them."

"There's a fortune in money involved, so Mr. Guggenheim doesn't like to leave any proof that his wife's lawyers could get ahold of," Mimi explained evenly, as though it was a mere legal consideration.

"When did you become so worldly?" I asked. She had changed — she seemed older, more sophisticated — and I didn't like it.

"I've been traveling the world for over half a year, Jane, and I've been with Ninette, who was a cabaret singer in

Paris before she met Mr. Guggenheim. So yes, I am *world-lier* than when I left. I don't think that's so bad."

"Well, I do!" I said, raising my voice. "You've been dazzled by Ninette and her crowd. You think the way they live is all right just because they're rich. I don't think they're happy or good. You never used to care so much about money. What is it you think money will do for you?"

"Ha!" Blythe laughed. "What *won't* it do?"

"I'm not talking to you!" I snapped.

"Money protects a person from the world," Mimi replied forcefully.

"Why do you need protection from the world?" I demanded.

"Why can't you get this through your head, Jane? Because I'm black!"

"No, you're not," Blythe insisted.

"I am!" Mimi shot back. "I have been to Europe and even to Northern Africa. It's not like America. Although I did observe instances of racism in France and other places, people of color are not second-class citizens *everywhere* in the world."

"Then why are you worried about telling Victor about your background?" I asked.

Mimi sighed deeply. "Because he wants to live in America, and so —"

"I don't want to talk about all this," Blythe said

insistently, clasping her hands over her ears. "They fought the Civil War before we were born. Slavery is ended, and everyone should treat everyone fairly."

"You're as naive as Mother, Blythe," Mimi commented.

"I don't care. All I want to know is how Mimi intends to get me on the *Titanic* with her," Blythe said.

"What are you talking about?" Mimi asked, startled.

Blythe threw off her blanket and crossed to Mimi, perching on the arm of her chair and grabbing hold of her hand. "You have to; you must get me on that ship. It's my dearest wish in the whole world."

"Since when?" I challenged.

"Don't you remember? I told you how I longed to be on that ship, Jane. Mimi, you said Ninette has a maid; I'll be the maid's assistant — as long as I don't have to wear a uniform. I wouldn't like that. Better yet, I'll be *your* assistant! I'll be the companion of the companion. I'll sleep on the floor. It doesn't matter as long as I can be on the *Titanic*. Did you know they call it 'The Ship of Dreams'? I read that in a magazine."

Mimi gazed down at her thoughtfully. "I suppose you're old enough to be a mother's helper," she considered.

"Yes!" Blythe cried. "I love helping mothers!"

"When have you ever helped a mother with anything?" I countered.

"I help our mother."

"Ha! Barely! You have to be prodded and reminded just to pick your petticoats off the bedroom floor."

"Well, this would be different," Blythe replied. "I could do it."

"In France I spoke to a woman who was very nice. We met at the ticket office of the White Star Line there when I was picking up our tickets. She had been sent tickets for the liner *La France* but when she learned that her two little girls would not be allowed to take meals with her and her husband, they changed the *La France* tickets for ones on the *Titanic*. Her first-class tickets on the *La France* cost the same as second-class tickets on the *Titanic*."

"That's nice, but what does it have to do with me?" Blythe asked, a touch impatiently.

Mimi smiled. "I'm getting to that. Juliette — that is her name — asked if I knew of a nanny who might want to take care of her two little girls for the duration of the trip because she is pregnant with a third child. I said I didn't, but I took her name and address just in case I heard of anyone."

"I'll do it!" Blythe exulted.

"You're only thirteen," I reminded her.

"Nearly fourteen, and Mimi will be there. Can you phone her, Mimi?"

"I have no phone number, but I could send a telegram."

Emma appeared in the room, rubbing her eyes, her long hair in her face. "What's going on?"

Blythe leaped from the chair onto Emma, hugging her happily. "I'm going on the *Titanic* with Mimi!" she revealed. In the moonlight her face glowed, luminous with happy excitement.

Emma scowled. "We should all go home together on the boat we came over on."

"That's a great idea," I agreed. "We can get Mimi a ticket."

"I don't want to be on that old tub," Blythe said. "We should *all* go on the *Titanic*."

We debated this for another half hour, but clearly no one was going to change her mind. Emma returned to her guest room on the second floor. One by one, Mimi, Blythe, and I drifted off to sleep.

Some hours later, I was roused from sleep by the repeated banging of a shutter outside the window. A howling wind had risen while we'd been sleeping. Once awake, I needed to use the bathroom, which was on the second floor, and so I got off the couch.

When I came out of the bathroom, I noticed that the door to the room Mother, Amelie, and Emma were sharing was open. Mother and Emma slumbered, but Amelie was not in her bed. Looking down the dark hall, I saw no sign of her.

Hurrying down the stairs, I checked the kitchen but she wasn't there. It was only when I came back to the living room that I noticed the front door was slightly ajar.

Had Amelie gone out? But where? Why?

I grabbed my coat from the stand and threw it over my nightgown. Moving fast, I slipped, barefoot, into my high-button boots by the front door, not even bothering to fasten them.

Out in the dark, empty street, the ocean wind blew my hair in front of my eyes and made my coat flap open until I clutched at it. Looking in every direction, I saw no sign of her.

Not knowing what else to do, I headed down toward the beach and crossed the road to the boardwalk. The ocean gusts were fierce there, whipping my hair and clothing. Thankfully the full moon illuminated the beach, enabling me to spot Amelie's lithesome silhouette down at the shoreline.

Was she crazy? What was she doing there all alone in the dark? It was certainly far from warm.

With my head down, I set out across the beach, treading with determination despite the sand pouring into my boots. In the middle of the beach, the sand made it too hard to walk, so I stopped to pull off my footwear.

At the moment I pulled off the second boot, I looked over to Amelie. In the next second, I flung the boots and raced across the beach at full speed.

The lunatic was walking into the ocean!

By the time I reached her, she was thigh deep in the crashing, white, foaming surf.

"Amelie!" I screamed. "Amelie!"

She never turned. Was she ignoring me? Was the howling wind carrying my voice away?

"Amelie!"

She continued forward and was quickly to her waist.

Tossing off my coat, I headed into the white foam. The freezing water sent a painful shock from my toes to my head. It sucked the breath from my lungs.

I forced myself to move forward through the crashing surf, dancing about to avoid being knocked over. "Amelie!" I called.

She kept going.

I couldn't swim, but neither could she. There was no choice but to go after her. Pushing my way through the wind and the water, I hurried toward her. "Amelie, you're going to get us killed!" I shouted, desperate to get her attention.

It was impossible to make headway with the wind and water pushing me back.

Finally . . . finally, I got close enough to yank her arm. With physical strength I'd never experienced before, I pulled her back to shore, though she resisted me every step of the way, her back to me, pulling to go out to sea.

When we were knee high, I pushed her forward so hard,

she fell down. I stumbled onto her, falling into the frigid water.

"Amelie! What are you doing?!" I screamed.

A freezing wave hit us both in the face.

When I shook off the water, I really saw Amelie up close for the first time that night. Her eyes were wide and she gazed at me without recognition.

The sound of a voice crying out made me turn to the shore. Blythe was there, also in her nightgown, jumping and waving her arms. Mimi was racing down the beach, blankets bundled in her arms.

In the next minute, Blythe was crashing through the surf toward us. "Help me get her up!" I commanded. Together we were able to get her out of the water. Mimi met us with a wool blanket opened wide to enfold first Amelie, then me.

My teeth chattered uncontrollably and yet Amelie was strangely serene. "She's sleepwalking again," Blythe realized as Mimi spread the blanket over my shoulders.

"Why does she do it?" Mimi asked. She shook Amelie. "Wake up!" she shouted. "Wake up!"

"Don't do that," I said.

Amelie blinked hard and then began to cry.

"Are you awake, Amelie?" I asked.

She nodded as the tears streamed from her eyes.

"Why are you crying?" I asked, though I knew she wouldn't answer me.

Amelie's tears escalated into huge, rolling sobs. She was nearly hysterical.

Mimi took hold of her shoulders firmly. "Come on; let's get home. It's freezing out here."

We made our way across the beach without saying anything more. As soon as we opened Agatha's front door, though, we heard horrifying screams from upstairs. "That's Emma!" Blythe cried as she, Mimi, and I raced to the second floor.

The door was still open and we found Mother trying to subdue Emma, who thrashed wildly on the bed, shrieking with terror. "Emma, wake up!" Mother shouted. "You're dreaming! Wake up!"

She threw Mother off with the elevated strength of the truly terrified and desperate. Her eyes were like saucers. Her arms swept back and forth rapidly. "Help me, Mother!" she screamed. "Help! I'm drowning!"

"You're not drowning, Emma!" Mother yelled. "I'm here. You're dreaming!"

Agatha bolted into the room, mudpack and sleep bonnet on. "Who's drowning? What's happening?"

"Emma's having a nightmare," I told her.

"A waking nightmare," Blythe added.

"Oh, the night terrors," Agatha said.

Amelie came into the room, dripping water everywhere. I wasn't sure if she was awake or asleep.

Only then did Mother and Agatha look at us closely. "You're wet!" Mother cried, aghast. "Where have you been?"

Before we could answer, Amelie got onto the bed and put her arms around the frantic Emma. Like a blind person, Emma felt her wet hair and wet face and slowly seemed soothed.

"We have to get her out of that wet nightgown," Agatha said, but Mother held up a hand to stop her. Emma laid her head on Amelie's shoulder. Together they lay down on the bed and quickly drifted back to sleep.

"Now what do you suppose that was about?" Mother asked.

Chapter 20

The next day, the five of us were all laid flat with illness, ranging from Emma, Mimi, and Blythe with sniffles to Amelie and me, who had raging fevers, congestion, and a total lack of energy. Fortunately Mother and Agatha were well and tended to us.

They both left by midmorning because Mother was giving a lecture titled "Spiritualism, a Science We Do Not Yet Understand."

For my part, I lay deep in feverish dreams. I dreamed of ships passing in the night, going faster than was possible. I was all alone on a huge liner. I saw Mimi dressed in a bride's dress on another ship. She waved a lace hanky as she receded quickly from me. I cried out to her not to leave. I saw Blythe on another ship with twenty children dancing around her. Tesla and Thad flew overhead in a small, flying automobile, which was probably how I imagined Tesla's flivver plane. Strangely, as happens in dreams, Aunty Lily was with them and she was driving. When I looked down, Emma and Amelie were happily doing the backstroke in the ocean. Amelie called to me to join them, in a voice very like Emma's.

From time to time I would wake, parched. Cousin Agatha was always nearby to pour me a glass of water from her cut-glass pitcher. She placed cold towels on my forehead as I returned to my delirium of dreams.

By suppertime, I was cooler. "Thank heavens, darling," said Agatha, handing me toast on a plate. "You'll soon be better now. Amelie is still quite feverish, though."

I ate the toast and then went upstairs to see Amelie. In her room, an orange and pink sunset was pouring into the window. Emma sat on the bed beside Amelie, who slept. I sat beside her.

"What's it like with her when she's not channeling or making predictions through you?" I asked.

"It's just talk. She says something and I hear it in my mind, and then I answer in my mind and she hears it in hers. I never have to speak out loud to her."

"It's strange, Emma."

"Not to me. It's the way it's been all my life. I like it. It's comforting to be so close to another person. I'm never lonely."

Mimi and Blythe came in. They'd sent a telegram to Mrs. LaRoche, the Frenchwoman Mimi had met who was looking for a nanny. "I hope she wants me," Blythe fretted, her voice thick with congestion. "You told her I love children, didn't you, Mimi?"

"Since when do you love children?" I scoffed.

"I was one until very recently," Blythe replied.

"Shh!" Mimi hushed us. "Let's let Amelie sleep."

"Can you see her dreams?" I asked Emma in a whisper.

"Sometimes, but not right now."

We went downstairs just as Mother came in with Agatha, who had driven to London to get her. Mother was aflutter with all the news from the conference. W. T. Stead was the most gifted psychic she had ever met — an absolute genius of extrasensory perception. The way he communicated with Julia, his spirit guide, was amazing. "That Mr. Weiss kept trying to expose him as a fake but he never could!"

"Mother, are you in love with Mr. Stead?" Blythe asked. I was glad she posed the question, because I wouldn't have had the nerve, but I was also wondering.

Mother colored a brilliant red, which wasn't at all like her. "Heavens, no! He has a wife and six children. They live out on three acres in a place called Grainey Hall. He has merely rented the town house for the conference. We are dear friends and colleagues."

I directed my next comment to Mimi. "It matters to a decent person that a person he or she fancies might already be married."

"Who says I fancy him?" Mother objected. "He is a

brilliant, brilliant man. And kind. But there is no romance."

No matter what she said, I had the feeling that she had been disappointed to discover he had a wife, let alone six children.

"In a speech today he recounted three premonitions he's had in his life which were fulfilled. He alluded to a fourth which is yet to come," Mother told us.

"What is it?" Emma asked.

Mother gazed at us intensely and held a beat for one of the dramatic pauses that had become a trademark with her. "He would not say. He didn't want to be accused of bringing about that which he had predicted."

"Did Dr. Conan Doyle come back?" I asked Mother.

"Yes, but the poor man seems to have aged ten years. He is now completely converted to spiritualism, however, and sat for several readings. I did a vibrational reading for him."

"You touched the man who writes Sherlock Holmes!" I gasped.

"Only his vibratory field, and it's very erratic, I fear. I cautioned him to be careful of his health."

"Mother, can you truly tell anything at all by doing that?" Mimi demanded.

Mother cast a withering glance. "Would I do it if I could not?"

Mimi shot me the most subtle look of exasperation, no more than a lifted brow and a quivering eyeball, but it was enough to make me bite down on a grin. How I had missed her!

By the next day, even Amelie was almost all better, though she stayed in bed while we went to the convention with Mother. I saw Mr. Weiss writing in a notebook, appearing very engrossed. Intrigued, I sat down beside him. "Have you found evidence of fraud?" I asked.

He spoke swiftly, as if eager to be back to his writing. "Oh, there's a great deal of trickery going on here. Yes, indeed. Some of these people are so good at it that I cannot see how they are doing it at all."

"If you can't detect a trick, then maybe it's legitimate," I offered.

"It can't be done, so it has to be a trick," he countered.

"Isn't that a preconceived notion tainting your research?" I argued.

"It's plain common sense, if that's what you mean."

"Are you writing an article claiming that the conference is full of frauds?" I inquired. I was surprised to discover that I was slightly alarmed by this possibility. Was I becoming a believer, or did I simply like the people involved and not want to see them embarrassed?

"Someday I will write that article, but right now I am recording all the tricks I have witnessed here. One man can throw his voice to the corner of the room and thereby appear to be talking to a ghost. It's the greatest demonstration of ventriloquism I've ever witnessed. Another woman can swallow metal objects and silently regurgitate them at will, thus appearing to produce keys and bracelets and all sorts of things from the spirit world. It's amazing!"

"If you're not writing an article, what will you do with the information?" I asked.

He grinned at me. "I will only become the greatest magician the world has ever seen; that's all! My fame will be even greater than it already is."

"I know who you are!" I cried as the reality burst upon me. "You're Harry Houdini, the magician!" I'd seen his picture in the papers. He would have himself chained hand and foot yet escape from a sealed case of water before he drowned.

He stood abruptly and bowed. "At your service," he said gallantly.

"Why are you using a fake name?" I asked.

"It is my real name. Harry Houdini is the fake name." He tucked his notebook under his arm. "Good-bye, Jane," he said.

I watched him leave, not quite believing I'd actually met the world's greatest magician. His convincing skepticism made me once again uncertain about the spiritual realm.

The next day, Mimi received a return telegram from Mrs. LaRoche who said she had already put Blythe's ticket in the first-class mail. Needless to say, Blythe was in a state of exaltation. However, it quickly turned into a state of absolute panic when she considered that her wardrobe wasn't nearly grand enough for the greatest of all luxury liners, the *Titanic*.

"You're just a kid nanny," I reminded her.

"And you'll be in second class," Mimi said.

"That won't matter. You'll get me into first class, won't you? I mean, for meals and parties and things?"

"I don't know if I can," Mimi told her.

"Well, I'll find a way in — but not in these horrible dresses I own. Oh, this is a disaster!"

Chapter 21

April ninth was the last day of the conference. Mimi and Blythe would leave on the *Titanic* that morning, while Emma, Amelie, Mother, and I had tickets to sail on the twelfth on another ship. We would meet Blythe and Mimi in New York.

"Your European trip is over, so will you be coming back to Spirit Vale with us?" I asked Mimi that evening as we walked along the boardwalk.

She wouldn't meet my eye. "I don't know. It depends."

"On what?"

"On how things go with Victor."

I sighed. "Suit yourself," I grumbled.

Now she looked straight at me. "Don't be that way, Jane. Why do you have to make this harder than it already is?"

"It's not hard for you," I countered angrily. "You do just as you please. You dumped me off in a strange city and then left me to go home alone to face the consequences."

"We went there for your sake, in case you don't

remember," she came back at me. "And you met Thad. You ran off to lunch with him, as I recall."

"Yes, lunch, Mimi — not Europe!"

"You don't understand," she insisted.

"I understand selfishness when I see it." I don't know what made me be so peevish with her. Oh, but maybe I do — it was the idea of her leaving again. Tomorrow she would be gone and she was telling me she didn't know if she was ever coming back. And this time she was taking Blythe with her. Even though I'd see Blythe again in New York, the whole thing just gave me a bad feeling.

Mimi turned and walked back toward Agatha's without even waiting for me. For the rest of the evening we were icy to each other. Everyone must have noticed as we sat around the table having Agatha's trifle pudding for dessert. I'd been outspoken enough about my feelings, so I supposed they pretty much figured out what was going on.

"Mr. Stead has invited us to breakfast in the morning. I hope you girls can be civil to each other and not ruin the event," Mother cautioned.

Mimi and I didn't look at each other but stared down at our desserts without responding.

"Darlings, remind me to get petrol in the morning for the trip to the dock," said Agatha.

"I'm sorry, dear. I forgot to tell you. William, Mr. Stead, will accompany them by train to Southampton," Mother said. "He's also leaving tomorrow on the *Titanic*. President Taft himself mailed him first-class passenger tickets directly from the White House."

"You won't be seeing us off?" Blythe questioned, pouting.

"We'll say our good-byes at Mr. Stead's conference house. It will only be for a few days," Mother said.

"Almost a week," Blythe corrected her.

Mimi pushed her chair back and picked up her dish. "I'm not quite finished packing. How about you, Blythe?"

"I'm in desperate need of help," she replied. "Do you think I could borrow some of your things? Ninette's bought you such pretty clothing, and I'm almost your size."

"Not nearly," I put in.

They both shot me looks of annoyance.

"I have a few dresses you could borrow," Emma offered. "And you have some nice ones, Amelie. Could Blythe borrow some?"

Amelie looked up from her pudding and nodded.

Blythe's smile was forced. "Thank you both, but I'm sure Mimi has more clothes than she can even pack."

Mimi sighed with tolerant exasperation. "Later we'll go see what I've got."

"Agatha," Mother said, stirring her tea in a distracted way, as Emma, Amelie, and I took our dishes to the kitchen, "have you ever read anything by an author named Morgan Robertson?"

Agatha tilted her head thoughtfully. "I can't say that I have, darling. Why?"

"He was at the conference — a charming man. I only just met him and I can't recall reading any of his books, but his name seems so familiar and I simply can't stop racking my brain trying to remember where I know it from."

"Why does it matter so much?" I asked, returning to the parlor.

"I'm not sure," Mother answered absently, clearly still stewing on the question. "It just seems important for some reason."

"I'm sure it will come to you," Agatha commented.

"That reminds me," Mother said, looking at Mimi and Blythe. "Be cordial to Mr. Stead on the ship, girls, but do not occupy too much of his time. When I told him you would be on the *Titanic*, Mr. Stead did his utmost to convince me this was not a good idea. He urged me to have you take another ship."

"I can't!" Mimi cried. "I *must* take the *Titanic* with Ninette and Mr. Guggenheim. They're my employers. I'm being paid to keep Ninette company."

"And I don't want to take some dumpy, dull other ship!" Blythe put in. "To travel on the *Titanic* is a chance of a lifetime. It wouldn't be fair to prevent me from going! Why did he say that?"

"He wouldn't say, but many socially prominent people

will be on board. The only reason I can think of could be that he wants to be free to associate with them without being distracted by looking out for your welfare."

"We won't bother him," Mimi assured Mother. "But there is no chance that we would pass up this trip."

"That's what I told him," Mother said.

"It's strange for him to object so much to their presence on the ship," I remarked. He'd been so friendly to us during the conference that it seemed out of character to me.

"It struck me as a bit odd, as well," Mother agreed. "He ended our conversation with a peculiar statement. He said, 'Mimi is a woman and Blythe will be considered a child. That will affect the outcome.' When I asked him what outcome he was referring to, he brushed it off, saying he was just working out a problem in his head."

We arrived at Mr. Stead's breakfast at seven thirty in the morning on April tenth. Mr. Stead was entering the building as we all pulled up, jammed into Agatha's motorcar. He explained that he had gone to his home in the country to spend the night before his departure with his wife and children.

It was a lovely buffet spread, and we all ate heartily. We were not the only ones there. Agatha joined us at Mr.

Stead's invitation. Quite a number of other guests attended, but they were all on their way by nine.

Mimi and Blythe were dressed to travel, their suitcases stowed in the front lobby closet. Blythe was like a baby peacock strutting her new finery, a navy blue jacket and a blue sailor-style dress with a dropped waist, both borrowed from Mimi. Her brimmed hat was truly cute. Mimi was the picture of elegance in a rose brocade, ankle-length dress with a solid rose jacket.

Mr. Stead was quiet during breakfast. I assumed he was tired from the rigors of the conference or maybe apprehensive of the upcoming peace conference. We all left the buffet table and at Mr. Stead's invitation joined him in the study to await the horse-cab he'd ordered to take them to the Waterloo train station. From there they would take the train to the *Titanic*.

The study was lined with bookcases and papers. "I've slowly brought so many things from home," he commented when he saw me looking at them. "Somehow I shall have to get all this back to the country when I return from the United States and give up my lease on this place."

"Have you learned anything valuable from this conference?" Mother asked him.

"Your daughters have convinced me that there will, indeed, be a world war. I now believe that Mr. Taft's attempt to sidestep or prevent it will probably be in vain."

"Why go, then?" I asked.

"One must try one's best despite the evidence," he replied sadly. "It is always possible that what we do affects the future. It may be that in a future where we do nothing there will be war, but if we try to stop it, the outcome will change. My spirit guide, Julia, has implied as much to me, though she hasn't stated it directly. At the very least, perhaps the misery will be lessened or shortened due to our efforts. One must always try."

"You are a good man," Mother told him.

"I'm just a man with many questions," he replied. "All my life I've been driven to seek answers."

It heartened me to hear him say that since I, too, had a million questions, took nothing for granted, and was always seeking. Sometimes I thought something must be peculiar about me that I was so driven. To hear Mr. Stead say he felt the same made me see myself as less odd.

Much less encouraging was his conviction that Emma and Amelie — or should I say Queen Victoria? — had convinced him war was coming. I didn't want to think about what a world at war would be like.

Soon the horse-drawn cab arrived to take Mr. Stead, Mimi, and Blythe to their ship. "We will see you soon." Mother bid them good-bye with hugs. "Mimi, you watch out for Blythe."

"She won't have to," Blythe objected.

"I will," Mimi promised, speaking over Blythe.

I hugged Blythe good-bye, but when Mimi approached

for a hug, I didn't make a move to enfold her in my arms. "Good-bye, Mimi," I said stiffly, avoiding her hurt gaze. "I suppose we'll see you in New York."

"Come, ladies," Mr. Stead urged. "Our cab waits."

Mother, Agatha, Emma, and Amelie went out to say more good-byes at the curb, but I stayed behind in the study, dropping into a high-backed leather armchair. Now that Mimi was gone, I let my anger at her become what it had truly been all along: bitter sadness and disappointment. Dropping my head, I began to cry.

Minutes later, someone entered the study and I quickly brushed my tears away. It was Mr. Robertson inquiring for Mr. Stead. "You've missed him, I'm afraid. He's left for the *Titanic*."

He nodded somberly. "So he decided to go, after all."

"What do you mean?" I asked, suddenly alarmed by the seriousness of his expression.

He held a large paper envelope tied in string. He placed it on Mr. Stead's desk and began to untie it. As he worked the string, Mother, Agatha, Emma, and Amelie returned.

Mother gasped sharply when he produced the contents of the envelope. "Now I remember why your name is so familiar!" she cried. "I read that book on the train from New York to Buffalo many years ago."

Standing, I looked to see what Mr. Robertson held. It was a slim novel with a picture of an ocean liner on the cover. Its title was *Futility*.

"In your novel, the ocean liner sinks, if I'm correct," Mother recalled.

"I'm afraid it does," Mr. Robertson confirmed.

Mother leaned heavily on the desk as though she needed its support to keep from fainting. "And the ship is named the *Titan*."

"Yes," he said. "I urged Stead not to travel on it. He himself has made predictions of his own death by drowning. It's preoccupied him for many a year."

"He never spoke of it to me," Mother said. "I thought it was ice he feared."

"He entertained both possibilities. It is a matter of public record. In 1886 he wrote an article titled 'How the Mail Steamer Went Down in Mid Atlantic by a Survivor.'" He strode to the bookshelf and pulled down a magazine, *Review of Reviews*, that Mr. Stead had founded and edited. "This is a story he wrote in 1892 featuring a character that was clairvoyant."

He quickly found the page he wanted and began to read: "'I was saying,' said Mrs. Irwin, 'that last night, as I was lying asleep in my berth, I was awakened by a sudden cry, as of men in mortal peril, and I roused myself to listen, and there before my eyes, as plain as you are sitting there, I saw a sailing ship among the icebergs. She had been stove[d] in by the ice, and was fast sinking.'"

The quaver in Mother's voice made me realize she was trembling. "An iceberg, you say?"

"Yes. The ship collides with an iceberg and sinks," Mr. Robertson said.

"What is the name of the ship this book is about?" Emma asked.

"The *Majestic*," Mr. Robertson told her.

Majestic. Titanic. It was much too close for me to feel comfortable about it. But I clung to logic. There was no sense in jumping to irrational, panicked conclusions. "Think about it," I said, trying to convey a cool rationality I didn't really feel. "These ocean liners have been growing bigger and bigger steadily. That could be cause for concern. Icebergs are a known hazard in the northern Atlantic. And these ships all have names that are similar: the *Gigantic*, the *Olympic*. It's logical that anyone who thinks about the nature of these liners might come up with a similar scenario as these."

I took a concluding breath, feeling satisfied with my dispassionate assessment of the situation. Sherlock Holmes — if not Dr. Conan Doyle — would have been proud.

"That sounds sensible, my dear," said Mr. Robertson, "but the *Titanic* is considered unsinkable. If there were not an element of supernatural prophecy and clairvoyance in these stories, why would they be about an unsinkable ship sinking?"

"It's only a fear," I suggested.

"When I wrote *Futility*, it came to me like a waking dream. There was nothing logical about it," Mr. Robertson insisted.

"It's the fourth prophecy," Mother said to Mr. Robertson, much alarmed. "In his speech the other day, he said he had documented a fourth prophecy. This has to be it."

"I believe you are correct, madam. He and I discussed this only two nights ago." He pulled open the top drawer of Mr. Stead's desk and took out a hardcover sketchpad. "He showed me these drawings he's been making while in a trance state over the course of the last ten years. He is quite a good artist, but that is hardly the point here."

He opened the book of Stead's sketches and showed Mother. A tortured, anguished cry came from her. Dropping the book, she covered her face with her hands. Agatha rushed to support her as she wilted to the side.

Frightened but overcome with curiosity, I retrieved the book. Emma and Amelie crowded me on either side, looking down at the pages of charcoal sketches along with me as I slowly turned them.

One drawing was a full-length self-portrait of Mr. Stead flailing helplessly under the water, his suit and tie floating around him. Another sketch showed a gigantic ocean liner sinking, its back half standing straight up at a ninety-degree angle. A third depicted an iceberg with some people climbing onto it while others floated in a frigid ocean.

"Let's go! Right now!" I cried, all my misgivings about clairvoyance swept aside. "We can't let Mimi and Blythe get on that ship!"

*C*moke billowed from under the hood of the motorcar as
Agatha sped into Southampton at twenty miles an hour,
as fast as her automobile would go. As soon as we got close
to the dock, she had to slow down because there was a
huge crowd of people milling in the streets of the plain,
working-class town with its square, brick buildings. Some
were laden with bundles, trunks, and suitcases. Others
carried nothing and had probably come out simply to witness the maiden voyage of the reported wonder that was
the *Titanic*.

"Oh, heavens!" Mother cried. She'd caught sight of the
immense ship at dock.

The ship was, indeed, a sight to behold. My first impres-
sion was of a gigantic tiered wedding cake. The enormous
ocean liner boasted white stacked decks above a great
black hull that seemed to stretch on forever. At the very
top were four very large smoke funnels. It appeared to be
as tall as any building in London or New York City.

The train station connected directly to the ship and
cranes were loading cargo and trunks from the train directly

into the liner's cargo hold. "Maybe we're not too late, dar-lings," Agatha said as she sharply turned the steering wheel in the direction of the station. As soon as we arrived, I jumped out of the back and ran to a stationmaster to ask if they were unloading cargo from the nine thirty train from Waterloo; I was told that the nine thirty had already arrived and had been unloaded.

Before returning to the automobile, I stopped but a quick moment to let my heart slow down. It wasn't possible that we wouldn't reach Mimi and Blythe in time to stop them from leaving. I couldn't consider that possibility for even a second or I would fall to pieces.

When I gave everyone the bad news, Agatha turned the motorcar back toward the ship but was again stalled in a thick crowd of people moving forward. Although the *Titanic* was supposed to be the most luxurious liner of all time, the people in this crowd were clearly not wealthy. The women's dresses were unstylish, their hair disheveled — some wore unattractive scarves — and they carried heavy bundles while they tried to manage messy children. The men, too, wore frayed, patched coats.

Agatha pulled the motorcar aside and turned it off. Getting out, we struggled through the crowd on foot. Emma, Amelie, and I made better progress than Mother and Agatha. When once we paused to wait for them, Mother waved us forward. "Go! Go!" she shouted. "Try to catch up with them before they board."

With much breath sucking and squirming past, even sometimes crawling under legs, my sisters and I finally reached the boarding gateway. The gangways leading to the ship looked like wooden bridges with waist-high railings. The top gangways were occupied with rather grand-looking passengers, the middle gangways had less fancy passengers, while the lower one was packed with the people I guessed to be the third-class passengers. They were boarding the lower decks of the ship.

We went to where the people were showing their tickets and having their names crossed off a list. I tried to get the attention of the uniformed purser at the entrance to the gangway who was checking names but couldn't distract him from his task no matter how hard I tried.

As an alternate, I located a uniformed officer, another seemingly junior purser, for he was not much older than me, with a clipboard and asked if Mimi or Blythe Oneida Taylor had boarded. He checked the passenger list and found their names. "They're here, all right, on the ship already. First and second classes have already boarded. Third-class steerage passengers are going on now."

I tried to impress upon him how urgent it was that I board the ship, just to talk to them, but he insisted it was impossible. I argued with him that it was of utmost importance. "Has there been a death in the family?" he asked in a tone that made it sound like he might accept this one reason to let us on board without tickets.

"Yes!" Emma cried, before I could even formulate a response. "Our father has died." That was true enough. No one could fault her for lying. I quickly banished an inadvertent smile as Amelie subtly rolled her eyes at the lie.

"Let me speak to my superior," he said. "Come with me." We followed him back to the man checking names and tickets. The junior purser instructed us to stand a distance off while he spoke to him. As they talked, the purser at the gate kept shaking his head, refusing, it appeared, to let us board without tickets.

Emma tapped my shoulder but I was too intent on watching the two men debate to take my eyes from them. It didn't look good. When I finally turned to say this to Emma and Amelie — they were gone!

Casting about frantically looking for them, I eventually spotted my sisters up ahead. They had somehow sneaked past and were on the gangway and now stood shoulder to shoulder, their heads bent low. Almost imperceptibly, Amelie glanced back over her shoulder and quirked her head, indicating that I should follow them. But how?

I couldn't be too long about it, because once the officers ended their discussion and turned their attention back to the passenger line, there would be no getting past them. At that moment, a white-bearded man of military bearing in a white uniform with epaulets and a captain's cap walked past with two other white-uniformed officers. "That's Captain Smith," someone in the halted line realized. The line pushed forward, breaking form, as people tried to gain Captain Smith's attention with various questions.

It was my moment and I grabbed it, ducking low and scooting up the gangway. Just as I reached it, the line of people on the gangway moved forward. Others were admitted behind me.

We'd done it! We were on, though we dared not revel in our victory for fear of drawing attention. And besides, the job was not done yet. We still had to find Blythe and Mimi.

As we crept forward with the crowd, I craned my neck, scanning the upper gateways trying to find Blythe and Mimi. When we went into the ship, people were busily trying to locate their rooms, crowding past one another in the narrow halls.

I saw a steward locking a gate, closing off a stairway that would lead to the upper decks. "Why are those being locked?" I asked.

"Third-class passengers can't leave steerage," he informed me.

"Well, we must get up," I told him.

"Sorry," he said, looking none too sorry.

Nodding, I took the twins by hand and moved them out of the steward's hearing. "We've got to find a gate that's still open," I said to them. "Hurry, follow me." Nearly running, I rushed farther down the hall. When we were around a bend and out of the steward's sight, I yanked at a gate and was relieved to find it had not yet been locked.

We climbed the narrow stairs toward the upper decks until we came out — quite by mistake, because we really had no idea of where we were going — onto the second-class outdoor walkway. A sign read: SECOND-CLASS PROMENADE. FIRST- AND SECOND-CLASS PASSENGERS ONLY. We were dressed better than most of the passengers in steerage; I hoped that fact would enable us to move freely into second class where we might at least find Blythe.

As I stepped onto the deck, I began to have second thoughts about our mission. It was almost inconceivable that this ocean liner would sink; it was so massive and sturdy. For it to be plunged under the water would be as if an entire town had sunk under the ocean.

I estimated that the ship was probably bigger and contained more people than all of Spirit Vale. Most of the people were not here on this particular part of the promenade at the moment, though. We were at the back of the ship, and the others were crowded at the bow and on the opposite side, waving good-bye.

Standing there, my emotions began to spin wildly. Like so many other times in my past, I was torn. Swept up in the conviction of Mother's panic, I had been so convinced that getting my sisters off this ship was the most important thing on earth. But now, faced with the immensity, high level of efficiency, and utter solidity of the vessel, a feeling of being almost ridiculous was beginning to descend upon me.

It was not a good feeling.

A man walked by in a heavy overcoat with a cap pulled low over his face. I noticed him casually only because the heaviness of his coat seemed excessive for the pleasant weather.

Turning to Emma and Amelie, I was about to suggest that maybe our being on the ship wasn't the best of ideas and that we should leave. But when I turned to them, both were locked in a rigid fixation on the man in the heavy coat.

Emma's mouth opened and a voice came out, though she seemed to be barely moving her lips. It was the slightly higher voice she used when Amelie was speaking through her. "He's the one," she said eerily. "He will bring death to this ship."

Beside her, Amelie had begun curling in on herself as she slowly sank to the floor, her hands over her bowed head, her head bending into her chest. It was as if she were trying to pull herself into a ball.

I swung my head back to get a better look at the man but he had turned a corner and was out of sight.

"Everyone must leave the ship now!" Emma cried and she began to shake uncontrollably. Her eyes rolled back in her head until only the whites showed. "I don't want to die! I don't want to die!" she screamed and then dropped suddenly and hard onto the floor.

Bending over them, I tried to shake my sisters into consciousness. "Come on; wake up! Wake up!" They didn't stir. I became worried that Emma had hit her head badly.

A young woman knelt beside me. She was Chinese. "I help," she said, her English heavily accented. "You wait. I get friend." She hurried toward the bow of the boat.

It was probably only a few moments but it seemed an eternity that I waited there beside the unconscious twins. Finally, the young woman returned, hurrying in front of a young man in a tweed cap, pants, and jacket. His blue tie flew out to one side in the breeze as he walked at a fast clip behind her.

Why was my skin suddenly tingling, gooseflesh forming on my arms?

It was the young man hurrying so quickly forward, with that same brisk, purposeful walk. . . .

As he came closer, I blinked hard into the sunlight at the young man.

Had I fainted, too?

Was this a dream?

It was Thad.

Chapter 23

He came to a sudden halt in front of me, then staggered back a few steps in surprise. "Jane?"

"Thad, what are you doing here?" It *had* to be a dream.

"I can't tell you exactly. Why are *you* here?"

"I can't explain that right now, either. It's a long story, and right now I need to get them some help," I said, gesturing down at my prone sisters.

"What's happened?"

"They're my sisters. As I said, it's hard to explain. They're breathing, but they fainted when they saw —"

I suddenly realized who it was they had seen.

"You're here with Tesla, aren't you?"

"Don't ask me that," he replied, looking away.

I didn't have to; I was now certain it was Tesla who had passed us by in disguise, not even willing to greet me. What was he up to that had caused the twins such overwhelming distress?

A horn sounded. I looked up at Thad in alarm. "Are we leaving? So fast?"

Thad nodded. "I think everyone's boarded. The third-class passengers were the last to come on."

"We have to get off the ship," I said.

"You're not booked for this trip?" he asked.

"No. Are you?"

He nodded. My heart sank. Our reunion would be painfully brief. Seeing him again reawakened all the longing I'd felt these last months. My efforts to forget him were undone in a second.

It wasn't right that we would be separated again soon.

"The boat's going to leave," he cautioned as the horn sounded once again. "If you plan to get off, you'd better go."

"I have to find Mimi and my other sister, Blythe. In fact, you and Tesla shouldn't be on this ship, either."

"Why not?"

"Oh, you'll think I'm crazy . . . but . . ."

"What?" he pressed.

"We've just come from a psychic conference, and have learned that this ship is going to sink," I blurted.

He stared at me skeptically. "I wouldn't worry about it, Jane," he said, suppressing a grin.

"I'm not exactly sure it's true anymore, either," I admitted. "But it's not worth taking the chance."

"And how are you getting those two out of here before the ship sails?" he asked.

"I don't know," I replied.

"I could carry one of your sisters. Maybe you and Li could carry the other between you," Thad suggested.

"All right. All right," I agreed. "Let's try it." Thad spoke to Li in Chinese and she nodded. She lifted Amelie under her arms and I took hold of her feet. Thad was trying to get Emma over his shoulder when a loud, shrill third blast blew.

"Where should we go?" I asked, utterly lost.

"I'm not sure. Let's carry them toward the bow."

As we got closer to the happy, waving crowd toward the bow, a uniformed steward approached us. "What's happened to these young women?" he demanded.

Thad, Li, and I looked at one another, speechless.

"They've fainted," Thad replied after a quick moment of indecision.

"Where are you taking them?" he asked suspiciously.

"We have to get off the ship," I admitted but, at that moment, a fourth deafening sounding of the horn obscured my words.

The ship lurched, knocking Li and me off balance. We staggered, with Emma still hanging between us.

The *Titanic* was moving!

At the same time, Emma and Amelie began to come to. "Ladies, are you feeling better?" the steward asked.

"I — I think so," Emma stammered drowsily.

"And you, miss?" he addressed Amelie.

"She doesn't speak," Emma told him.

"She seems much better," I offered.

"Very well, then," the steward said, satisfied and moving on.

"The three of us have no tickets," I told Thad. "What do we do now?"

He made no answer but his baffled expression said that he had no idea what we should do. "Just don't let them catch you, I suppose," he suggested.

"It might not be such a bad thing if they put us off for not having tickets," I said. Of course, there would be the problem of how to get home from France or Ireland — the places the ship would stop before New York — made especially difficult by the fact that the three of us had no money.

"This ship is not going to sink," Thad said confidently once again. He took a folded brochure from his back pocket. It had been issued by the White Star Line. "Read this," Thad said. "It says that the ship has been designed to be unsinkable."

As he spoke, there was a loud crack and a jolt as if the ship had hit something very large.

"What was that?" Thad cried, alarmed.

A wide grin swept over my face. I was hugely reassured at this sound, nearly giddy with relief, in fact. Would the ship sink right here and now? If it was going to sink, this was surely the place to do it, while it was still in the protected Southampton waters with hundreds of people onshore, watching. There were boats everywhere that would come out and help at a moment's notice. The ship's lifeboats would never even have to be used.

"Why are you smiling?" Thad asked me, looking perplexed.

"I'll tell you later," I said as the five of us hurried to the bow of the boat where many passengers were hanging at the railing, curiously watching the activity below.

It turned out that the *Titanic* was hardly out of port when it collided with a much smaller vessel called the *New York*. Neither was greatly damaged.

I *hoped* that the *Titanic* had sunk just a fraction, sprung a pinprick of a leak. I knew from my years in Spirit Vale that clairvoyance was not an exact science. I recalled the mediums in the town square: *I'm getting a J.R. — either initials or a junior.*

What if Mr. Stead and Mr. Robertson really possessed extrasensory perception, could truly predict that there would be a collision and some damage to this ship? Might not they be wrong about the severity of the accident?

Of course they could be! They had been right about the incident but wrong in the details of it.

This was what they'd predicted. It had just happened! Their premonitions had been accurate. But now it was over.

I didn't voice any of this, because I didn't want to think about it anymore. And, with the truth of hindsight, I realize now that I didn't want to risk having Emma tell me any differently.

As far as I was concerned, the danger had passed.

The *Titanic* was under way and there was no chance of getting off now. Our biggest challenge was to get to New York without being discovered and locked up for not having tickets. They probably had some sort of jail on the ship — they had everything else conceivable, so why not that? — and I didn't want to spend this trip sitting inside a windowless box.

Besides, if I was in jail, I wouldn't be able to spend time with Thad. Had all my dreams and longing for him somehow made this happen? At the moment, that was how it seemed to me. The force of my desire to see him again had somehow brought him back to me. I knew such thinking made no sense, but I'd also heard people say that if a couple was meant to love each other and be happy together, somehow it would happen.

Maybe all the events of the last few months had occurred for just one reason — to bring Thad and me together. Perhaps our being here on the *Titanic* wasn't predestination, but rather, destiny.

Chapter 24

We knew Mimi was in first class and Blythe was in second. Thad had a room in first class so I went with him to C Deck to search while Emma and Amelie remained in second class with Li to look for Blythe.

The moment we got to first class, I immediately felt my dress to be shabby compared to the gorgeous dresses and day suits I saw parading past. When I mentioned it, though, Thad just smiled. "You look better than all of them. They need all that stuff because they don't have what you do."

"What do I have that they don't?" I asked, immensely pleased by his compliment.

"You know what," he said as we hurried down the hall. "That certain something. You know, inside."

What a letdown!

"You're saying I'm smart?" I surmised unhappily. I knew I wasn't a raving beauty like Mimi, but I had hoped he was working up to a more thrilling bit of praise than *smart*.

"Not *only* smart," he said. "Stop fishing for compliments. You know what I mean."

I *didn't* know! I had no idea! And I'd have given anything to hear him say what this special something I possessed was — but since he was onto my attempt to get him to compliment me, I would probably never know. And it occurred to me: If he thought I was so "special," why hadn't he written?

After walking through a labyrinth of thickly carpeted hallways unsuccessfully looking for Mimi, Thad guided me into an empty room on A Deck. It was filled with elegant tables and upholstered chairs. Heavy moldings surrounded a huge chandelier at the center, and its many windows were draped with velvet curtains that matched the swirling brocade pattern of the thick wall-to-wall carpet. "This is the reading and writing room," he told me.

As I examined the linen stationery embossed with the ship's letterhead that was offered free for the taking, Thad pulled out a chair for me beside a highly polished round table. I sat and he took a chair beside me. "I'm so glad to see you again, Jane," he said.

"I thought you were going to write to me," I reminded him. I hadn't planned to be so direct, but the words tumbled out almost on their own.

He pressed the tips of his fingers together and studied them for a long moment before speaking. "Jane, when we first met I didn't realize you were only sixteen."

"But you said I was *smart*."

"I said more than smart."

"Then what's the difficulty?"

He leaned back and studied me with a mixture of amusement and frustration. "You're blunt, aren't you?"

"I just want to know why you didn't write," I said.

"It just didn't feel right to be corresponding with a girl your age."

"Even a smart girl?"

"Jane!"

"My birthday is in four days," I told him. "I'll be seventeen."

"I'm twenty," he reminded me. "Seventeen does sound better than sixteen, though."

"You make too much of it," I insisted. "There's not much difference between us at all."

He thought about this a moment. "Let's forget about it for the time we're on the ship," he suggested. "I'm surprised to see you, but really glad."

I laid my hand lightly on his, an overly bold gesture perhaps, but it felt right. "I'm really glad to see you, too."

We left the reading and writing room and set back out to continue looking for Blythe and Mimi. "You still haven't told me why you and Tesla are here," I reminded him as we walked along the second-class promenade, checking every deck chair for signs of them.

"Okay, here's the thing," he began earnestly. "You can't tell anyone that Tesla is on board."

"Who would I tell?" I questioned. "Besides, doesn't the White Star Line already know? He must be on the ship's roster."

Thad shook his head and offered me his arm to hold. It felt wonderful to be walking arm in arm there like a real couple. He bent closer in order not to be overhead. "He's traveling under the name Emil Christmann."

"Why?"

He bent closer still, leaning in until we were nearly nose to nose. This closeness thrilled me. I was drawn to the warmth of his body. "John Jacob Astor the Fourth is on the *Titanic*," he revealed, speaking very quietly. "Tesla is determined to talk to him while he's a captive audience on the ship. Tesla has a couple of inventions to pitch to the guy. He's even brought some prototypes to demonstrate. He doesn't want the press catching wind of any of this."

"Is he worried they would file a report from France?" I asked.

"No," Thad said, shaking his head. "They only take on passengers in France and Ireland. No one gets off. The problem is that there's a Marconi room on board."

"Marconi the inventor?"

"Yeah, it's named after him. It's a room where they send telegrams. It drives Tesla crazy that they call it a Marconi. He's suing the guy for stealing his ideas."

"He told me about that," I said.

"It should be the Tesla room. If Tesla was allowed to do his work in peace, ships would be able to speak from ship to ship by now. Anyway, the ship is crawling with reporters writing reports and articles about the trip. One of them could send a telegram ahead. Some capitalist in America might steal the idea and set up a rival manufacturing plant before we even land in a week from now."

"All these new inventions make things move so fast these days," I commented.

Thad laughed drily. "This is just the beginning. At the rate things are being invented — even with all the delays — everything will keep moving faster and faster. You'll see."

"What kind of delays?" I asked.

"Competition, lack of money," Thad answered. "Tesla has lost years of research because he always needs money guys to back him. And the money men only care about something if it can make them more money. Tesla can't manufacture any of his inventions, but big shots have the money to jump on it."

"Why is he so desperate for Astor's money?"

"He likes Astor, thinks he's a good guy, a smart guy. He's invented a few things himself. Tesla trusts him."

"From what I've heard, I guess that's important," I remarked.

"Trust is important to Tesla. It's important to everybody, I guess."

"How do you know Li?" I asked.

"From when I was in China. I told her father I would escort her over from England to America to work with him in his restaurant. She's in second class, so you and your sisters can squeeze in with her."

"Maybe. Perhaps we can also bunk with Blythe or Mimi," I suggested, throwing my arms wide with frustration. "Where could they be?!"

Back in the hallway, we found a steward who was willing to check the roster and located Mimi's room. We knocked on her door but got no response. I wrote her a fast note on *Titanic* stationery:

I AM ON BOARD WITH TWINS. MEET YOU HERE AT 3 AND I WILL EXPLAIN. JANE.

After I'd slipped the note under the door, I felt we could stop searching.

Thad and I climbed up narrow stairs to the first-class promenade. We stopped by the railing to gaze out over the water. "You know, Jane, I've been thinking about trust since we talked about it just before. Do you feel you can't trust me because I didn't write after I said I would?"

I kept my eyes on the ocean. I didn't want to say anything hurtful but I wanted to be honest, too. His not writing had caused me a lot of pain. Did I trust him? I was madly happy to see him — but did I trust him completely?

"I don't know," I replied.

Chapter 25

I had looked out over the water. It seemed like a long time before either of us spoke. I was dying inside, worrying that my words had been too harsh. I feared losing him again but I had to speak the truth. He had hurt me deeply. The past winter had been so difficult — hoping for a letter every day and never receiving one.

"I'm sorry if I hurt you," he said softly. "I wanted to write. I did put one thing in the mail to you."

I gazed up at him, surprised. "I never received anything," I said.

"I sent you a book," he replied.

"*You* sent it?" I questioned. "I thought it was Tesla who did."

"Are you disappointed it was me?" he asked.

"Not one bit," I said. "Why didn't you add a note?"

Thad shrugged. "It was a way of writing without writing, I suppose."

"Was there a reason you sent me *The Time Machine*? Why that particular book?"

"Have you read it yet?"

"I'm nearly done but I've left it back at my cousin's house, I'm afraid. Hopefully Mother will bring it with her and I can finish it on the train ride home from New York. Why did you send it to me?"

Once again he looked out to sea, but then faced me as though he'd made his mind up about something. "I might as well just say it, Jane. I've never met a girl like you, one I can talk to so easily. You've been on my mind. A lot. Tesla has been working on an invention and in my mind — my imagination — I keep talking to you about it."

This was all too wonderful! Here I'd believed he'd completely forgotten me, and all the while he'd been wanting to talk to me, to tell me everything that was important to him. While he'd been imagining speaking to me, I'd been doing the exact same thing. In a strange way, it was as if we'd never really been apart.

"In your imagination, did I understand what you're talking about?" I asked.

"Not at first," he admitted. "But slowly I explained it to you and we had amazing conversations about it. I even imagined that Tesla asked us to test it, and you and I traveled to —" He cut himself short.

"Traveled to where?" I pressed.

He didn't answer.

"Did you imagine we traveled in time?" I guessed. "Did we travel forward or back?"

He stared at me, stunned at my words. "How did you . . . how could you . . . ?"

"Tesla talked to me about time travel that day when I interviewed him in the park," I explained.

"It's all theory, Jane. Sending you that book was my way of talking to you about it."

"I'm so happy that you did, and now I regret not having finished it," I said. "Thad? If finances are so bad for Tesla, how are you two staying in first class?"

"Tesla sold a patent he held on an electric car to an automobile manufacturer. He thinks the company is going to produce the cars, but I think they wanted the patent so they could make sure it never is produced. A lot of people are going to make fortunes in oil when motorcars get into big-time production. They're already investing. This war that's coming —"

"I hope not," I interrupted.

"It's coming, and part of the reason for it is because it's going to be a land grab for oil," he said with assurance.

"And that's where Tesla got the money for this trip — from selling the patent for a car that doesn't use oil?"

"Exactly. Our room is C-93. We're both in there."

An eight-man band began to play lively music there on the deck. "That's called ragtime," he told me. "It's the newest thing. Come on. I'll show you how to dance to it. I just recently learned it myself."

He took hold of my hand and together we hurried to a

spot near the band where other couples held one another close and did a bouncy sort of strut in unison. "I have to put my arm around your waist — is that okay?" he asked.

I hoped to high heaven that I wasn't blushing as I nodded that it was fine — much better than fine. He held me so close that we were cheek to cheek, ankle to ankle. The dance was fast, which didn't leave time to feel too awkward, and before I knew it I was smiling so hard that my face ached a little. At one point Thad began turning us in dizzying spins without ever letting go of his hold on me.

It was such breathless fun!

How had I come to this? This morning I'd expected a quiet day. Now I was on the greatest luxury liner of all time, out in the middle of the ocean, spinning joyfully in the arms of the person I'd been longing for over the last seven months.

Complete heaven!

At three that afternoon, Thad and I stood outside Mimi's cabin door. I raised my hand to knock, and the door opened before I even connected with it. "Jane, why are you here?" Mimi asked anxiously. "Is something wrong?"

"No. Well, not anymore," I said. At that moment, Mimi saw Thad, and her eyebrow couldn't help but rise.

"So have the two of you run off together?" she asked.

Thad blushed furiously, and I hastily said, "No — we just met. I mean, we met again while I was looking for you. He's not the reason — you're the reason we're here. You and Blythe."

"I think you'd better explain," she said, drawing us both into the room.

Her room was so luxurious! Her four-poster bed was high off the floor and covered in a satin spread. The dresser gleamed with polished mahogany wood that held a crystal vase with the most gorgeous bouquet of flowers. Everything about the room was . . . well, first class.

I told her everything that had happened, and the more I spoke, the more perplexed her expression became.

"Jane, it doesn't make sense," she commented when I was finished. "Why would Mr. Stead get on this ship if he thought it was going to sink?"

"I don't know," I admitted.

The feeling of being ridiculous was returning.

"Perhaps he predicted a different ship was going to sink," Thad offered gallantly, probably sensing my mortification. "His ship was called the *Majestic*. Maybe it's a ship yet to be built."

"It could be that, or maybe the accident we had earlier was what the prediction foretold," I said.

"That little bump?" Mimi scoffed. "How about this scenario: Mother's imagination got the best of her, and all of you became swept up in her panic."

"Most likely that's what happened," I had to agree, feeling extremely foolish. Then I recalled Emma and Amelie's shouting fit on the ship deck. "Why would the twins faint when they saw Tesla, though? They made it sound as though he was responsible for sinking the ship."

Mimi threw her arms out in frustration. "Those two have gotten as bad as Mother. One of them sleepwalks into the ocean in the middle of the night. The other one thinks she hears her twin talking in her head. They've both been converted by Spirit Vale — that's why they do what they do."

"You're being harsh, Mimi," I remarked.

"I'm sorry, but I'm done with this spiritualism craziness. I've lived my whole life with it and it's just nutty," Mimi cried. "See all this?" She gestured around at the lavish room. "This is the life a person can enjoy, free of the spirit world, the Beyond, the other side."

"Don't you believe in life after death?" Thad asked.

"Yes, *after* death — not hopping back and forth *between* life and death," she answered.

"Maybe on the other side spirits can time travel back to a moment when they were alive," I suggested, *The Time Machine* still on my mind.

"Time travel? Jane, don't — please!" Mimi pleaded. "If you became as crazy as Mother and the twins, I couldn't stand it."

"All right," I agreed. I honestly didn't want to think

about anything more than being on this remarkable ship with Thad all to myself. I had one week to convince him that I was not too young to be a suitable female companion for him, and it seemed I was making good progress.

Mimi knew where in second class Blythe's cabin was located and took us there. The twins and Li met us at the door, having also located her room. When we knocked, she called for us to enter. Her room, while not as spectacular as Mimi's, was still extremely nice.

From the look on Blythe's face, you'd have thought *we* were ghosts — she was that surprised to see us. After explaining why we had come, she rocked back on the bed and laughed. "I have the craziest family!"

"It's not crazy," Emma insisted. "The predictions are real." Amelie nodded in agreement.

"What did you see when Tesla passed?" I asked Emma.

Emma shook her head in bewilderment. "Amelie was speaking through me."

"Amelie, do you still believe this ship will sink?" I asked her.

Amelie wrapped her arms around her head and ran from the room. I looked to Emma for an explanation, but she only raised her shoulders in a gesture of confusion.

"She doesn't know," Mimi insisted. "This is the trip of a lifetime. We're all here together, so let's enjoy ourselves."

*B*lythe was free for the day because her family, the LaRoches, were boarding at Cherbourg, France, in the evening. Mimi was also available since Ninette was coming on board in France, as well.

Around noon, a bugle blew, announcing that lunch was being served. The twins, Li, and Blythe went off to the dining salon that both first- and second-class passengers could use, hoping it was too soon for anyone to realize that the twins didn't belong.

"I'm meeting Victor for lunch," Mimi told us.

"Something tells me you don't want company," I guessed.

"If you don't mind," she said.

I turned to Thad and asked if he was free for lunch and he said that he was.

"No, I don't mind. Go see the love of your life," I teased Mimi. Truthfully, I was happy to be alone with Thad.

"Where's Tesla?" I asked as Thad led the way to one of first class's several restaurants.

He wasn't sure. He speculated that Tesla might be in the cargo hold guarding his prototypes. "Most of his inventions could fit in your pocket," he said. "But he brought something on board as big as a wardrobe."

"What is it?"

"He worked on it this whole month while we were in England waiting for Astor to show up. There wasn't much for me to do, since he wouldn't even let me in the same room with it. He said it was too dangerous. The thing was all crated up to travel before I finally got into that rented lab."

"Will he show it to Colonel Astor?" I asked.

"No," Thad said. "He's just bringing that one back to America."

"Can't you tell me what his inventions are?" I pleaded, dying of curiosity.

"You won't write about it in one of your journalistic articles?"

"I swear!" I said, meaning it.

We were standing in front of the Ritz restaurant. Glancing inside, I saw it was extremely fancy with stained-glass windows, caned chairs, glistening dishware, and starched, white linen napkins folded into cone shapes. "Where can we go? I don't want to be overheard," Thad told me.

A thrill ran through me — Thad was going to tell me Tesla's secret . . . which meant he trusted me.

"I know where we can go," I said. Stepping inside the restaurant, I asked the man at the front podium if we could have our meal delivered outside onto the first-class deck, and he assured me that would be fine. Thad ordered the grilled mutton chops with mashed potatoes and I requested the chicken à la Maryland.

We went out and settled into side-by-side deck chairs where we could talk in private. We sat facing each other, our knees touching. "Tell me what he's going to present to Astor," I said in a whisper as I leaned so far forward that my ear was almost to his lips.

"All right, here it is," he agreed. "His first idea is to use his Tesla coil to create a magnifying transmitter which would beam up frequencies between New York and England over the seas. The transmitter would get the frequencies vibrating and it would create a natural luminescence. It would create an artificial effect like the Northern Lights."

"He'd create lighted shipping lanes for the ships to follow," I realized.

"Smart girl!" Thad praised me.

Not only smart, I thought mischievously.

"Ships would be able to see where they were going at night like never before. The chances of them colliding would be greatly reduced," he continued.

"How brilliant!" I remarked.

"That one would require a big investment of equipment,

even though he knows how to do it. His second idea, though, fits in your coat pocket. It's a small little machine that can shatter anything it's aimed at. Tesla told me that if he set it to the right vibratory frequency, he could split the world in half."

I suddenly knew what it was. "The earthquake machine!" I whispered excitedly.

"Yes, right! You saw it for yourself."

"What use does it have?" I asked. "Why would Colonel Astor want to invest in it?"

"It would change the face of ocean travel — make it incredibly safer," he said. "The North Atlantic is a maze of icebergs. Ship captains have an awful time navigating through them, especially at night. Some of the icebergs are much wider under the ocean, and the navigators can't even know how massive they are under there."

"How would the earthquake machine help?" I asked.

"It could shatter icebergs," he revealed. "By setting the machine to the proper frequency measured by approximate size and distance, a ship could shatter any icebergs in its path."

This was so thrilling — to be here on the first-class deck of the greatest ocean liner in the world, with Thad entrusting to me secrets of immense importance. We were so close, both emotionally and physically, speaking in low tones. I couldn't imagine ever being apart from him again.

Overhead, the squawk of a seagull diverted my attention for the briefest moment. As I turned and my eyes flickered up to the bird, I caught sight of nearby movement and a man ducking behind a door.

It took no more than a second for me to realize why the man seemed familiar.

The door was still ajar and Thad was still talking. "The trick to calibrating it correctly is to measure the distance times the velocity at which the ship is traveling and then to —"

I cut him off by abruptly leaping into his lap and covering his mouth with a kiss. I couldn't allow Thad to continue speaking for a second longer.

His lips were warm and tasted of the salty ocean air. At first he pulled back a little, startled. But in the next second he put his hand flat on my back to draw me closer while he returned the kiss.

It would have been tempting to forget the man lurking at the door, but I knew we couldn't. Nuzzling Thad's neck with my nose, I whispered to him. "Don't look, but the man who threatened me and Tesla in the park is hiding behind the door."

While we were talking, our backs had been turned away from the door. I'd caught sight of the man lurking there only when I'd turned to glance at the seagull. The moment I moved, he ducked back behind the door.

It was still open a crack. I guessed he was still there.

Drawing out of our lovely kiss, Thad eased me off his lap and then suddenly sprang at the door, yanking it open. There was no one there, but I heard the clatter of the man retreating quickly.

In a flash, Thad was off after him, chasing the man back into the ship.

I followed Thad, nearly knocking down the waiter who was approaching with our lunch on a tray. "Sorry! We'll be right back," I told him as I dashed away.

For a few minutes, I could see Thad, running full out. Then he turned a corner. I ran to keep up, but it was no use. When I turned, he was not there.

In the next moment, though, Thad returned, panting hard. "I lost him," he told me breathlessly. "How much do you think he heard?"

I admitted that I didn't know. Thad wanted to go to his and Tesla's room. "The device is there," he confided. "I think I locked the door, but I want to be sure."

He took hold of my hand and we hurried together toward cabin C-93 where he was staying with Tesla. The door was closed but unlocked. When we realized this, we exchanged a worried look. Cautiously, Thad pushed it open, motioning for me to stay back.

The cabin had been ransacked. Clothing and bedding were tossed all over; drawers hung open.

I hovered tentatively in the doorway as he crept stealthily into the disheveled room, lunging at drapery, dramatically throwing wide the twin doors of the wardrobe, flinging open the washroom. When he was satisfied that no one was there, he waved me inside. "Lock the door," he said as he knelt and took a metal case from under the dresser.

I sat on one of the torn-apart twin beds and watched as Thad unlocked the case with a tiny key and lifted out an alarm-clock-sized mechanism very similar to the one I'd seen Tesla smash so long ago. "It's still here," he noted with obvious relief.

"Thank heavens for that," I said.

"Me and my big mouth!" Thad rebuked himself. "Why did I have to go blabbing all that stuff to you in such an open area? I wonder how much that guy heard."

"You were speaking quietly," I said, which was true.

"Good thing you stopped me. I like the way you did it, too."

I could feel warm embarrassment rushing into my face. "It was the only thing I could think of. I guess, if our lunches had arrived sooner, I could have shoved a dinner roll in your mouth. That would have worked, as well."

"I'm so glad you didn't," he said with a smile. "But I'd like to check something, if you don't mind."

"What?"

Stepping close, he wrapped me in his arms and bent to kiss me again. I melted toward him, returning his kiss, matching his intensity.

This was our real first kiss, and it was everything I'd imagined during the drawn-out, cold months I'd been longing for him.

When we drew apart, he kept me close, looking into my eyes. "What were you checking for?" I asked softly.

"I wanted to see if kissing you was really as wonderful as I thought it was out there on the deck."

"And?"

"Even better."

I pressed my forehead into his shoulder as he held me close. I was flooded in happiness as we stood there in the ransacked room, momentarily forgetting everything but each other.

"I should lock this up with the valuables in the ship's safe," he said after a few more moments of this bliss.

I looked up at him and smiled. He smiled back. "You're right. We should do that right away."

After we had done that, we went to the cargo hold to find Tesla. He was dressed in the long coat and cap I'd seen him in on deck. Scribbling busily in a notebook, he was sitting on a wooden crate marked ORANGES beside a much larger, rectangular crate. I assumed it was the secret device Thad had told me about. It was marked: FRAGILE. USE EXTREME CAUTION IN HANDLING. DO NOT OPEN UNDER ANY CIRCUMSTANCES.

"Ah, Jane, that *was* you I saw on deck. I was lost in thought and only realized I might have passed you much later," Tesla greeted me pleasantly. "What a coincidence that you are aboard this vessel, though the controversial psychologist Carl Jung would prefer to think of it as *synchronicity*, a converging of events in a seemingly random overlap which, in an actuality we do not yet comprehend, has an underlying meaning or purpose. Someday I would like to attempt an algebraic calculation of synchronistic coincidence. At any rate, what brings you here?"

I explained to him the events that had brought me and my sisters onto the ship. "It sounds silly, I know," I concluded.

He arose and began to pace agitatedly. "No, not silly in the least; a warning picked up from a distant dimension is never to be taken lightly. I know of Mr. Stead, a greatly respected gentleman. You say ice figures into his premonition?"

"He thinks he will die because of ice," I confirmed.

Tesla nodded thoughtfully. "He might, if I do not act."

Thad gave him the news about their cabin being ransacked and the thug on the ship. "I've locked the device in the ship's safe now," he added.

"Well done. This confirms that no time can be lost," Tesla stated with resolve. "I will make myself known to Colonel Astor tonight after he boards at Cherbourg. Perhaps a predicted disaster can be altered by judicious action taken in time."

"That's almost what Mr. Stead said, though in different words," I remembered.

Tesla wanted to discuss their plans with Thad, so I went to find my sisters.

I saw Mimi on deck talking to the same handsome, dark-haired man I'd seen with Mr. Guggenheim and Ninette at the Waldorf-Astoria. Based on looks alone, I could see why she was in love. He was as breathtakingly handsome as I remembered him.

Victor noticed me hovering and bade Mimi good-bye with a quick kiss.

"Mimi, I'm sorry we fought," I said. "I just miss you so much. I really want you to be happy."

She hugged me. "I'm sorry, too."

"How are things going?" I asked her.

"Oh, I love him, Jane," she answered. "He says he loves me, too, and I believe him."

"That's great!" I cried.

"I still haven't told him about my background, though."

"He won't care, Mimi. If he really loves you, he won't care. Are you sure he really loves you?"

She nodded uncertainly. "He just now asked me to marry him," she revealed.

I gasped, my hand flying over my gaping mouth. "What did you say?"

"I will give him my answer tomorrow."

"What will your answer be?"

"I don't know. I have a lot of thinking to do."

That evening we came to port at Cherbourg. The ship didn't actually dock, but rather, smaller boats carried passengers out to it.

Blythe stood on deck with Mimi, Emma, Amelie, and me, looking for the LaRoche family. Mimi was fairly confident that she would recognize Mrs. LaRoche when she saw her again and, indeed, she did, excitedly pointing the woman out to us. She was attractive, with dark eyes and nearly black hair piled on top of her head. When she caught sight of Mimi, her face lit with a lively smile.

We hurried over and they hugged like old friends. Mimi introduced Blythe first and then the rest of us.

Speaking English with a heavy French accent, Juliette LaRoche reached behind her full skirt and drew out a little girl who was so petite and precious she might have been a doll come to life. She had the same olive skin and dark hair and eyes as her mother. She wore a lacy white frock with a matching bow. The lace on her little white socks matched that on the collar of her dress. "This is Simone," Juliette said, and the girl smiled shyly. "Louise, my younger daughter, is with my husband," she explained.

Just then a handsome man with a mustache and in a long, dark coat joined her. He held a precious little girl in his arms who was a slightly younger version of Simone. "This is my husband, Mr. Joseph LaRoche," Juliette said.

I tried not to stare. Emma and Amelie remained composed also. Mimi and Blythe, though, could not even make a pretense of calmness. Their flabbergasted expressions gave them away instantly.

"I see that you are surprised that my husband is a black man," Juliette said, taking it in stride. "Is this a problem for you?"

"Not at all," said Blythe, recovering from her surprise enough to take Louise from Joseph LaRoche. "Not one bit."

Mimi, for once, was speechless. I could tell it was anything but a problem for her.

This seemingly happy couple was, perhaps, a view of her own future.

Chapter 27

$\mathcal{M}$imi was quickly preoccupied with Ninette after she boarded in Cherbourg. Dressed in the latest Parisian finery, she greeted Mimi as though she were her long-lost sister, and I instantly felt that familiar pang of annoyance and jealousy that had plagued me in New York.

The biggest excitement, of course, was the arrival of John Jacob Astor the Fourth, his young bride, and his adorable Airedale, who was named Kitty despite the fact that it was clearly a dog. In the buzz of excitement surrounding their arrival, I heard someone say that Colonel Astor was worth more than thirty million dollars! I couldn't imagine such wealth.

I would have thought that a person with that much money who had just come back from a European tour with his new young wife would look carefree and happy. Astor didn't, though. He had a serious, almost scowling demeanor, as though great concerns weighed him down. His wife was very pretty, I thought, in her big, floppy, striped hat. The difference in their ages was, indeed, pronounced.

Thad was at my side and seemed to be the only one not dazzled at the sight of the famous Astors. "Why does one guy need that much money?" he asked sourly.

"So he can fund Tesla and make the world a better, safer, more humane place," I suggested optimistically.

Thad's crabbed expression slowly softened until he smiled. "All right. Hold on to that thought."

That night Li let the three of us stay in her room. We couldn't bunk with Mimi or Blythe since their employers didn't know we were there without tickets and probably wouldn't have liked it.

Li told the steward she was cold, and he brought her a pile of extra blankets, which Amelie and Emma snuggled into on the top bunk. I wrapped into another blanket and settled in on the floor. We were lucky because Li was supposed to have had a bunkmate rooming with her but she'd apparently missed the boat.

"You have good young man," Li said to me, leaning on her elbow in her bunk. "Thad wonderful to me and my family."

"Have you known him long?"

She nodded. "My parents cook for his family back in China. They good people. They lend my father money to open restaurant in America. You love him?"

"I'm not sure yet. I haven't spent much time with him," I answered. Did months of talking to each other in our minds count? Probably not, though it felt like it should. I'd spent so much time thinking of him, going over every inch of his face in my thoughts, carrying on imaginary conversations, that it felt as though I'd known him much longer than I actually had.

"You love him," Li declared, speaking confidently. Then, with a wide yawn, she turned and fell asleep.

I knew she was right.

The next morning, Thad rapped on the door and entered with a wonderful-smelling box filled with hot chocolate and pastries. "Good news," he said as we huddled over our steaming cups. "Tesla has talked to Astor. Tonight, he'll speak to him about creating lights on the shipping lanes, and then Astor agreed to see him again about the earthquake machine."

"When will that be?" I asked.

"Not sure," Thad replied, wiping croissant crumbs from his lips. "He said he needs a time when there's a lot of ice around so he can demonstrate."

Amelie looked up sharply at Emma.

"Ice?" Emma echoed, looking worried. "Has anyone seen Mr. Stead?"

"Not yet, but I think we should look for him today." I turned to Thad. "Has that creepy guy shown up again?"

"No," he replied, "but unless he somehow sneaked away at Cherbourg — which would have been hard to do — he's still around somewhere."

There came another rap on the door, and Blythe came in with the two little LaRoche girls. I offered hot chocolate. Blythe was full from breakfast, but we got some cups for the little girls. Blythe was thrilled to have discovered that second-class passengers could eat in the same salon with the first-class passengers. "Mimi and Ninette had breakfast with Madeleine Astor," she told us excitedly.

"Madeleine Astor is younger than Mimi," Thad supplied. "She's eighteen!"

"Who cares?" Blythe dismissed the remark. "Our Mimi is hobnobbing with the rich and famous."

"Mmm," I said pensively. I was wondering how much hobnobbing she'd be doing if they knew her secret.

"Do they allow Mr. LaRoche into the salon?" Thad asked. "Have you noticed that he's the only black person on the ship?"

"Thad!" I scolded, nodding to the LaRoche girls.

"That's all right. They only speak French," Blythe said. "Mr. LaRoche has an engineering degree from a French university, but he can't get any work because of his color. And do you know why he and the girls are the only black people on this ship?"

"Why?" Emma asked.

"They won't let black people buy a ticket in England or America. They tell them they're sold out. The only reason he's on board is because his white wife bought the tickets."

"That's disgraceful!" I cried.

Blythe nodded in agreement. "Mr. LaRoche is from Haiti and his family is very well-to-do there. He and Juliette and the girls are traveling back to his home to live."

"Haiti! What a coincidence. That's where Mimi is from."

"Mimi?" Thad questioned, which required me to go into the whole story.

Li shook her head sadly. "It too bad the way people can be," she remarked. "My father he thinks white people crazy," she said, tapping her forehead.

"That's why a man like Tesla who is for all the people can't get off the ground," Thad commented.

That morning we went to Queenstown, Ireland, to pick up more passengers. It was cold but the sky was a startlingly crystal blue.

As in France, they came out to the *Titanic* by boat, so we never actually docked in Ireland. I got to stand on deck and at least see the lovely lush green hills and pastures the country is so justly renowned for.

Thad was in with Tesla, preparing for their first demonstration of the device to illuminate the night skies. Blythe was occupied with the little girls while Emma and Amelie did a tarot reading for Li in the cabin.

I was beginning a stroll on the deck when Mimi caught up with me. "Jane, I've just come from Victor, and the most wonderful thing has happened."

"What?"

"I told him about . . . me."

"And?" I asked, although a smile was already spreading across my face. I could tell from her expression that it had gone well.

She took both my hands in her own. "He doesn't care! He laughed, in fact. He said because he's Italian, people make derogatory cracks, and he just ignores them. And seeing the LaRoche family has made me feel so much braver about it all. I see how happy they are, and how beautiful their little girls are. Juliette did the right thing to marry the man she loved and not worry about the rest."

Words didn't seem enough, so I hugged Mimi, truly happy for her. "When will the wedding be?" I asked once we separated.

"In three days."

"Three days?" I cried, aghast.

"We'll be married on the fourteenth. It's the day before your birthday, I know. You don't mind, do you?"

"I don't care about my birthday. It just seems awfully soon," I replied.

"We want to be married before we get to New York. Mr. Guggenheim has asked Captain Smith to marry us on board the ship, and he has agreed. He and Ninette want us to travel with them to Italy almost as soon as we reach New York. They've offered to get us a stateroom together — a sort of honeymoon. It's the only way we could afford one."

"Mother will be hurt, if you marry without her there," I pointed out.

Mimi considered that for a moment. "When we return from Italy, we'll have a second ceremony in Spirit Vale. Every ghost in western New York will be invited."

"That would probably make her feel better," I agreed. "It would be spectacular to be wed on the *Titanic*."

"Ninette will give the banquet afterward. It will be so much better than any wedding we could give for ourselves. Much, much grander!"

"Can I invite Thad?" I asked.

"Of course — invite Tesla, too."

I couldn't believe everything was happening so fast. I almost got caught in the whirlwind of it. But then I realized that, with Mother not here, I had to ask the most important question of all.

"Mimi," I said, "you're sure Victor is the one?"

Mimi took my hand. "I know it seems sudden, Jane, but Victor and I have spent all our free time together for the last seven months. We've become so close, and I love him with all my heart."

"And he loves you, too?" It sounded as though he did, but I had to be sure.

"I know he does," she confirmed.

Victor must have been waiting for his cue to join us, because he appeared a moment later. "So, does she approve?" he asked, smiling.

"How could she not?" Mimi replied.

"Only if you promise to treat my sister like a queen," I said.

"I will," he promised, "because she is a queen, the queen of my heart." He turned to Mimi and told her he had to go lay out Mr. Guggenheim's evening clothes. "But after dinner, I will dance with you under the moonlight," he told her before sweeping her into a passionate kiss.

I didn't want to stare, so I turned and watched the ocean waves until a tap on the shoulder made me turn back. "Good-bye, my sister to be," Victor said. "Maybe you and your boyfriend will join us dancing tonight."

"Oh, Thad's not my boyfriend," I protested.

"Sure he is," he insisted. "I've seen you walking together. I know the look. After all, I'm in love, also."

"Are you in love with Thad, Jane?" Mimi asked when Victor had left.

"I think it was love at first sight," I admitted. Once the words were spoken, I knew they were true.

"And here you are together with him on this ship — all quite by accident," she said happily. "I knew this would be a wonderful trip, but I never imagined everything would work out this well. No wonder they call it the *Ship of Dreams*."

If only it *would* work out. Mimi had passionate kisses and a wedding date. I'd experienced my first kiss. And I had Thad back in my life. It was perfect — too perfect. The perfection of it all made me uneasy somehow. But I scolded myself for feeling this way. There was no sense worrying over nothing.

Mimi and I hurried inside to tell Blythe, then Emma and Amelie. Blythe was over the moon with excitement, but Emma and Amelie were more subdued in their response.

I took Emma aside into the hall. "What's wrong?"

"We've been having bad dreams," Emma said. "We still think this ship is going to sink."

"When?"

"We don't know. But we have a dream and we are both underwater, floating. Our skin is blue and our hair floats everywhere around us."

"The two of you are there?"

"We're not sure. Each of us only sees the other."

I scowled, perplexed. "Do you see anyone else?"

"There are lots of other people floating, but we can't tell who they are. It's too dark."

I didn't want to imagine what Emma and Amelie were seeing in their shared nightmare. It was too awful. But I'd had horrible nightmares, too. I'd once dreamed that the evil Dr. Moriarty, Sherlock Holmes's archenemy, was trying to kill me — and that certainly wasn't about to happen. Perhaps the twins were simply having a nightmare that sprang from all the talk of the ship sinking.

I took hold of her hand. "Let's locate Mr. Stead. I want to know what he thinks of this," I said, pulling her along.

We found a steward with a passenger list who directed us to Mr. Stead's stateroom on D Deck. Before we arrived there, I caught sight of him in the reading and writing room. As we approached him, it was obvious that he was confused by our presence there, though he greeted us cordially.

We explained the series of events that had brought us onto the ship the day before. "So my question is this: Did you predict the sinking of this ship? And, if so, why did you get on it?" I asked.

He sighed deeply and frowned. "I don't know," he said.

"You wrote a book about it," Emma said. "Mr. Robertson showed us."

"True," Mr. Stead said. "But at the end of the text, I

added a note that said the following: 'This is exactly what *might* take place and what *will* take place if the liners are sent to sea short of boats.' And, the *Titanic* is woefully short of lifeboats."

"But it's unsinkable," I reminded him.

"That is merely an untested claim," he said.

"Did your spirit guide, Julia, tell you the ship would sink?" Emma asked.

"No. She has been oddly silent on the subject," he said. "She only told me that I would face a great test."

"But you have made other predictions," Emma reminded him.

He nodded. "I honestly don't know if what I wrote was an example of clairvoyance or the working of my logical mind exploring the possible consequence of an overpopulated ocean liner with an insufficient number of lifeboats."

"But you doubted your prediction enough to get on the ship," I pointed out.

"I thought about it long and hard," he agreed. "When my ticket came from President Taft for this particular ship, it was as if the time had come for my great test. I sensed it. Perhaps the test is of my faith in the supernatural. Maybe it is in my ability to enact a change for world peace. Either way, I couldn't say no simply because I was frightened. Not to go to this conference would mean I failed to attempt to work for peace."

"You could have taken another ship," I said.

"Julia has predicted my death by ice. On the other ship, I might have slipped on a dropped ice cube and hit my head. There is no sense trying to outwit fate."

I admired his courage. "My sisters are dreaming they will drown," I told him.

"Maybe they will — thirty years from now. Maybe they are simply afraid of the ocean, and this anxiety finds its way into their dreams."

I remembered how the twins disliked the ocean. "I think that must be it."

After we left Mr. Stead, I sensed that Emma felt better. On her way back, I suggested to her that Amelie might even have gotten upset at the sight of Tesla because some buried childhood memory of the terrifying earthquake had reawakened at the sight of him.

"That does make sense," Emma agreed.

We would try to put the whole thing out of mind . . . if we could.

Chapter 28

After that, everything became about planning Mimi's wedding. It was scheduled for Sunday night. It was the only time Captain Smith was available, since he was obligated by tradition to sit with the most elite of the first-class guests during dinner.

In the next two days, I lost a lot of the animosity I'd felt toward Ninette because she included me in planning the spectacular reception that was to follow Mimi's wedding ceremony. The ship's kitchen was already at work preparing a sumptuous dessert buffet and a three-tiered wedding cake.

On Thursday night, Ninette pulled a straight white crochet dress with a dropped waist from her wardrobe closet and, claiming that she had never worn it, handed it to Mimi, who proclaimed it "Perfect!"

But Ninette disagreed. "Not nearly good enough. Last night I dined with Sir Cosmo Duff Gordon and his wife, Lucy. Lucy is a dress designer with shops in New York and London. She's designed for the royal family! I'll commission her to design new gowns for all of us. She told me she's got yards and yards of gorgeous fabric in the cargo hold. She's bringing it to her store in New York, but now it will be all used up by the time she gets there. Oh, well; she can get more. Of course we'll have to invite Lord and Lady Duff Gordon. You don't mind, do you, Mimi? They're not bad company."

"The more, the merrier," Mimi agreed happily. Ninette and Mimi discussed the color and decided on a pale lavender for the bridesmaids, who would be Emma, Amelie, Blythe, and me.

"Jane, as maid of honor, you'll need a special dress," Ninette said.

I looked to Mimi to check if this was true. She hadn't mentioned it. Maybe she wanted Ninette to take that spot. "Really?" I asked her.

"Of course, really," Mimi said. "You're my closest sister, aren't you?"

My eyes misted up, but I didn't want to make a big fuss. "Won't all new dresses cost a fortune?" I asked, quickly wiping my eyes.

"Ha!" Ninette hooted. "Benjamin has ten fortunes. He'll never miss it. And Mimi will look like a goddess in a dress designed by Lady Duff Gordon."

"But who will make the dresses?" I asked.

"*Chérie!*" she cried, laughing at my naiveté. "Third class is teeming with seamstresses and tailors who would die for the chance to make the extra cash."

"Can they work that quickly?" I questioned.

"Of course they can!" Ninette said confidently. "There are hundreds of them down there."

By our third day out at sea, Emma, Amelie, and I were finally relaxed that no one would question our presence aboard the ship. In fact, the stewards had gotten so used to seeing us in Blythe and Mimi's rooms that they greeted us with friendly nods when we passed them.

Mimi sent an invitation list that included Mr. Stead as well as Colonel Astor and his wife. "Imagine the wedding present you'll get from them!" Blythe cried when she heard they were coming.

Besides the Astors and Duff Gordons, the list also included many other wealthy friends of Ninette and Mr. Guggenheim's, including a Mrs. Brown, whom some called "vulgar" behind her back but who I thought was a lot of fun, always telling funny stories and laughing at them louder than anyone else in the room. They also invited a very sweet elderly couple, Mr. and Mrs. Straus, who had started a magnificent department store called Macy's that I remembered passing on the way to the Waldorf-Astoria.

"And we must invite the movie actress Dorothy Gibson," Ninette insisted.

"Why must we?" I asked.

"Oh!" Ninette cried. "Because she is famous and beautiful, and vivacious — *très jolie!* What a reception this will be!"

Li was also invited, and so were the LaRoches. I didn't see much of Tesla, so I extended his invitation through Thad. By the afternoon before the wedding, I still hadn't heard if he was coming. I needed to know; since he was a vegetarian, I wanted to make sure they served something he would enjoy eating.

"Has Tesla told you if he plans to come?" I asked Thad.

"Oh, I'm sorry. I forgot to tell you," Thad replied as we walked along the deck. "Yeah, he'd like to come, but he and Astor will have to duck out so Tesla can demonstrate his next invention to Astor."

"Does it have to be that night?" I objected.

"Apparently so; that night the ship will be in the perfect location for Tesla's demonstration."

"Why?" I pressed.

"Tesla has been spending a lot of time in the telegraph room. He's driving the operators mad wanting to know about every message received from other ships at sea. They've thrown him out more than once, but he just keeps coming back. He's determined to know if the ships are sending any warnings."

"Warnings about what?" I asked.

"Ice. He's demonstrated to Astor that his machine can shatter a vase, but Astor wants to see if it can really break up an iceberg."

"Does Tesla expect we'll have a problem with ice?" I asked.

"He's hoping so," Thad replied.

Thad was supposed to spend the rest of the day working with Tesla but Tesla had one of his spells that forced him to lie silently in his darkened cabin. Thad immediately came and found me in Li's room. "Jane, come out. We can spend the day together," he called through the door.

I answered with a hot curling rod in my hand. I had been making a futile attempt to make curls in Emma's fine hair. "I can come back later," he said when he saw the rod and Emma seated on a stool, her hair down around her shoulders.

"No, Jane, you go out with him," Emma offered with a resigned sigh. "My hair was just not meant to curl. I'm going to give up on this and go find Amelie out on deck."

I gave her shoulder a quick pinch of thanks. She knew how much I wanted to spend the time with Thad.

I noticed he was wearing a blue wool pea jacket. "Is it cold?" I asked.

"There's a cold wind. Wear a coat," he advised.

He and I hurried together up to the first-class deck. The sky was a field of blue with fat clouds rolling lazily in it. Thad took hold of my hand. "Is this all right?" he checked.

Smiling, I nodded. It was more than all right. To be walking hand in hand with Thad on the deck of the *Titanic* was perfect happiness. A brisk breeze whipped past, pushing us forward. A woman's feathered hat blew past us like a great winged bird sailing by. Thad leaped for it, snapping it out of the air.

A woman laughed and clapped in delight. "Well done, young man. Thank you ever so much." It was jolly Mrs. Brown.

Thad handed her the huge hat.

She returned it to her head, jabbing a long, pearl-headed pin into it, attaching it to her mountain of hair. The boa of black feathers at her neck ruffled in the wind. "Maybe it wasn't a good idea to wear all these feathers in a stiff wind," she said with a chuckle. "Don't be surprised if you see me airborne off the bow of the ship."

This image made me laugh. "I hope not," I said, smiling.

"Aw, don't worry about me. Nothing ever happens to me. I was born under a lucky star," she said good-naturedly.

"Do you think there is such a thing?" Thad asked her.

"I'm sure there is, young man," she replied. "I can tell you're lucky."

"How can you tell that?" Thad asked.

Mrs. Brown threw her head back and let out the most raucous guffaw I'd ever heard. "Could it be more obvious? Look at this lovely young woman at your side! Don't you see the stars in her eyes when she looks at you? Could you be any luckier?"

I was beginning to blush, but then I noticed that Thad was red as Mrs. Brown's hat. Smiling broadly, Mrs. Brown thumped him on the back. "Ain't love grand?" she said as she began to walk off. "I hope you enjoy every second of it, kids."

We couldn't help but laugh.

"It is grand," Thad said more seriously once our laughter had subsided.

"Love?" I asked.

He nodded and stepped closer to me. "I love you, Jane."

Peering into his blue eyes, I tried to read his expression. Was he telling the truth? It took only a second to decide that he was.

I rested my hand on his sleeve. "I love you, too."

He lowered his head and I tipped my chin up to meet his warm kiss. This kiss felt different than yesterday's kiss. This kiss was like a promise, tender and heartfelt. It was slow and deep.

There was something flowing between us. Was it energy? Electricity? Spirit? Whatever it was made me feel so connected to Thad in a way I had never felt with another person, not even my sisters.

When we were done kissing, he kept his arms around me. My cheek rested against his chest, enjoying his warmth. "I feel like such an idiot when I remember that I almost let you get away from me," he said softly. "Mrs. Brown is right. I'm so lucky to be on this ship with you."

"I don't know if it's fate or luck," I said. "I'm just so happy to be here with you. I never want this trip to end."

Thad took a folded white piece of paper and a pencil from his pocket. Opening the paper flat, he began to write. "What are you doing?" I asked.

"You'll see." On the paper he wrote these words: *Thad loves Jane.*

Then he began creasing the paper. I quickly realized he was making another of his paper gliders.

With a quick pitch, he launched it over the side of the ship. A current of wind instantly snapped it up, whirling it in a circle before it leveled out straight.

Thad loves Jane. How wonderful it sounded.

"It's out there now," he said, putting his arm around my waist. "There's no taking it back."

*O*n the morning Mimi was to marry Victor, I met Thad for breakfast inside the dining salon. "So, this is the big day for Mimi," he said.

"It is," I agreed, smiling. "And for Tesla, too." Dropping my head, I checked around for any sign of the thug in the derby hat. Thad had caught a glimpse of him the day before, but he'd ducked out of sight before Thad could get ahold of him. When I was sure he was nowhere near, I whispered to Thad, "Has Tesla heard any more about the . . . you know . . . ice?"

Nodding, Thad spoke in an equally low tone. "Last night at ten thirty a ship called the *Rappahonnock* sent a severe ice warning."

"I hope it doesn't disrupt Mimi's wedding," I said.

"Don't worry — Tesla will have his device ready to bust up anything that gets in our way. That thing can crash buildings and take down bridges. What's a little ice?"

I remembered well what Tesla's earthquake machine could do and felt less worried.

After breakfast, we strolled on the first-class deck once again. Sometimes at the back of the boat — the stern — we would look down at the small outside deck given to the third-class passengers. It was called the "poop" deck. It was often crowded with children or men playing soccer.

That morning, there were only a few children playing. "Where are they all?" Thad wondered.

"Probably inside, putting last-minute touches on the dresses for the wedding," I guessed.

"Jane," Thad said seriously, "we have to figure out how we can see each other once we get home. I've been given a second chance with you and I don't want to be stupid again. I couldn't stand to be without you."

"I don't want to be away from you, either," I replied. The very idea of it made me heartsick. "We live miles apart but . . . I just had a thought. It's crazy. . . ."

"What?" he asked eagerly.

"Oh, I was just thinking . . . if my article on Tesla wins, I'll be living in New York City. I'll probably hear one way or the other when we get home."

He grasped my hands excitedly. "That's it! You'll win. You *have* to win," Thad said. "It will solve the entire problem."

"It would be wonderful, but we can't count on it," I cautioned.

"It's a sure thing! Once Tesla sells his inventions to Astor tonight, there will be a huge amount of interest in him and the invention. The timing on your article is phenomenal. It's bound to win!"

"You're pretty sure Astor will like what Tesla shows him?" I asked.

"He'd be crazy not to! It'll make his fortune even bigger than it already is."

I looked out at the choppy, white caps of the ocean and imagined Thad and me together in the city — on our own and wildly in love. I could almost see us kissing on the sidewalk, in restaurants, in museums — arm in arm and kissing endlessly.

And then that annoying part of me that felt fearful when everything seemed so perfect kicked in. "What if I don't win the contest and Astor doesn't want to fund the inventions?" I asked.

Thad was undaunted. "I'll get a job with Westinghouse Company in Buffalo. With references from Tesla, they'd be sure to hire me."

"You'd leave Tesla?"

"I'd convince him to move. He likes Buffalo. But, if I had to, I'd leave him — for you, I would."

"But you want to design planes," I reminded him. "Does Westinghouse do that?"

"Westinghouse invests in new inventions. It will be all right."

Being with him like this was everything I had always dreamed it would be.

Thad pulled me into his arms. "Jane, I can't be without you," he said, his voice filled with passion. "I don't ever want to be apart again. Do you feel the same?"

"See the ocean, Thad," I said. "That's what my love for you is like."

Don't ask me how I could be so sure after such a short time together that I would love Thad for the rest of my life. But I was absolutely certain of it.

Mr. Stead thought all of us had the potential to be psychic and predict the future — at least a little. Gazing up at Thad, I saw my own future.

"We could be engaged when we get home," Thad offered. "It could be a long engagement, if you don't feel ready for marriage. I don't care, really."

I reached up and kissed him with all the passion and love I felt.

"Does that mean yes?" he asked.

Tears of happiness swept into my eyes. "Yes! Yes!"

Chapter 30

Thad took me for lunch in one of the first-class restaurants. We sat in lovely wicker chairs at a beautifully laid table with sparkling china. We must have looked like two happy fools, because we just sat there grinning at each other, too blissfully in love to even need to speak much.

I was engaged to Thad. I'd said the word *yes* and it felt like the smartest thing I'd ever said.

"Let's not tell anyone we're engaged until after Mimi's wedding," I suggested. "I don't want to take away from her excitement. She should be the center of attention."

"All right," he agreed. He smiled into my eyes and I smiled back.

Everything was so perfect!

The rest of the day was spent down in third class with the many seamstresses Lady Duff Gordon had hired to make the dresses she'd designed. What a different world it was down there, compared to the splendor of first class, and even second class. I'd hardly given it a look when we first came on board, but now I paid more attention, peering into the many open doors of the various cabins.

The cabins were tiny; some had two bunk beds so that a family of four could squeeze into the small space. There were almost no windows at all. People lived from their suitcases since there was only one narrow dresser in each room, and after four days at sea, many of the rooms had grown quite disheveled. People called to one another from across the halls and moved freely in and out of one another's rooms. It reminded me a bit of a floating village.

The work station for the dresses had been set up in the rear section of the third-class eating kitchen, which consisted of rows of wooden tables and benches. There was no shortage of sewing machines, since a great many of the third-class women were shipping the machines to New York, where they intended to make their living from them. Those not working on a machine were occupied with handwork such as cutting and pinning or hand stitching buttons and collars and hems.

My sisters were all there for their dress fittings. I ached to tell them about Thad and me, but held firm to my decision to keep it a secret until after Mimi's wedding. It was only fair that she should be the one everyone was thinking and talking about. It was her wedding day, after all.

"It seems more fun down here in third class," Emma said, standing on a table in her bare feet as a seamstress, a plump Italian woman with her hair caught up in a red bandanna, pinned the hem of her bridesmaid dress. She had resigned herself to the fact that her fine brown hair would not take a curl, and so had braided it prettily in a thick plait that started high on her head and ran down the back of her neck.

Amelie nodded in agreement from the chair where she sat, arm outstretched across a table while a seamstress sewed on one of the many covered buttons that ran up the side of her dress's narrow sleeve. She'd swept her hair — equally as fine as Emma's — into a graceful coil at the nape of her neck.

"How can you say that this is better?" Blythe cried. She looked so comical with her hair set in a blizzard of white rags just waiting to produce gorgeous curls that would be swept atop her head for the wedding. "I'm so glad we're not crammed in down here. It's too warm. There's no air."

Mimi stepped out from behind a makeshift dressing room that had been constructed from sheets tossed over a stack of chairs. She was wearing the white wedding gown Lady Duff Gordon had designed just for her.

We all stared at her, mouths agape in stunned admiration.

In fact, the entire room, which had only a moment before been abuzz with animated female chatter, was now silent.

The dress was utterly modern and completely breath-taking. It had none of the ballooning, flounced skirts of traditional dresses but was all fluidity and smooth lines. It was made from a snowy white satin that shimmered from its straight-cut neckline all the way down the form-skimming body to the end of its long skirt that swirled around Mimi like a glowing cloud on the floor. The long sleeves started just below Mimi's shoulders and were made from the most exquisite white lace.

The lush, creamy white sheen of the dress was in dramatic contrast with the luxurious black pile of shining hair atop her head. Ninette's private hairdresser had whipped it into an a breathtakingly elaborate style, complete with glistening crystal ornamental hairpins.

Mimi was nothing short of magnificent. She looked like a princess from a fairy tale.

"You could be on the cover of a fashion magazine," Blythe murmured reverently.

"You like it?" Mimi asked, and was answered by a wave of applause. She beamed with pleasure. I hoped I would always see her looking so happy.

The wonderful moment was abruptly interrupted by a man careening into the room. It was the thug with the derby hat, though now he clutched it in his hand as he ran to the far end of the kitchen.

Thad raced into the room after him.

The man scrambled up onto a table, attempting to climb through an open high window leading out to the poop deck. Thad raced across the room and lunged at his legs, pulling him back down.

With a forceful swing, the man punched Thad in the face, knocking him down, and then raced out of the kitchen.

The women nearest to Thad surrounded him. One blotted his face carefully with a wet cloth to wipe away the blood. Another came with a towel filled with ice from the kitchen. I hurried to his side. "Thad, are you okay?"

He dabbed his sore nose tenderly and winced. "I can't tell if it's broken."

"No broken, just hurt very much," the woman who had wiped his face assured him in accented English.

"What happened?" I asked.

"I found him in our room and chased him all over the ship until he ran down here. The room wasn't even tossed around, so I think I must have interrupted him before he had a chance to steal anything. Tesla usually naps at that time. He would have been there if he hadn't had a sudden urge to go back to the telegraph room for the thousandth time."

"Do you believe that man would have hurt him?"

"I think that's what he was there for, yeah," Thad said.

"Let us hope that villain dives off the ship and never returns," said one of the women. Her comment was met with a wave of agreement.

I agreed with the sentiment, but thought it unlikely. More probable was that he would continue to lurk about on the ship until we docked. Thad, Tesla, and his inventions would be in danger until then. I was suddenly glad Tesla would be seeing Colonel Astor that night. The sooner someone else knew about the invention and its possible application, the less chance there was of someone else stealing it. I didn't want to see him lose out again as he had lost credit for the radio to Marconi.

Thad got to his feet, still holding the ice to his face. "Let me change out of this dress and I'll walk you back to the infirmary," I offered. "Then we should tell the ship's security that your room was broken into again."

I noticed purple bruises starting to form under both his eyes. "You need a doctor," I said anxiously. "I think your nose is broken."

"No, it's not," he disagreed.

I wasn't convinced, and touched it gingerly. With a howl of pain he jumped away from me. "Why'd you do that?" he cried. A line of blood ran from his right nostril.

"It *is* broken," I insisted. "Come with me. We're going to the ship's infirmary."

When we got there, the ship's doctor confirmed my theory: "Oh, it's broken all right." The blue purple color of the rings under Thad's eyes had deepened in just the time it had taken to get there.

I left Thad in the infirmary and walked out on the deck alone. Leaning on the railing, I gazed out once more at the rolling waves. The quietly steady hum of the ship's motors mixed with the crash of the water below. I found it very calming.

A strange thought came to me. I wondered if being on the ocean, traveling from one country to the other, was what it might be like for spirits in the Beyond — if indeed there was such a thing. One wasn't in England anymore but hadn't yet landed in America yet, either. One was just . . . floating. It was still possible to travel back and forth. Maybe some spirits didn't want to commit to either side and chose, instead, to float in between for a very long time. I could understand that happening. I would hate to leave all the people I loved.

Perhaps *I* would choose to be a ghost, given the chance.

Chapter 31

Mr. Guggenheim's status as one of the wealthiest passengers on the *Titanic* helped Ninette to secure the ship's amazingly beautiful and luxurious Grand Ballroom for Mimi's wedding ceremony. The reception would be held there, as well. There was plenty of room for both in the enormous room.

All was set for the wedding. Mr. Stead had agreed to give Mimi away, and when she appeared on the curving Grand Staircase with its ornate ironwork decoration under the spectacular glass dome overhead, you could hear people gasp, amazed by their appearance. Mr. Stead was the picture of stately dignity in his tuxedo. Mimi stood beside him like royalty. Her dress seemed to glow and her veil was held in place by a wreath of white roses that encircled her head.

The photographer whom Ninette had located on board flashed a photograph and the ship's eight-man band began to play "The Wedding March."

"Wouldn't Mother just love to see this," Blythe whispered to me.

"We'll say it was a small, plain ceremony," I whispered back.

When Mimi joined Victor in front of Captain Smith, they made the most striking couple imaginable. The happiness that was so evident on both their faces made them all the more radiant. The civil ceremony was brief and to the point, but Captain Smith was a man of such dignity and authority that the plain words when spoken by him seemed to take on a deeper meaning.

The party began with the band striking up a song that the band leader, Wallace Hartley, said was called "Ragtime Mocking Bird," written by a popular songwriter named Irving Berlin. That set the tone wonderfully and put everyone in a festive mood.

My sisters and I stood on a receiving line with Mimi and Victor and greeted all the guests. I was happy when Thad came along, purple under eyes and all.

"Does it hurt a lot?" Blythe asked him.

"I'll live," Thad told her.

Tesla came along after Thad. He didn't shake hands as the others did — afraid of germs, I guessed — but bowed politely. "A lovely wedding, Jane. You will excuse me if I nip out with Colonel Astor later? We have business to conduct that cannot be postponed."

"Of course. Thad told me you had to go," I said. "Best of luck with everything."

The line passed with many people I didn't know

greeting us politely. Mr. Guggenheim was reserved, though Ninette hugged me like we were sisters and I found that I didn't mind. Mrs. Brown nearly swept me off my feet with her enthusiastic embrace. "What a hoot to have a wedding on a ship!" she said.

Madeleine Astor came by looking slightly greenish. "Is this ship rocking?" she asked me. I told her I didn't feel it. "It's the pregnancy," she said.

"I didn't know you were having a baby. Congratulations," I said.

"Thanks, but it's making me sick to my stomach. They say the feeling will pass."

Li looked pretty in a narrow, embroidered, traditional Chinese silk dress. "I am so happy for you all," she said.

I hugged her warmly. "We wouldn't be here to see it if it wasn't for your kindness to us," I remarked.

Once the line had finished, I got to enjoy the party — which meant searching out Thad and getting him onto the dance floor. I no longer wanted to deny that he was my boyfriend. After all, he would soon be my fiancé — my betrothed, my intended! I wanted to embrace it — and him.

Thad and I danced to songs like "The Society Bear," "All Night Long," and "Beans, Beans, Beans!" At one point, the band gently teased Colonel Astor by playing a funny song called "The Tramp That Slept in Astor's Bed" that had been popular back in 1894. It was about an earlier Astor who had lived in a house so huge that a homeless man had gotten in and lived there for several days without anyone realizing. Colonel Astor gave one of his rare smiles and waved at the band, indicating that he had not taken offense.

Breathless from dancing a ragtime number, I got off the dance floor and scanned the guests to see where everyone was. Tesla and Colonel Astor were still there with their heads close, locked in serious conversation. Blythe was sitting with Mr. and Mrs. LaRoche, along with Mimi and Victor. Mr. Stead was talking to Captain Smith, the Strauses, and Mrs. Brown. But where were Emma and Amelie?

I quickly located them on the Grand Staircase. Amelie was shaking and Emma was trying desperately to calm her. "Uh-oh," I said to Thad. He was right behind me as I hurried toward them.

"She's having a vision," Emma said, holding on to Amelie's quivering shoulders. "I'm trying to block it out. I don't want to ruin Mimi's wedding."

"No, you don't want to do that," I agreed, knowing how impatient Mimi had become with this sort of business and how embarrassed she would be in front of all these people.

Emma's eyes suddenly glazed over and I could tell she'd lost the struggle to resist Amelie's voice. "Get in the life-boats!" she shouted. "Get in now!"

The band played on but everyone stopped dancing and talking. All eyes were on us.

Captain Smith stood and looked at us questioningly.

I glanced at Mimi and saw how horrified she was.

"We have to get them out of here," I said to Thad.

"I'll carry Amelie," he suggested, stooping to lift her slumped body.

"Sorry, everyone," I announced. "My sisters are afraid of ocean travel and they're overtired from the day. Please go back to what you were doing."

"Yes! Yes!" Captain Smith agreed reassuringly. "All is well. No cause for concern."

Li joined me as I hurried Emma out, still shouting and struggling to be heard. By the time we got them to Li's cabin, she had calmed down. Amelie was snoring as Thad set her down on one of our bedrolls on the floor, so I assumed she was no longer sending messages to Emma.

"I stay with them," Li offered as Emma curled up on the bed and fell instantly asleep. "I also tired."

I thanked her and we left. "I'd better get back. Tesla wants me with him for the demonstration," Thad said.

"Can I be there, too?" I requested.

"I'll ask," he replied.

Thad and I returned to the wedding to discover that Tesla and Colonel Astor were already gone. We left and went to the Astors' stateroom, but no one answered our knock. On a hunch, Thad decided we should look for them in the telegraph room, and that was where we found them.

Tesla saw us and smiled when we entered. He took out a pad and began to read from it. "Nine o'clock this morning, the *Caronia* warns of ice. At eleven forty, another ice warning from the *Noordam*. The *Baltic* reports ice at eleven forty-two. The *Amerika* checks in with an ice warning at one forty-five this afternoon. At seven thirty the *Californian* telegraphs to warn of ice. At nine forty the *Mesaba* sent an ice warning. And most recently, the *Californian* telegraphed again to warn that they were encountering heavy ice."

"I told the *Californian* to *shut up* for heaven's sake," the telegraph officer said. "All these ice warnings are jamming up my lines."

"Which of these is the closest ship?" Tesla asked him.

"The *Californian* is only a few miles away from us."

"So if they were experiencing ice less than a half hour ago, we have to be encountering ice, as well," Colonel Astor concluded. "Can you contact them and see what their conditions are right now?" he asked the telegraph operator.

The operator looked annoyed, but didn't dare refuse the ship's number-one passenger. He tried to reach the *Californian* but soon shook his head. "I can't get any response," he reported. "Come to think of it, their telegraph operator usually signs off at about eleven thirty and it's eleven thirty-three now."

"Thirty-three, an auspicious number," Tesla remarked. Thad had once told me Tesla had a superstition about things divisible by three: He thought they were good luck.

"I think our moment has come," he continued. "Shall we go on deck to see if we have any potential problems with ice?"

"Did you say *ice*?" We all turned to see who had spoken.

Mr. Stead stood in the doorway, his face ashen.

Chapter 32

Fifteen minutes later, Colonel Astor, Tesla, Mr. Stead, Thad, and I were out on the first-class deck. The night sky was brilliantly clear, a blue black field crowded with stars — some of which seemed distant and others astoundingly close. We could hear the muted sound of the band still playing at the wedding reception inside. I shivered in the night air, and Thad draped his jacket over my shoulders.

We peered into the darkness but saw no sign of ice.

Two officers joined us. "Officers Fleet and Lee," Colonel Astor greeted them. "Seen any ice, gentlemen?"

"No, but Captain Smith stationed us out here tonight with specific orders to be on the lookout for it," Officer Lee replied.

"Hold on!" cried Officer Fleet. "Look out there!"

In the distance something glowed like a giant phantom in the darkness.

"We should be able to steer around that without a problem," Lee said. "Let's go tell Officer Murdoch at once."

"Officer Murdoch takes command at night," Colonel Astor explained to us. "He's an extremely able seaman."

Tesla waited until they were gone before taking his earthquake machine from its case and handing it to Thad to hold. He did some quick calculations on a pad. "I believe we are traveling at a speed of approximately twenty-six knots," he murmured.

"That is what Captain Smith told me the other night at dinner," Colonel Astor concurred.

I felt a flutter of nerves. Although I'd experienced it nearly thirteen years earlier, I well remembered the power of that small device. "Should we stand back?" I asked.

"No need," Tesla assured me as he took the device from Thad.

We were quickly nearing the iceberg. It surprised me how fast it had gone from being a white spot looming in the distance to becoming an alarmingly large, jagged white pyramid just off the right side of the ship. "We're going to hit it," I said quietly to Thad.

I saw worry in Thad's eyes, and he looked to Tesla to see when he planned to make his move.

Mr. Stead folded his arms and remained calm, but his eyes were locked intensely on the iceberg.

Colonel Astor must have been concerned, too. "All right, Tesla," he said. "Let's see what this invention of yours can really do. Your moment of truth has arrived."

I sensed that the ship was beginning to steer away from the iceberg and felt a tremendous relief. Thad took my hand and squeezed it, smiling a little; he, too, must have been reassured that the situation was being handled.

Tesla held his earthquake machine toward the ever-larger iceberg and turned a dial.

Instantly I clutched my head with both hands. That high whine that had made my brain feel like it might melt, the sensation that had occurred during the quake so many years ago, had returned full force. I grabbed for Thad and he held me tight, but he, too, was cringing in pain.

"Something is wrong!" Tesla cried. He tried twisting the dial but it was jammed. "This device has been tampered with!" He scratched something sticky off the bottom of the device. Taking a tiny screwdriver from the case, he undid the minuscule bolts holding the device together. "Some sort of rubbery gum has been poured into this," he observed. "How could this have —"

"Turn it off, would you, Tesla?" Colonel Astor implored through a painful grimace. "Talk later."

"I can't."

"Throw it in the ocean," I suggested desperately, my teeth chattering.

"No," he said, "it might kill everything down there or create a whirlpool. The entire ship would be sucked under."

"Smash it, then," I said, remembering when he'd done it before.

The ship's outer railing suddenly started vibrating. A small crack began to split the wooden deck right under my feet.

Tesla stared at the device as though he were in a trance. In the next second he came out of it and began pounding the device on the side of the ship with a fury I would not have thought him capable of.

"Thank God!" Colonel Astor exclaimed when the thing finally lay in smithereens at our feet.

"We need to discover what damage has been caused," Tesla said urgently, hurrying toward the ship's bridge. We all followed him, moving quickly.

When we reached the bridge, we were told to get out. It was clear that some emergency was under way. We crowded in the doorway of the bridge as Officer Murdoch shouted at his helmsman, "I said hard astarboard! Didn't you hear me?"

"The ship won't turn as it should," the helmsman replied in a panicked voice. "The rudder isn't responding properly."

Captain Smith brushed past us without a word and demanded to know the situation. Officer Murdoch told him that the rudder was not turning correctly. "Whatever caused all that vibrating just before might have affected it."

"What was that?" Captain Smith asked.

It was a terrible moment for me — for all of us, probably.

Should we reveal what the earthquake machine had done and risk putting Tesla in peril of arrest? It seemed to me that we had to.

We felt a bump and all of us at once tottered back several steps. Thad caught hold of my elbow to keep me steady.

"We've glanced off the side of the iceberg," Officer Murdoch announced.

Tesla stepped just inside the bridge and spoke. "That vibration you experienced was caused by an invention of mine. I was attempting to shatter the iceberg by vibratory waves. Someone tampered with it, and it vibrated at a rate much higher than intended."

Captain Smith listened to him without comment and then turned to Officer Murdoch. "Send someone to get Thomas Andrews, the ship's designer. Tell him to meet me below. I'll want his assessment of the damage."

We hurried back to the wedding to tell the guests what we knew. The wedding had been scheduled to end at eleven thirty and most of the guests had already left. Blythe and the LaRoches were gone. The band was packing up its instruments and soon departed, too. Mimi and Victor were saying good-bye to the few guests still in the process of leaving. Soon only the Astors, Mrs. Brown, Mr. Guggenheim, Ninette, Mimi and Victor, and Thad and I were left.

"Jack, where were you?" Mr. Guggenheim asked Colonel Astor.

Everyone gathered to listen as Colonel Astor told them that we'd hit an iceberg and that the captain was assessing the damage.

"We felt the impact," Mrs. Brown said, "but we weren't worried. This ship is unsinkable. What was that strange shaking, though? It gave me quite a headache while it was going on."

"I was demonstrating an invention of mine," Tesla admitted.

"What are you — some kind of mad scientist?" Mrs. Brown asked.

"It would seem so," Tesla replied despairingly.

"I am sure there is nothing for us to worry about," Ninette spoke up. "This is the *Titanic*."

I noticed Mr. Stead was standing off by himself at the bottom of the Grand Staircase. Leaving Thad's side, I went to him. As I approached, I heard him speaking rapidly in a very low tone. When he noticed me, he stopped talking in this way. "Julia has come to me," he said. "This is the test of which she spoke. My destiny is before me at last, and I must meet it in the right way. Tell your sisters, tell everyone, to prepare to leave right away." He hugged me in a fatherly way and then held my shoulders, speaking to me urgently. "Go immediately. There is not as much time as everyone is saying." Having said that, he hurried up the Grand Staircase.

I told everyone what Mr. Stead had told me. "He's a brilliant journalist except when it comes to all that Julia nonsense," Mr. Guggenheim pronounced. "I, for one, am not going to get into a panic before the captain advises me to do so, which I don't believe will happen."

"John, I'm not feeling well," Madeleine Astor said. "Can we go to our room now, please?"

Saying good-bye to us, Colonel Astor put his arm around Madeleine's shoulders and escorted her out.

"I'm with Mr. Guggenheim," Mimi said. "I'm not going to worry about a little bump in the night."

"Mimi, please get ready to get on a lifeboat," I argued with her. "I believe Mr. Stead, and I'm scared."

"Don't be scared," Victor tried to comfort me. "This crew is very capable. Anything that needs to be done will be done."

"I must lie down!" Tesla blurted. "I'm having one of my flashes. I can taste the air. I can see all the food smells in this room. It's overwhelming me." Without waiting to get to his room, Tesla climbed atop a table and lay down on his back, shutting his eyes.

Mrs. Brown bade us good night. Mimi and Victor said they would go with her. "Don't be up late, Jane," Mimi advised. "Get some sleep. It's nearly midnight."

"Let's go on deck and see what we can find out," Thad suggested. Leaving Tesla asleep on the table, we went and discovered the crew pulling tarps off the lifeboats. We looked at each other anxiously. "You alert your sisters. I'll go wake up Tesla," Thad said. "We'll meet back here in fifteen minutes."

Chapter 33

$\mathcal{B}$ack inside the ship, stewards were already getting passengers out of their rooms and instructing them to put on heavy coats and gather only the necessities they would need on the lifeboats. People complied grudgingly, many complaining that the ship was putting them through a safety drill in the middle of the night. No one seemed too worried. Their confidence in the ship's safety was that great.

By the time I reached Blythe's room, she was in her nightgown, throwing some things in a bag for the still-sleeping LaRoche girls. "Is it cold out there?" she asked me. "Should I bring coats?"

"Absolutely, and wear one yourself," I told her. She looked so young to me there with her hair all tumbled around her shoulders, so thin in her ruffled white gown. A surge of affection for my baby sister formed itself into a lump in my throat. I held her tight. "You'll be all right, won't you?" I said.

"Of course," she replied calmly. "I'm in charge of Louise and Simone. I have to be all right."

"Don't forget your life belt. There's one for each passenger in every cabin," I said as I left. Of course Emma, Amelie, and I didn't have one, since we weren't officially on board.

I then went to find the twins. Li was pacing the room when I got there. "When I wake up, Amelie is gone," she blurted the moment she saw me. "Emma say she sleepwalking and go to find her."

"You go. I'll find them," I said. "Dress warm. Bring your life belt. This isn't a drill, Li."

Where could Emma and Amelie be? Would they get to the lifeboats on time? Mr. Stead said he was worried that there weren't enough of them. I decided to look for them on deck.

Thad was there to meet me. "Where's your coat, your things?" he asked.

"Where are yours?" I countered.

"I never got to my room because I couldn't wake Tesla up. I only left him so I could meet you, but I have to go back for him. I have time because they're loading women and children first. You should get on a boat right now."

I spied Mimi, still in her wedding gown with a heavy coat over her shoulders. "Where are Blythe and the twins?" she asked, rushing up to me and Thad.

Looking around, I pointed to Blythe, who was already on a boat with Juliette LaRoche and the little girls. Mr. LaRoche stood on deck, handing his wife the bag Blythe had packed and some other supplies. Juliette lunged forward and wrapped her arms around his neck. I could tell he was murmuring words of assurance to her as he settled her back down into the boat. After that, the attending officer gave a signal and the boat was lowered out of sight.

"Amelie is sleepwalking," I told Mimi. "Emma has gone to find her."

I'd never heard Mimi swear before, but she did right then. "Where could they be?" she asked, turning in a circle in her search for them.

Victor joined us, also still dressed in his wedding tuxedo. "Mimi, find a place on the next boat," he urged.

"I can't go until my sisters are safe," she told him.

"Yes, you can," I said.

"No, I'm the oldest. I'm in charge. I just can't."

"They'll be all right. I'll see to it," Victor promised.

"Hey!" Thad cried suddenly, pointing.

We all turned and were instantly bewildered. He was pointing at an old woman in a large, flowered nightgown wearing a ruffled cap who was getting into a lifeboat. Before we could question him about it, Thad had bounded over to the woman. Everyone gasped as Thad yanked the cap from her head, revealing the old woman to be the hired thug who had undoubtedly wrecked Tesla's earthquake machine.

The man took off and Thad chased after him. Victor

sped away to help. All of them turned a corner and disappeared.

The same eight-man band that had played at Mimi's wedding assembled on deck. They broke into another ragtime song. I presumed it was to help keep everyone calm, and it did seem to help. It created the feeling that everything was under control.

Emma rushed up to us. "Thank God!" Mimi cried. "Where's Amelie?"

"I've looked everywhere. I can't find her," Emma cried frantically.

"We'll spread out in three directions," Mimi decided. "Whether you find her or not, be back here in exactly ten minutes."

We agreed and set out to find Amelie. I moved into the halls, walking against the tide of people heading for the lifeboats. I was jostled and had to struggle to get through. Eventually I realized I was outside the Grand Ballroom and decided to check if Amelie had gone there, maybe trying to return to the wedding in her sleep.

As I ran down the Grand Staircase, I saw at a glance that no one was there except Tesla, who was still laid out on a table. I had to try to wake him but as I approached, he startled me badly by unexpectedly sitting bolt upright.

He looked straight at me, not seeming a bit surprised at my presence. "Jane, I've had one of my dreams. I know a way to right this entire situation. But it's in the cargo hold. Come with me. I'll need your help."

"Are you sure?" I asked, doubtful that this was the best use of my time at the moment.

"You doubt my flashes?"

"Maybe."

"My dear, one can think clearly, but one can be quite insane and still think deeply. I have had a deep thought."

"All right," I agreed, persuaded more by his conviction than his words. "I'll go with you."

At the top of the staircase, we met Thad. His face was badly scraped. "He got away again," he reported. "Victor's gone back to wait for Mimi and force her into a boat if he can."

"Come, Thad," Tesla said. "We'll need you, too. The device is very heavy."

We knew that the cargo hold was below in third class, so we headed down. When we got there, we encountered a locked gate that barred our way in.

What I saw through that gate horrified me.

Water was rushing through the hallways. The people in third class crushed up against locked gates shouting to be let out.

"Hold on," Thad said, running back up the stairs. He'd

spotted what might be a key cabinet, but it was locked. Forcefully smashing it open with a jab of his elbow, he quickly located a ring of keys.

We had frantic and frustrating moments as he tested each key until one finally clicked in the lock. Then we were nearly trampled by the stampede of terrified passengers charging up the stairs.

At first, we flattened ourselves against the wall to let them pass, but more and more kept coming through, since all the other exits were locked. Finally, we had to push our way down the several steps to third class.

It seemed like so much insanity to be going *toward* the very situation that these people were fleeing. The knee-deep water was frigid and instantly seeped into my shoes and soaked my dress.

"This way!" Tesla directed us, slogging through the torrent of freezing water.

We followed him to the flooded cargo hold, an immense, warehouse-like room where cars and furniture stood side by side. Boxes and trunks had already broken apart, their contents floating like colorful seaweed. An open jewelry box sailed by, its dazzling contents — sapphire rings, diamond bracelets, golden earrings — as in need of rescue as the passengers above.

There was no time to pay attention to it. Tesla found what he was seeking, a very large crate stacked high on top of other crates. "Thank God, it's not wet," he cried.

Thad jumped up on some boxes and began pulling at the crate, but it was too heavy. Tucking the hem of my skirt into my waistband, I scrambled up to help him.

"Here, I found this!" Tesla called, reaching to hand me a crowbar. "Don't try to bring the crate down. It's too heavy and it will get wet. Just open it up. It will work just as well in a horizontal position."

Thad took the crowbar from me and began cracking open the slats of wood. "What is this machine?" I shouted down to Tesla.

"Haven't you guessed?" he asked. "It's my time machine. I'm going to transport this entire ship forward in time so that other ships will have a chance to get here. Surely the *Titanic* has sent out calls for help by now."

"They have," Thad confirmed. "The *Carpathia* is not far, and neither is the *Californian*, if they can be reached before they resume their morning telegraph operation. The captain has sent up a number of flares."

"Could we send the ship back to the past and change what happens?" I asked.

"Theoretically, maybe," Tesla answered, as he began to climb up on the boxes to us, "but I don't know how to do that yet. I can only go forward."

We got the crate open. Tesla slowly climbed alongside of it. With Thad's help, they pried open the door. Inside was a chamber big enough for two or three adults. "Normally, one would enter the chamber, but in this case

I'm going to turn it high with the door open. Hopefully the frequency will emanate out and take the entire ship forward."

"Will this hurt?" I asked.

"Maybe," he admitted, "a little. But it's worth it to have so many more people saved. All these steerage passengers don't have a chance unless one of the big ships arrives much faster than they will get here otherwise. It's just a small hop forward, but it will be significant in its consequences."

After that, everything happened so fast. Tesla began turning dials.

Thad clutched my hand.

"Jane!" Mimi splashed into the cargo hold.

"Mimi, why aren't you on a boat?" I shouted.

"I couldn't leave without you."

There was a loud, loud humming.

The room became a blaze of blinding, ultrabright, white light.

In the next moment, I was flailing in icy water, gasping for breath. A chair floated by, and I grabbed onto it to keep myself afloat.

At first, I was so shocked by the freezing water that I couldn't even think. People floated by, many with

wide-eyed, horror-filled stares, and my brain couldn't make sense of it. Who were they? Why were they floating in the ocean? Why was I?

Slowly my body temperature adjusted and rational thought and memory returned, but it was still hard to make sense of everything.

Where was the ship?

How could a vessel so enormous have sunk so completely that no sign of it remained?

Off in the distance, dark forms hovered in the water. Why were they just standing out there? "Help!" I yelled, waving my arm. "Help me!"

"Jane!" It was Tesla, several yards away. He was floating on an overturned table. Using his arms to paddle, he moved toward me and pulled me on with him.

"Have you seen Thad or Mimi?" I asked.

"Not yet," he replied. He pulled a small light from his pocket. I assumed it was another of his inventions and didn't even bother to question it. He shone it around the dark waters.

What we saw was too horrible to describe. Colonel Astor and Mr. Stead were blue-faced and still. They clutched the same piece of a floating door. Soot covered Colonel Astor, which led me to guess that one of the ship's funnels might have hit him.

A man I guessed to be Mr. LaRoche lay facedown in the water, his arms spread in front of him. I saw a great number of the women who'd worked as seamstresses on our dresses just this morning.

I spied Victor floating there, and had to turn away. Poor Mimi. How would she ever get over this?

Once again I began searching for Thad and Mimi, but couldn't locate them.

And then I saw two figures in lavender bridesmaid dresses. They lay side by side on another floating door. They appeared to be sleeping, eyes closed.

"My sisters!" I told Tesla urgently.

We both began paddling frantically until we were beside them. Tesla reached out from our floating table and felt Emma's pulse, then Amelie's.

I waited only a moment for his response but it felt like a hundred years.

"They're alive," he said, "but barely."

"Help!" I shouted at the dark forms of the lifeboats hovering out there. "Help! Help! Help!" I screamed until I was hoarse and then called even more. Tesla shone his small light at them.

A dim light that looked like a match flickered, burned for a second, and was gone. But it wasn't as far away as the others. Tesla shone his beam on it and kept it there until a familiar face came into view.

It was Mrs. Brown, and she was rowing. So were a number of the other women in the boat with her.

Before long, the lifeboat was close enough that Mrs. Brown and the other passengers could pull Emma and Amelie on board. I noticed the quartermaster of the boat looking out to sea, not even acknowledging us. "He didn't want to come back for you," Mrs. Brown explained as Tesla and I climbed on. "So I threatened to throw him overboard; then the ladies and I commandeered the boat."

"Thank you! Thank you!" I said, my teeth chattering uncontrollably from the bitter cold.

"Sure thing," Mrs. Brown replied as she draped her sable coat over my sisters.

"Mimi and Thad are out here somewhere," I told her, peering anxiously out into the darkness. And Blythe, I had to hope, was still safe in her boat with the LaRoche women.

The water was so frigid. We had to find Mimi and Thad. Why hadn't they materialized beside me and Tesla? Where were they? I was sick with worry. "Mimi!" I shouted at the black ocean. "Thad!"

"I don't see them, but they're in luck," Mrs. Brown said. "Look at that."

In the far distance, something glowed and streamed across the sky like a comet. "Is it a shooting star?" one of the rowing women asked.

"I hope not," said Mrs. Brown. "I'm thinking it's a flare from a rescue ship."

Emma opened her eyes and clutched for my hand. Grasping it, I sat beside her. "It's okay. You're safe," I assured her.

"No," she said with a chilled quiver. "Jane, I don't want to leave." Her voice was so faint I barely heard her.

"Of course you do, Emma. A ship is coming for us. We're going to be saved."

"No, not that," she said, shaking her head slowly. Her voice was so nearly inaudible I had to bend low to hear her. "I won't leave," she whispered hoarsely. Then her eyes closed and her head lolled over.

"Emma, wake up!" I shouted. "Emma! Emma!"

I kept shouting at her until Mrs. Brown drew me away. "She can't hear you anymore," she said softly. "She's in a better place."

"No!" I shouted, tears exploding from my eyes. "Emma! No!"

I didn't want her to be in a better place. I wanted her with me, right there in the freezing lifeboat — alive.

Chapter 34

I don't remember much about the trip to New York on the *Carpathia*. Amelie slipped into unconsciousness before we were even on board. Since she was one of the more critically ill, they found a cot for her; many others had to sit up or lie on the floor. The doctor said she was in a coma.

The official report was that Emma had died of hypothermia, meaning she'd frozen to death, but the doctor allowed that she no doubt had many broken bones and other internal injuries. Amelie had two broken legs and frostbite on her toes.

Blythe saw what had happened to them from her lifeboat. Through the course of the first day on the *Carpathia*, she made five attempts to tell me what she'd witnessed, but each time couldn't get through the entire horrific tale without breaking down in heaving, racked sobs.

That night, as I sat on a wooden chair beside Amelie sleeping on her cot, Blythe came in and sat at the foot of the cot. Once again she tried to tell me what she'd seen. She took a deep breath to calm herself and began.

At about two in the morning someone remarked that

there was a person walking way up high near the funnels. Blythe looked up and knew instantly that it was Amelie and guessed she was still sleepwalking. Then she spotted someone else climbing after her.

"It was very hard to see, but I knew it had to be Emma," she recalled miserably. "She reached her, too. But just as she did, the ship seemed to snap in two and the front end sank into the water very fast. The front funnel broke off and flew toward the water. At the same time, Emma and Amelie went flying into the air."

An image from last year flashed in my mind: Amelie on the roof, silhouetted against a field of stars; Emma dreaming she was flying through the night. Had they some-how known what would happen to them?

I didn't want to think of them hitting the water from so high up. It must have been horrible. "They were so injured, yet they hung on for an hour and a half more," I said.

Once again Blythe dissolved into deep, pain-racked sobbing. "I pleaded with the lifeboat captain to go back to look for them. I begged and begged, but he wouldn't. He said it was too dangerous. He said if I didn't calm down, he'd knock me out. Really, Jane, I tried all I could."

I put my arms around her and together we rocked as tears ran down my cheeks. "Shh. Shh. You did all you could. No one could have done better."

"Do you really think so?" she asked through her tears.

"Yes! I know you did."

Shutting my eyes, I let the tears fall, not even trying to control them.

Blythe and I sat there holding on to each other for a long time. Finally, I realized she'd fallen asleep on my tear-drenched shoulder.

I settled her onto the cot at Amelie's feet and covered her with a blanket. Then I went out on deck to search once more for Thad and Mimi. I hoped with all my heart that they'd been rescued. The intensity of my need to find them was so strong I felt as though I could almost will them to appear.

People from all the different classes sat mixed together out on the deck. The *Carpathia*, I learned, had picked up 750 passengers. Fifteen hundred other passengers and crew members had died.

Fifteen hundred souls lost!

Revised lists of who had lived and who had died were going up hourly as bodies were retrieved by the *Californian*, which had shown up much too late to be of help to anyone.

Thad and Mimi were, as yet, unaccounted for, and so I continued to search. I hoped maybe they were passed out, like Amelie, and no one had identified them. I read a story once where a person was hit on the head and had forgotten his own identity; *amnesia*, I think they called it. I let my inventive mind work overtime to come up with stories in which they survived.

I came upon Juliette LaRoche sitting on a deck chair, holding both Simone and Louise as she stared out at the ocean. I'd learned from Blythe that she already knew her husband, Joseph, was dead. The pain in her eyes was heartbreaking to see. "Blythe is sleeping," I told her. "Can I help you in her place?"

She smiled sadly. "No, thank you. I have lost the best husband on earth. No one can help me."

Tesla came by and saw me with Juliette. For a moment I looked at him hopefully, but his expression told me there was no need to even ask if he'd seen Mimi or Thad.

Louise started to whimper, and Juliette went to find the girls something to eat. I got up and walked the deck with Tesla.

"I never dreamed it would turn out like this," he said. "I will never be able to forgive myself."

"Thad and I are the only ones left who know what really happened," I said.

"Then you must tell," he said.

I shook my head. "The man who tampered with your earthquake machine is to blame. And I think he must be dead. I haven't seen him anywhere, and we'll never know who he was working for."

Mother met us at New York Harbor, having gotten onto another ship almost immediately after the *Titanic* sailed. Her face looked like it was permanently swollen from days of relentless crying. She had contacted the White Star Line and learned of Emma's death and Amelie's condition. She knew Blythe and I were safe and Mimi was missing.

When Blythe and I came down the gangplank, she rushed to us through the waiting crowd, gathering us both in her arms. Her emotional tears, at once happy and tortured, set Blythe and me off in a matching torrent yet again.

"And Mimi?" she asked. "Anything?"

I shook my head and a stricken cry came from her like I've never heard. It was as though someone were choking her while she screamed. And then she swooned. A man nearby steadied her gently to the ground. In moments, she regained consciousness but dropped her head into her hands. "I don't know how I can go on," she murmured.

Amelie was brought to Saint Vincent's Hospital. We stayed with her around the clock, performing all the duties required to keep her fed and clean.

"Mr. Stead was right; he died by ice," Mother said as she and I sat around Amelie's curtained-off bed with the amber lights turned down low, while Blythe slept curled in an armchair nearby. It was late and most people were asleep.

"I heard he was very dignified," I told her. "They say he went to the ship's library with Colonel Astor, where they sat together and waited for the end."

"He was a dear friend," Mother remarked.

"Mother? Jane?"

Mother and I both looked up quickly to Amelie.

Had she spoken?

"Mother?"

We sprang to her. "Amelie! We're here, darling," Mother said excitedly. "How do you feel?"

"My mouth is dry. What happened? Where am I?"

"We'll tell you everything later," Mother said, no doubt not wanting to upset her. "You're talking, dear."

"Emma is talking."

Mother and I looked at each other, shocked.

"You know about Emma?" I asked cautiously.

"I *am* Emma."

Mother gasped. "I know the difference between them," she said to me. "I've always been able to tell them apart. That is Amelie."

"Amelie is here, too," she said.

Blythe had awakened and quietly come to the foot of the bed, watching. "That's Emma's voice," she whispered.

"Emma said she wouldn't leave," I recalled softly.

"I haven't," Amelie said.

$\mathcal{B}$ack in Spirit Vale, we had a memorial service for Emma, even though she was very much with us. We had another one for Mimi. Although we had no body, she was presumed to have drowned.

Mother took down her sign and announced that she was done contacting spirits. "While that ship was sinking, the spirit world overwhelmed me with messages and warnings. At one point I was so frantic that I tried to jump overboard to swim to you. The ship's captain finally had me sedated. I never want to go through anything like that again."

Instead, she went back to working for Aunty Lily at the hotel, keeping books and managing things.

Another sign went up in front of our house, though. Amelie changed her name to Amelie-Em and became one of the most sought-after psychics in western New York. With the force of their combined personalities, Amelie-Em was a vibrant, forceful woman, not at all the fey, winsome girls they had once been. In fact, she became *the* force in Spirit Vale, much as Mother had been before them.

It seems strange to refer to one person as *them*, but

that's how we all came to think of Amelie-Em, almost as if they were Siamese twins attached at some psychic intersection of their metaphysical selves.

I grieved deeply for Mimi and Thad. Every day I had to remind myself that they were really gone, because, no matter how hard I tried, I couldn't believe it. I constantly spoke to them both in my mind. I even imagined that I heard answers, though I suppose I was only imagining what they might say. If I ever told myself I had to let go of them, the pain was crippling and I couldn't do it.

Mimi had been my dearest friend. Thad was my greatest love. How could they be dead? It was too cruel. I couldn't bear it. Most of my days were spent in my room, crying. My only pleasure was sleep because there I could see them in dreams so vivid they were like visits in another time and place.

I never stopped feeling their loss, but in May I got word that my article on Tesla had won me the internship at the *Sun*. Mother did not immediately agree to let me go. But I desperately needed to get out of Spirit Vale, where everything reminded me of Mimi. In the end, my relentless pleading wore her down and she consented.

"Take me with you," Blythe pleaded.

I couldn't, though I promised she could visit often.

Everything about working for the *Sun* was thrilling. Well, maybe the work was less than stimulating. I read endless reams of copy, checking for typographic errors like missed commas. I sometimes aided the art department in inserting small type that had been missed in the first go 'round. I often returned to my room in a town house owned by an elderly couple in the West Twenties with ink on my hands and face. To get there, I had to pass a building with black-gated windows and a black wrought-iron fence that was the Astor Counting House. Every time I went by, the pain of the previous April came back to me anew. I soon found a new way to go.

One evening I went down to Chinatown to see Li in her father's restaurant. I got to the front door but stopped before going in. I hadn't realized this was the same place I'd eaten with Thad. I clamped a handkerchief to my face to soak up the rush of tears as I hurried away. That night I cried myself to sleep, curled in a ball in my small room.

Those six months were a time of bitter loneliness for me. I spent my days alone in the museums and reading. I had finished every Sherlock Holmes adventure and so began reading them over again beginning with "A Scandal in Bohemia," the very first, written in 1891. It surprised me how my perception of Holmes had changed since I first encountered him. Where I had once thought him to be a god of dispassionate reason, someone I should emulate, I now saw his very human flaws. He was moody and irritable. He had no friends other than the understanding Dr. Watson. Even his fervid attention to detail began to strike me as abnormal.

I kept reading the newspapers, too. There was a hearing held in the Waldorf-Astoria to determine what had gone wrong with the *Titanic*. A panel declared it had been too large a ship with too small a rudder. There was no mention of the crack in the rudder. I wondered if they ever even knew about it.

One day I came upon an article written by George Bernard Shaw in a paper called the *Daily News and Leader* claiming that the heroism of the people on the *Titanic* had been exaggerated and romanticized. I was outraged! I remembered seeing the playwright outside Stead's rented town house and recalling he was supposed to have been a good friend of his.

A day or two later I came upon a rebuttal written by none other than dear Dr. Sir Arthur Conan Doyle. He said, "It is a pitiful sight to see a man of undoubted genius using his gifts in order to misrepresent and decry his own people." He was Stead's real friend, and I thought more highly of him than ever I had before.

I also kept clipping accounts of Tesla and the rumblings of war in Europe.

That year, Tesla had more money worries. His creditors at Wardenclyffe Tower were demanding their money back. With Colonel Astor gone, Mr. Boldt demanded twenty thousand dollars in back rent. Tesla sold him the scrap metal from the tower to pay his debt. Eventually Tesla was forced to move out of his beloved Waldorf-Astoria. I had no idea where he was living.

Tesla was nominated for the Nobel Prize in science that year for his work with high-frequency resonant transformers, but when he heard he would have to share the award with Edison, he said he wouldn't accept the nomination. He could have certainly used the money from that award, but once again he was too principled to compromise.

When the time came for my internship to end, my editor asked if I'd like to stay on as a paid assistant. I jumped at the chance. The couple I was staying with said I could stay on if I started paying rent, and I agreed.

That would have been the rest of my life.

But then, something remarkable happened.

Chapter 36

NEW YORK CITY, AUGUST 1914

I worked at the paper for the next two years getting more and better assignments. By the time I was nineteen, I was reviewing theatrical events for the paper. This was a lot of fun, although I begged my editor ceaselessly to allow me to cover more substantial news stories.

One story I was dying to be assigned was a piece on the quarrel between Dr. Conan Doyle and Harry Houdini. They had been friends at the time of the conference in London, and now they were the bitterest enemies. Dr. Conan Doyle was a leading champion of spiritualism, while Houdini remained its most vocal disbeliever. Conan Doyle publicly claimed that Houdini was in fact a psychic who did his amazing feats by means of metaphysics.

I pleaded to interview them both for the paper and was told that maybe, if they both came to New York at the same time, I could interview them.

The other topic I wanted to write about was the one on everyone's mind — the war.

The conflict that Mr. Stead had been so worried about had erupted. In June there had been an assassination in the city of Sarajevo — a twenty-year-old Yugoslavian shot the Austrian archduke and archduchess. Because of this, Austria-Hungary declared war on Serbia in July. Then Russia got into it, siding with Serbia, and France joined them. Germany came to the aid of its ally, Austria-Hungary. Britain got into it to side with France and then Japan honored its alliance with England and came on board. It was just as Stead had predicted — a world at war.

I read that Arthur Conan Doyle, although fifty-five, joined the Crowborough Company of the Sixth Royal Sussex Volunteer Regiment and served as a private. I recalled Amelie-Em's prediction and wondered if he had signed up to be with his son, Kingsley Conan Doyle, who had joined the British Army.

The United States was still not involved in the war, though some political columnists at the paper said it was only a matter of time until we were. Germany had already accused the United States of sending England war supplies — an accusation that was probably true. They threatened to torpedo any of our ships found in British waters. Sinking ships was something I didn't even want to think about.

"How can I cover entertainment when so much is going on?" I complained to my editor one evening after filing a particularly insipid article about a doggie fashion show at Madison Square Garden.

As I spoke, an assistant came in and dropped a paper on his desk. As I rambled on about how silly and boring such events were, my editor ignored me and read the paper. "Would you look at that, Jane?" he said, putting down the typed article so I could see it. "Those Germans are going to force us into this infernal war one way or the other. A naval ship just picked up a man and a woman floating off the coast of Nova Scotia — right in the middle of the ocean without a boat or anything in sight. They think they're spies, and the Germans knew our guys would pick them up. How dumb do they think we are?"

He kept talking, but I was no longer listening. My eyes were glued to the photographs accompanying the story. Both the young man and the woman were wring- ing wet.

The woman had long, thick, jet-black hair.

Someone had blackened both the eyes of the young man.

"What is it, Jane?" my editor asked, noticing my stunned expression. "You look like you've seen a ghost."

"Maybe," I said quietly, and then I exploded into action, nearly throwing myself across his large desk. "You have to let me go to Nova Scotia to cover this story. You *must!*"

"Well," he considered tentatively, "I don't have anyone else I can spare right now and since you're so bent on —"

"Thank you!" I cried.

He handed me the sheet of paper. "All the information is here. See accounting for some expense money and you can leave in the morning."

"I'm leaving right now! Right now, tonight!"

Was it possible?

$\mathcal{M}$y train has pulled into the station and I am now writing in a motorcar on the way to the Halifax Police Station where the prisoners are being held. My heart is beating so hard I have to stop to take deep breaths to calm myself.

I think I know what might have happened. I hope so, at least.

Tesla's time-travel device threw him and me two hours and forty minutes into the future. For some reason, it sent Thad and Mimi two years and four months forward in time.

I hope I am right.

Am I just wishing, making up more stories in my head?

Please, let me be right.

I am now sitting on a bench at the police station waiting. The wait is endless.

Footsteps approach.

I am shaking.

Mimi bursts into tears when she sees me. She is dressed in dry clothes but her wrinkled white wedding gown is draped over her arm. "I don't know what's happened, Jane. I'm so confused," she says. "What happened to the ship?"

I weep with joy. "Mimi! Mimi!" I gush as I hug her tight.

"Jane, you look different," Mimi observes, stepping out of my embrace, twirling a long strand of her loose, unbundled hair. "You look older, somehow. What's happened?"

"I'll tell you everything on the way home," I promise, throwing my arms around her again.

Thad steps into the room, his eyes still swollen purple, an expression of complete confusion on his face. But when he sees me, his face shines with joy.

"Jane, you're alive!" he shouts, taking me into his arms. He sweeps me into a passionate kiss. I am too happy to bother caring that we are in a very public place.

I am in his arms. He is back.

For me, years have passed. For Mimi and Thad, only minutes. It is too great to be true. Yet it *is* true. I turn to the policeman in the corner. "I'm not dreaming, am I?" I check.

"No, miss," he assures me.

Now we are on a train traveling back to New York. Mimi is very quiet, deeply sad to learn that Victor is dead. I have told her how Emma seems to be with us still, and that seems to console her in some way.

They are not a day older than that terrible night in 1912. Their time in the water was brief, so their health is good. The authorities have grilled them with questions and have decided that they are not spies, after all. Though, when asked, I could offer no plausible explanation of how they came to be there, the fact that I knew them and could vouch for them as Americans facilitated their release.

"Victor said he would take me to Haiti," Mimi mentions. "Maybe I'll plan a trip there myself. Would you come with me, Jane?"

"Yes, of course, I will," I assure her.

Thad holds my hand and I point out to him that we are now nearly the same age, and he smiles. He puts his arm around me as I snuggle close.

As the train rumbles on, I think of Tesla saying that we are all inevitably traveling into the future — a future full of doubt and uncertainty. I remember also what Mr. Stead said that morning in the study — that the things we do can change the future.

Tesla's time machine, by throwing us forward in time, had changed Mimi's future, Thad's, Amelie-Em's — and mine, as well. If they weren't alive, my life would be very different; on the inside if not the outside. It wasn't the big save he had wanted, but it was the world to me.

I am here with Thad and Mimi. My heart is full with joy and gratitude at their return. This gift fate has unexpectedly given makes me feel I might explode with love for the whole world.

Jiva is Shiva.

Like the ocean, life is vast and mysterious.

It makes me excited to travel forward into the future regardless of its uncertainties, knowing that what I do makes a difference.

Yawning sleepily, I rest my head on Thad's shoulder, ready for whatever is next as we roar on into tomorrow.

Author's Note:

WHAT'S REAL IN *DISTANT WAVES*?

This novel is a work of fiction. However, it is based on certain historical facts. Maude, Mimi, Jane, Emma, Amelie, and Blythe Oneida Taylor are fictional, as is Thad. Quite a few real-life characters appear here, although I have imagined their dialogue and actions. I began to compile a chapter-by-chapter article on what was true and what was imagined in this novel, and it soon began to rival the length of the story. With the need for brevity in mind, here is a quick overview of the true history used here.

The home where Maude conducts her séance really existed and is open to the public. **The Old Merchant's House** is known to some as "the most haunted house in New York." It is located at 29 East Fourth Street in Manhattan. It became a museum in 1936.

In 1835, Seabury Tredwell, a wealthy merchant, moved into it with his family: a wife, two sons, and six daughters. The youngest member of the family, Gertrude Tredwell, lived in the house until she died in the upstairs bedroom in

1933 at the age of 93. Her older sister Julia Tredwell died in 1909, twenty-four years before Gertrude. Their sister Mary Adelaide Tredwell Richards, one of the only two daughters ever to marry, died in 1874.

The Fox sisters, Kate, Leah, and Margaret Fox, whom the Tredwells and Maude talk about, really existed. The story Maude tells about them is true. In 1848, the sisters were living in Hydesville, New York, in a house that was already considered haunted. They heard unexplained sounds and attempted to contact the ghost making them. They claimed they did make contact, and later it was verified that a peddler named Charles Rosma had died in the house.

The sisters were celebrities in their day. By 1850, they were giving public séances in New York City and are credited with starting the movement known as **spiritualism**. They were later discredited when it was discovered that some of the strange thumps and bumps the public heard were created by the sisters cracking their finger and toe joints.

It is said that **Abraham Lincoln** always had a strong belief in the spirit world as well as a belief in visions and predictions. He saw an image of himself in a mirror once that led him to believe he would not live through his second term in office — which, of course, he did not.

In 1862, Lincoln's twelve-year-old son, William Wallace Lincoln (Willie), died. Historians say it was the greatest blow Lincoln ever suffered. He often talked about how his son's spirit was always with him.

Though Lincoln was not publicly associated with spiritualists, his wife, **Mary Todd Lincoln**, embraced them. There is a famous story about a spiritualist named Nettie Maynard who was purported to have caused a grand piano in the White House to levitate off the floor while trying to contact Willie Lincoln.

It is documented by police and fire records of the time that an **earthquake did occur outside the Manhattan laboratory of Nikola Tesla** at 46 East Houston Street. Years later, in 1935, Tesla revealed to the *New York World* newspaper that he had accidentally caused it while experimenting with vibrating frequencies in his lab. Tesla told the reporter:

"I was experimenting with vibrations. I had one of my machines going and I wanted to see if I could get it in tune with the vibration of the building. I put it up notch after notch. There was a peculiar cracking sound. I asked my assistants where did the sound come from. They did not know. I put the machine up a few more notches. There was a louder cracking sound. I knew I was approaching the vibration of the steel building. I pushed the machine a little higher. Suddenly all the heavy machinery in the place was flying around. I grabbed a hammer and broke the machine. The building would have been about our ears in another few minutes. Outside in the street there was pandemonium. The police and ambulances arrived. I told my assistants to say nothing. We told the police it must have been an earthquake. That's all they ever knew about it."

Nikola Tesla was born in 1856 in Austria-Hungary. He was perhaps the greatest scientific genius of the last century, but he's not as well-known as **Albert Einstein** or **Thomas Edison** because he was not very practical, nor was he a good businessman. At age twenty-eight, the six-foot-four Tesla arrived in New York with four cents in his pocket. With a letter of recommendation from home, he went to see Thomas Edison, the man who had introduced electricity to Manhattan in 1870. They soon fell into conflict over theories and business practices. Edison did offer Tesla money to refurbish his generators . . . and when the job was done, he claimed that he had been kidding. After Tesla quit, he had to dig ditches for the Edison Company for a while in order to support himself. Tesla had no respect for Edison's methods, claiming he relied on guesswork and had no background in sound mathematical or scientific practice.

The most famous argument between Tesla and Edison centered on a disagreement about whether alternating electric (AC) current was more efficient than direct current (DC). Tesla favored alternating current, while Edison believed in direct current. By 1887, Edison launched a propaganda war to convince the public that AC current was unsafe. He filmed a rogue elephant being electrocuted with

AC current in order to horrify the public and have them associate their horror with AC current. Eventually, though, the public embraced AC current as more efficient, less expensive, and safer.

After this, Tesla returned to his lab to work on high-frequency vibrations. He felt that this would have many practical applications, particularly the efficient and safe transmission of energy. He wanted to reproduce the vibrations of sunlight, which he believed would create virtually free electricity for humanity. Jumping off from this, he began work on the wireless transmission of energy and is credited with laying the groundwork for today's wireless technology. All the inventions and theories mentioned in this novel, such as the Teslascope, Tesla coil, and Tesla turbine and the fact that Tesla believed viruses could be shattered with vibrations, are true. He did move to Colorado Springs, built a radio tower, and attempted to contact extraterrestrial life. He did this because he believed that his tower had picked up signals from outer space. This tower eventually burned to the ground. Some speculated that this was done by agents of Edison or his financial backers, though this has never been proven. Others believe it was either lightning or the high voltages of electricity Tesla was experimenting with that caused the fire.

In 1900, he built another radio tower in Shoreham, Long Island, in New York. This tower, however, was a failure, and was foreclosed by the bank in 1908. He sold the scrap metal to **George C. Boldt**, manager of the **Waldorf-Astoria hotel**, to pay back the rent he owed for staying at the hotel for almost twenty years.

Many believe that he was experimenting with **time travel** as early as 1895. In the 1930s, Tesla was involved with a group at the University of Chicago investigating invisibility and the possibility of moving through the time-space continuum. For more on this work, research **the Philadelphia Experiment**.

Tesla died in 1943 at the age of 86. He continued to feed all the pigeons in Bryant Park until his death. Tesla's later years were spent working on such concepts as free energy, radar, electric cars, rocketry, and electric current therapy.

Tesla was *not* on the *Titanic* — or, at least, not that we know of. Emil Christmann, Tesla's alias, *was* the name of a real person on the passenger list. Also, Tesla *was* working on experiments to light shipping lanes in the Atlantic and to improve ship-to-ship communications. He did not propose a means to shatter icebergs with vibration, but given his extensive work in the area and his belief that the world itself could be split in half if the right frequency was found, such a device is certainly within the realm of possibility.

On the train to Spirit Vale, Maude Taylor reads a book called ***Futility***. It was a short novel published in 1898, fourteen years before the *Titanic* sank. It is eerily prophetic. The author, **Morgan Robertson**, called his ship the *Titan* and described it as "the largest craft afloat." In the novel, the ship has its first voyage in April and has a collision with an iceberg on that journey. Its publisher later renamed it *The Wreck of the Titan: A Nineteenth-Century Prophecy*. This novel can still be found and ordered online.

Spirit Vale is a fictionalized version of **Lily Dale**, in the town of Pomfret, about an hour south of Buffalo, New York. This community of spirit mediums was founded in 1879. By the early 1900s, it was a thriving center of spiritualism, as well as a political meeting place for those supporting women's suffrage. **Susan B. Anthony** was a frequent visitor, and **Frederick Douglass** came with his suffragist second wife. Many celebrities of stage and the early movies also came in search of a way to contact deceased loved ones. For more on Lily Dale, read *Lily Dale: The True Story of the Town That Talks to the Dead* by Christine Wicker.

Sir Arthur Conan Doyle was born in Edinburgh, Scotland, in 1859 and died in 1930. He first debuted his famous detective tales in *Beeton's Christmas Annual* in 1887, and in 1890, Sherlock Holmes appeared in a story featured in *Lippincott's Monthly Magazine*. The character became so popular that it became a regular series in the *Strand* magazine in 1891.

Arthur Conan Doyle was interested in spiritualism. His novel *The Land of Mist* deals with the subject, and in 1926 he wrote a book titled *The History of Spiritualism*, in which he praised the work of two noted spiritualists. His son **Kingsley Doyle** did die as a result of wounds inflicted at the Battle of the Somme in World War I. And, as in the novel, he was also friends with the great magician **Harry Houdini**.

Harry Houdini was born **Ehrich Weiss** in 1874. At the point we meet him in the novel, he had not yet legally changed his name but was using it in his magic act. Unlike his friend Arthur Conan Doyle, Houdini never changed his mind about spiritualism, maintaining that it was no more than trickery and fraud. He even claimed to have learned some of his own magic tricks from spiritualists. In the 1920s, he turned much of his energy to proving that spiritualists were fakes. He was a member of a group called Scientific American that offered cash prizes to any medium who could prove true abilities. Houdini made sure this prize was never awarded by continually uncovering tricks that confounded everyone else. His friendship with Sir Arthur Conan Doyle was broken due to Houdini's zeal in uncovering mediums. Conan Doyle came to believe that Houdini himself was a spiritual medium. The two men became public antagonists. After Houdini died, Conan Doyle dealt with this in his novel *The Edge of the Unknown*, published posthumously in 1931.

The psychic conference conducted by **William Stead** is a fiction. But W. T. Stead was a respected journalist involved with spiritualism and was a passenger on the *Titanic*. Although he had predicted the sinking of the *Titanic*, and predicted his own death by ice, he boarded the ship to attend a peace congress at Carnegie Hall in Manhattan at the invitation of United States President William Taft. He died that night, just as he had predicted. He spent his last hours in dignified resignation to his fate, sitting in the first-class drawing room with his companion **John Jacob Astor**.

The LaRoche family really existed. Joseph LaRoche went down with the *Titanic*. His wife and daughters survived. I imagined Mimi as Haitian and of mixed race, and then discovered the LaRoches' story — one of the most exciting discoveries of many I made while writing this book.

Colonel John Jacob Astor the Fourth also died that night on the *Titanic*. At the time, he was one of the richest men in America. He was returning to New York with his much younger, pregnant second wife, **Madeleine Force**. Along with his cousin, William Waldorf, he owned the Waldorf-Astoria, the world's tallest hotel at that time. He let his good friend Nikola Tesla stay there for minimal rent. The two men had been friends since the 1893 Chicago World's Fair, and later Astor, along with George Westinghouse and others, was a major backer of Tesla's Niagara Falls Project. He was an amateur scientist who held a patent on a moving sidewalk and who had written a futuristic novel. At the time of his death, he and Tesla were talking about the commuter flivver plane that Tesla was developing, part helicopter and part plane. It is said that Astor, a dog lover, freed all the dogs from the kennels so they would have a chance to survive the sinking of the *Titanic*. Madeleine Force survived the sinking and went on to have his son.

Mrs. Brown was never known as Molly Brown, but rather Maggie. She became known as Molly only after her death, because of a 1960 stage musical, *The Unsinkable Molly Brown*. Born Margaret Tobin in 1867, she grew up impoverished and, at nineteen, married a poor man known as J.J. Brown. Although their early married life was lean, they had two children and Maggie was involved in the fight for women's rights. In the early 1890s, J.J.'s work with the Ibex Mining Company turned profitable when he discovered an ore seam in a mine. Mrs. Brown was on the *Titanic* because she was returning early from a trip to Europe, having received word that her grandson was ill. She was traveling with her good friends the Astors. After the sinking of the ship, she was widely praised for her heroism.

Millionaire **Benjamin Guggenheim** and his girlfriend **Leontine "Ninette" Aubart** really sailed on the *Titanic*. With them was their valet **Victor Giglio**. Mimi Taylor is a fictional character and was not engaged to him. Although Mimi was not really her companion, Ninette was rescued in lifeboat nine with the maid with whom she was traveling, and did not die until 1964 at the age of 77. Victor Giglio and Benjamin Guggenheim both went down with the *Titanic*.

The center of this novel, of course, is the sinking of the *Titanic*, which occured at two thirty in the morning on April 15, 1912, although it had been considered unsinkable. It hit an iceberg on its starboard side and immediately began taking on water. Its rudder did not crack, as seen in the novel, but a panel convened afterward at the Waldorf-Astoria did find that the rudder was too small for the massive ship and was the reason it could not steer away from the iceberg quickly enough. Its sinking is considered one of the worst peacetime maritime disasters ever. One thousand, five hundred and seventeen people died.

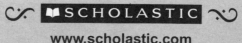